The handsome Russian took her arm firmly. "I am not to be refused," he said softly.

He led Susannah to a table and seated her ceremoniously.

"Two slivovas," he said to the waiter. Without speaking, he studied her closely. He found her provocative—quite a treasure to come upon in drab Sofia. Like fine bone china, she looked expensive and fragile, but he sensed that she would not break easily. Her eyes were watchful, even guarded. He saw the trembling hands and the way she avoided his eyes. He felt her fear.

Susannah swallowed the brandy down. The fiery sensation helped. When she was able to look into his eyes, she saw that the grimness that had marked his face a moment ago was gone entirely. *The face of mine enemy,* she thought, *is entirely too appealing.* It made him all the more deadly!

MESSAGE FROM ABSALOM
was originally published by Simon and Schuster.

Message
from
Absalom

Anne Armstrong Thompson

PUBLISHED BY POCKET BOOKS NEW YORK

MESSAGE FROM ABSALOM

Simon and Schuster edition published 1975

POCKET BOOK edition published March, 1976

This POCKET BOOK edition includes every word contained in the original, higher-priced edition. It is printed from brand-new plates made from completely reset, clear, easy-to-read type. POCKET BOOK editions are published by POCKET BOOKS, a division of Simon & Schuster, Inc., 630 Fifth Avenue, New York, N.Y. 10020. Trademarks registered in the United States and other countries.

TO MY MOTHER
WITH LOVE

Message from Absalom

Chapter 1

SHE RECOGNIZED HIM. He was wearing the blue coverall of a Bulgarian common laborer, but she recognized him nonetheless. Impulsively, she was starting to cross the cathedral toward him when the urgency in his eyes warned her. Turning quicky, she followed the guide across the sanctuary to the altar. When she could look again, he was gone.

Nine years had passed since she had last seen John Novak. He had come to her shop on Capitol Hill late one Saturday afternoon and quietly tapped on the door. She admitted him and heard his familiar whisper beg her help once again. Then, as before, she put the CLOSED sign on the front door and dimmed the lights. Playfully, he tossed her a small Chinese porcelain horse.

"Don't do that! It's valuable!" she exclaimed.

"I know. And you're much too concerned about it."

"It's supposed to be my living."

"And mine will be here shortly. Can we use your storeroom?"

"Of course."

They sat in silence, smoking, waiting. The knock they were expecting came in thirty minutes.

"The shop is closed," Susannah called to the man standing on the front step.

"I'm sorry. I was in the area and wished to ask, do you have any Ming horses?"

"Yes. I have just one. Please, won't you come in?"

Her two visitors talked for ten minutes. When the

9

stranger left, he took the horse with him. The trans-
action always signaled the importance of the information exchanged in the back room, so that day Susannah
watched the man with special interest. He was so
ordinary-looking she would never recognize him again.

Novak came quietly out of the storeroom. "Wish me
bon voyage," he said.

"Where are you going?"

"Away. It's a promotion. A substantial one."

"Congratulations."

"I'm not sure that is in order."

"Is it that sort of promotion?"

"Yes. I'm afraid so. This is good-bye, Susannah."

She held out her hand, but he smiled, put it aside and
stepped closer. His finger caressed her cheek, and bending his head, he kissed her very softly. "Don't stay in
this business too long, little one," he said. She followed
him to the door and watched him until he was out of
sight.

Nine years. His assignment must be nearly over. If
he had spent the entire time under cover in Bulgaria, he
must be very, very good. Oh, God, had she given him
away?

As they followed their guide around the cathedral,
Susannah looked at the other members of her tour party.
They were tired, their eyes a little glazed, but the women
still held tightly to their big purses. Aggie Taliaferro had
given up altogether and was slumped against a pillar.
Miss Tillie's nose had begun to twitch again.

"Now, there's a *man!*"

Susannah's eyes followed the jerk of her companion's
head. Marlene Wells had seen a Turk this time. He was
big and d--k, with a look of cruelty in the eyes.

Susannah could not help smiling. "He probably beats
his women afterward," she offered.

"Hmmm, think so?" Marlene began to lag behind, her

eyes on the Turk. Susannah was relieved. The group was functioning as usual.

Dimitri was citing the statistics on the Alexander Nevsky Cathedral. As the group looked and turned and listened, Susannah glanced at the few people still in the sanctuary. They were intent—the tourists on the great dome, the charwoman on her mop and bucket. The guards at the door didn't stir as Dimitri led his group out and a party of Japanese filed in. In the small flurry of arrival and departure, Susannah studied the street and the grounds beyond. John Novak had disappeared. No one was interested in his whereabouts. Or in hers.

Chapter 2

WITH DIFFICULTY, Susannah unlocked the door to her room. Keys and plumbing didn't work very well in the workers' paradise, and now that the tour was nearing its end, she was losing her patience with the inconveniences and the drab accommodations. There were always enough hangers, though, and she paused in the narrow entry to hang up her jacket. She heard no sound. The hand that covered her mouth and jerked her head back against rough cloth was completely unexpected.

"Susannah?" The lips moved against her ear. "OK, now?"

She nodded and relaxed. She knew who it was.

Still, he held her. "I forgot how tiny you are."

She smiled a little and turned in his arms.

"I don't have much time," he whispered. "Don't ever say the Lord doesn't hear us. He sent you when I needed you most. You must do something for me. Come in here."

His words were barely audible. At her look of inquiry, he glanced significantly at the metal circle high up on the wall in the corner of the room. It had been painted over and was hard to see, but it was there, listening to every word. He stepped into the bathroom and turned on the faucet in the tub full force.

"You can hear through the wall," Susannah said.

"Everything. I know. I've been waiting for some time."

"How did you get in?"

"I was trained to pick locks. And so were you. Remember? I must be the only worker at the Georgi Dimitrov Machine Works who owns burglary tools."

She smiled. It was good to see him again. "What can I do for you?" she asked.

"You must get a message for me."

"John, I left the business five years ago."

"I'm glad you took my advice. Are you married?"

"No. Just too selfish. I was making money and decided not to share it."

"I knew you were always too serious. Susannah, you're here. There's no one else who can help me."

She hesitated. She really didn't want to get involved again. "It's important?" she said finally.

"The most important thing I've ever done."

"Are you in trouble?"

"I've been in worse situations."

He said it lightly, but she wasn't fooled. He had been twenty-nine when he left Washington. Now he looked fifty. There were deep lines in his face. His hands were enlarged and callused, his hair gray and dull. The coverall hung much too loosely on his body. She couldn't deny him.

"What do I do?" she asked simply.

"Down the street to the right as you leave the hotel, there's a sidewalk café. It's diagonally across the street from the library."

She nodded. The library had been pointed out to them that morning.

"Go there. Take a table for four in the back, against the wall, and order coffee." He picked up a paperback book from the vanity. "Take this with you and read while you wait. When your coffee comes, put the book on the chair nearest the door to the kitchen and place that enormous pocketbook on top of it. Pull the chair under the table, as though you don't want anyone to see your purse. When you finish, pick up your purse and walk away. Leave the book in the chair so my contact will have an excuse to speak to you. Take what he hands you, and come back here."

"Will he be expecting me?"

"I arranged it as soon as I saw you this morning. Talk about godsends . . ."

"Suppose someone from the tour sees me and wants to go along?" She was thinking of Aggie. Aggie could never turn down a drink.

"Try to lose them."

"Will you be here?"

"I hope so. If I have to leave, I'll try to get back tonight. If I don't, take the book home with you and call my old boss, Jess Simpson."

She paused. "John, I can't. He's dead."

Novak's jaw tightened. "Are you sure?"

"Yes. It was in *The Washington Post* the Sunday before I left. He died of a heart attack."

"So *that's* what happened! I bet it was no heart attack!" He spoke grimly. His eyes were distant until he made his decision. Then he looked down at her. "There's only one other choice. You must take it to the President."

"John, I couldn't possibly get in to see the President. You know how it is at the White House."

"Only too well. But there's no one else I can trust. There's a leak. I don't know where, but high up. Jess was the only one I was sure of, and now if he's gone . . . Do you know anyone in the White House?"

"Maryanne Knowles is still on the First Lady's staff. We were in school together. I see her occasionally in Washington."

"Does she have access to the family?"

"Well, yes. I think so."

"That's perfect. Better than I had hoped. Ask her to help you, but you must give the book to the President personally. Don't let anyone else have it. Page 51 is the important one."

"Suppose the President's staff intervenes?"

"If you have to send word in to him, say you have the message from Absalom."

"Absalom?"

He smiled with genuine amusement. "That, sweetheart, is the secret. Do you need to know?"

Her own smile broadened at the familiar phrase. "No. I suppose not. But will the President recognize the name?"

"Absolutely. He's followed this operation closely. In fact, if you can just get word to him, your problems should be over."

"Will anyone try to stop me?"

"God help you if they do."

"You make it sound very frightening. I'm afraid."

"You'd be a fool not to be. Just remember that no one will expect you to have it." He looked at his watch, a worn one with a faded cloth band. "Now it's time for you to go."

She took the book he had handed her and stuffed it into her purse. He stopped her at the door to the hall.

"You know," he said softly, "since I left, I've thought of you many times, especially when I'm alone at night. Why didn't you marry that character you told me about that day?"

"He married someone else."

"Are you sorry?"

"No. He turned out to be a stinker."

He smiled. For a moment he looked like the man she remembered. "I told you so. I've been cold for so long. If I come home, will you make a fire in that old grate of yours for me?"

"Of course. The place in Fredericksburg has a dozen fireplaces. We'll light them all."

"Just the one in the bedroom. I'll think of it while I wait. Good-bye, Susannah."

He turned off the water and flipped out the lights.

"I won't be long," she said. "Rest a little if you can."

He nodded, touched her hair briefly and moved back into the dark of the bathroom. She opened the door and stepped into the hall. No one was there. She reached around the inside of the door, pushed the lock on the handle and slammed the door shut. The lock clicked. She tried the knob. Satisfied that it had worked this time, she turned down the hall and walked quickly to the elevator.

Chapter 3

SOFIA'S YELLOW BRICK STREETS baked in the late-afternoon sun, yet Susannah was cold as she mounted the steps to the café. Only two tables held customers. They looked up as she entered and, seeing that she was an American, subjected her to that curiously intent appraisal she had learned to expect from East Europeans. It was never hostile or sexually motivated, and usually she didn't mind. Today it made her nervous. She felt conspicuous, even exposed, as she walked to a rear table and ordered coffee. Taking the book from her purse as Novak had instructed, she let her eyes slide over the other customers to the streets beyond. No one had followed her. No one seemed interested in her presence. The Bulgarians at the other tables had politely returned to their own conversations and were ignoring her. Still, she was tense and uneasy. It was an effort to sip slowly, to smoke two cigarettes, to wait until enough time had elapsed to make her departure seem normal. Finally she rose and, counting out the money, slid it under the saucer. Her back felt stiff. No one spoke to her. No one looked up as she began to walk away. For a moment, she feared the rendezvous had failed.

"Please, madam . . ." The voice behind her spoke hesitantly.

She turned slowly. "Yes?"

"Please. Your book . . . you forget . . ." He held it out to her: a rather worn paperback copy of Gogol's *Dead Souls*.

17

Susannah looked directly into his face. She had not seen him on the terrace or in the street. Perhaps he had been inside. He seemed to be Bulgarian.

"Yes, I believe I did. Thank you very much."

The man nodded, smiled a little and backed away.

"Thank you," she said again, then turned and walked on. When she looked back, he was gone.

Fighting the desire to run, she started back to the hotel. It was not far. Several of the tour members were sitting in the sun in the Grand Hotel's own sidewalk café. Dr. Weisenstein called to her. "Where have you been?"

Susannah looked at him sharply. He was smiling, seeking to be friendly. "Window-shopping," she answered simply.

"Find anything interesting?"

"Not down that way."

"There's a good shop down the street to the left, across from the Austrian Embassy. They have the native dolls."

"Perhaps tomorrow. It's a nap for me now."

They let her go without protest. Weisenstein was a know-it-all of Russian antecedents. He spoke Russian and German and claimed he could read Bulgarian. He had been mercifully subdued in Hungary. Fearing he would become a pest, Susannah had not mentioned her own fluency in Russian. Weisenstein could be very tiresome.

Impatiently, Susannah unlocked the door to her room, eager to see Novak step from the shadows. The room was empty. He had gone.

Worried, she crossed to the window.

At first she saw nothing. The golden domes of the cathedral glowed in the sun. People hurried below, some of them carrying round loaves of bread, all of them intent on going home. The street was quiet, although there seemed to be more police cars than usual.

A shout broke the stillness. Novak dashed from the side street into the square. Dodging from side to side, he tried desperately to elude the pursuer. A gun cracked. Novak stumbled heavily, but went on. Two more shots slammed him into the gutter. Blood poured from the wounds in his back and trickled slowly through the dust.

Blind fury shook her. "Damn you!" she cried. "God damn you all to *hell!*"

Brushing away the tears, she forced herself to watch. She must know what happened next. Weisenstein had rushed forward. He knelt beside Novak, fingers on the pulse of an outflung hand. Security police carrying rifles and submachine guns swarmed from the hotel into the street. Elbowing roughly through the crowding Americans, they prodded Novak with their weapons. When Weisenstein made an outraged protest, an officer pushed him rudely away so that he too stumbled into the gutter. The Americans began to back away then and, intimidated, permitted themselves to be herded into the hotel. Sofians hurried by, knowing enough to avert their faces. In a few minutes a pickup truck arrived. Novak's body was tossed into the rear and covered with a rough tarpaulin. Eventually an old woman came and hosed away the blood.

"Dirty stinking bastards!" Susannah gritted through clenched teeth.

She could hear the Weisensteins coming down the hall, protesting loudly. The two Endicott sisters from Georgia were with them, sobbing hysterically. Quickly, Susannah crossed the room and opened the door. Already a uniformed security guard blocked her way. Others were hurrying down the hall to other rooms. Still more guards escorted the Weisensteins to their room next door. They all carried submachine guns.

"What happened?" Susannah cried.

"They killed a man. Shot him in the back," Weisenstein shouted over the heads of the guards.

Menacing guns silenced his continued protests and forced the guests into their rooms. Impatiently, Susannah slammed the door, hurried into the bathroom and banged on the wall until Weisenstein answered.

"Herb? Who killed the man?"

"The security police, I think."

A rifle butt hammered on her door, ending their conversation. It didn't matter. She had learned what she needed to know.

Slowly she returned to the bedroom and sank into its only chair. Her position was serious. It was all too obvious that Novak's cover had been blown. His part of the operation was exposed, and its participants would be arrested or shot in short order. Even more serious, Jess Simpson's murder meant that the operation had been exposed at CIA headquarters as well. To Susannah, it seemed that a determined effort was being made to unmask the entire Absalom operation and that she was caught in the middle. She could hope to carry out Novak's assignment only if no one knew to whom he had entrusted the mission. The security police had run out of the hotel. They must have been close enough to their quarry to know that Novak had been there. But were they close enough to know that he had talked to someone? Did they suspect whom?

She rose quietly and opened the door. The guards were there, stationed to watch several rooms at once.

"I'm hungry. When do we get our dinner?" Susannah demanded indignantly.

Indifferently, they waved her back inside. She complied. At least for now, she knew that they were watching everyone.

She went to her purse and took out *Dead Souls*. Its title was grimly prophetic. Thoughtfully, she turned to the title page, seeking the publisher's address. Yes, it had been printed in New York, and while it was not her idea of literature to vacation with, her possession of it was not illogical. Then she read page 51 carefully, paying attention to the condition of the paper and the printing. Nothing seemed unusual. Even when the page was held to the light, it looked entirely normal. It must contain a microdot or a special ink. She sighed deeply and closed the book. It had become a grave responsibility.

Suppose the police learned to whom Novak had talked? To whom could she turn for help? The American Embassy? Novak had said there was a leak and he didn't know where it was. An embassy wouldn't be safe. There were too many people who could talk, and in a Communist country, the very embassy walls might conceal listening devices.

The tour guides? Olaf was a gentle, smiling young man who clouded quickly at the least unpleasantness. Assassination and double-dealing were beyond his comprehension. Dimitri, their local guide, was Bulgarian and therefore out of the question.

The tour party itself? Of the eighteen other members, Susannah thought only Frank Phillips was a possibility. He was a retired executive of a large multinational industrial corporation. Quick and knowledgeable, he had traveled widely and would be helpful in an intellectual crisis. But he had had one heart attack. In the event of danger, it would not be fair to ask him to risk another.

Gradually, reluctantly, she had to conclude that she must act alone. She had tasted the intrigues of clandestine operations. She had been taught self-defense and the use of weapons, but her covert job with the CIA had never become dangerous enough to require use of these skills. Her cover had been blown quietly and she had been transferred to an overt bureaucratic job on the Soviet desk. Although that position had not been secret, something had kept her from mentioning her CIA career to anyone in the tour party. To them, and probably to the Bulgarian Government as well, she was just another tourist. And therein lay her only chance. She must continue with the group and avoid any action that would call attention to herself. She could only wait and be watchful.

Her chair was too low for her to see out, so she rose and stood at the window. The square below had become an armed camp. The hotel had been cordoned off. Guards patrolled around it, their weapons resting easily for instant use. Others lounged and smoked, waiting for their turn at duty. Blue-and-yellow vehicles of Bulgarian police jammed the square, but the boulevards beyond were deserted. By some covert network, Sofians had learned of political trouble at the Grand Hotel and were staying away.

When she was too tired to stand any longer, Susannah pulled the room's only table to a good vantage point, climbed up on it and settled her back against the wall. Carefully she eased the curtain back and opened the window so that she could hear and see without being seen. She watched for a long time.

Chapter 4

SHE MUST HAVE SLEPT. When she jerked up-right, it was dark. Her watch said midnight. Below, the street was quiet. The guards were still there, but now there was no milling or smoking. They seemed to be waiting. Susannah lit a cigarette and waited too.

Half an hour later, the guards began to move about expectantly. Up the street a limousine rounded the cathedral and approached slowly. It stopped before the hotel.

The guards snapped to attention. The rear door was opened and a man in civilian clothes stepped out. He ignored the men clustering around him, turned back to the car and snapped his fingers. A black Doberman pinscher jumped down. It stood while the man caressed its ears. Then it sat quietly at its master's heel. Only then did the man turn to the guards and shake hands with the commanding officer.

They talked. Gesturing widely, the Bulgarian officer described the shooting and led the man to the place where Novak had fallen The stranger stood and looked, and reached for a cigarette. A match flared in the Bulgarian's hand. The newcomer did not acknowledge the favor. He stood for a long moment staring into the gutter. Then he turned and looked up. His eyes roamed over the buildings in the square. Carefully, floor by flood, he surveyed the hotel. His gaze paused on Susan-nah's open window. She moved back. A moment more he stood and looked. Then he nodded and walked briskly into the hotel lobby. The Bulgarians hurried ahead and held the door for him. The dog paced quietly at his knee.

When nothing more happened, Susannah thought of going to bed. The jangle of the telephone stopped her.

Hesitantly, she picked it up. It was Olaf. Their guide's soft English was a little uncertain, uneasy in the crisis.

"I hope I didn't awaken you. I am sorry for the inconvenience. The hotel will serve supper in the mezzanine dining room in fifteen minutes if you wish to eat."

"Yes, thank you, Olaf. I am hungry."

"The guard will knock on your door and escort you."

"Olaf, why—"

"Please, Miss Clarke. I don't know why just yet. It concerns the shooting this afternoon. As soon as I know, I will tell everyone."

"Thank you, then."

There wasn't time to change clothes, but Susannah washed her face and applied fresh makeup. She wished it could mask her fear.

When the knock came, Susannah suddenly knew panic. In planning her strategy for the remainder of the trip, she had neglected to decide what to do with *Dead Souls* right now. She hesitated. There was nothing about the book that would betray it to the casual observer. It would be all right to leave it here. She tossed it onto the bed and turned away. Fear crawled then in her stomach. She couldn't just leave it, at least not without taking some precautions. And there wasn't time for that now. Almost desperately, she snatched it up again and stuffed it deep into her purse. Her hands were shaking as she opened the door and confronted the guard.

They were a subdued and diminished group that

gathered in the ugly plush dining room. The Weisensteins, Marlene, Olaf, the Reynoldses and, of course, the Elberts, who could never resist food. Surprisingly, Aggie Taliaferro was there too, her shoulders hunched as though she were cold. All together, they didn't fill two tables. Their voices echoed through the big room. Susannah moved to the far side of the second table and took a chair with her back to the wall. It gave her a clear view of the mezzanine, where two security guards paced. Their revolvers were in plain view.

"Who's next door?" Susannah asked when she became aware of the clamor of voices in the adjacent dining room.

"The Japanese," Marlene said dryly. "Who else?"

Susannah managed to smile. It was a large group of businessmen from Tokyo, traveling without wives. Nothing ever dampened their appetites or their enthusiasm.

Service was slow. Awkward under normal circumstances, the waiters had now lost all semblance of efficiency. The group waited restlessly, munching bread. There was nothing to drink, and Mrs. Elbert called repeatedly for tea, hot tea. The waiters ignored her.

"Hell. There won't be anything to drink or to eat either," Aggie suddenly said. She pulled a flask from her tote bag, poured the cap full of Scotch, and drank it in one gulp.

"I think you have the right idea," Reynolds muttered, but Aggie didn't offer to share her liquor. No one else said anything. The silence became uncomfortable.

The waiter brought a tureen of soup and began spooning it into their bowls. He was flustered and served hastily, balancing the tureen on his left hand and ladling awkwardly over the diner's shoulder. When he had served her without spilling any, Susannah looked up in relief.

The mezzanine guards had come to attention, but again the stranger with the dog ignored the mark of deference. He walked past them to the entrance of the dining room. There he stood quietly, deliberately surveying its occupants. His eyes rested a moment on Susannah before he turned to the headwaiter standing at his elbow.

"Look at *him!*" Marlene murmured.

"You look. I'm eating," Susannah retorted, dropping her eyes quickly to her plate.

"Pass the salt, please."

As Susannah handed it down to Myrna Weisenstein, her eyes went to the stranger's face. Now he was sitting at a table for four in the far corner. Three waiters hovered about him. *He* didn't have to wait for his food. The dog lay at his side.

The Americans ate hungrily. At the other table, the Elberts slurped audibly. Olaf sat with them. Olaf always had to sit with the Elberts.

"What nationality do you suppose he is?" Marlene asked.

"Would it matter?" Reynolds asked teasingly.

"He's too tall for an East European," Weisenstein noted.

"Not tall by Texas standards," Reynolds said.

"He's good enough looking to be Yugoslav," Kitty Reynolds said.

"Russian," Weisenstein answered positively.

"Russians are swine!" Aggie said with feeling. Her voice rasped, carrying clearly in the empty room. Susannah looked up. The stranger had lifted his eyes from his dinner and was glancing over the faces before him. His gaze came to Aggie, paused and went on. Then he continued eating. There had been no expression on his face.

"I don't think so," Marlene said, daring to contradict Aggie. "All that wildness and passion couldn't have died with the Revolution."

"It didn't die. It was murdered," Aggie answered roughly.

Marlene wasn't listening. She was staring openly at the man, a speculative expression on her face. "Do you suppose he's really Russian?" she asked thoughtfully.

"Go ask him. I dare you," Reynolds said. His wife tugged his arm warningly.

"All right, I will," Marlene said, rising to the bait.

"Please." Olaf interceded at their elbows. "We have instructions to stay together at our tables."

"Oh, very well," Marlene conceded. "But I'll find out. Just you wait, Hank Reynolds."

The animated banter continued. Only to someone who knew them well did it seem a little forced. The stranger's level gaze observed them closely, examining each member of the group in sequence. It always returned to Susannah. She ate quickly, her dark head bent. When she finished, she laid her knife and fork precisely side by side on the plate and reached for her cigarettes. Reynolds held his lighter for her and she turned to dip the cigarette into the flame, cupping her hand to steady its sudden flicker. When she looked up, her eye fell on the Russian and noticed his unwavering scrutiny. She turned her chair a little sideways so that he was no longer directly in her line of vision. But that was a mistake too, for now he watched her openly. She could feel his gaze.

Russian! Of course he was Russian, she thought. Novak's operation didn't concern Bulgaria. He was merely using it as a base for operations against his target, the Soviet Union. It hadn't taken the Russians long to get their man to Sofia!

The Americans rose together. Marlene, black eyes flashing, went first. At the stranger's table, she slowed deliberately. Immediately alert, the dog raised its head, ears upright. A low growl rumbled in its throat. In that moment, while Marlene occupied his attention, Susannah studied the man. For once, she agreed with Marlene's assessment. Whatever else he was, he was handsome, with thick, well-cut black hair and no trace of the peasant in his face. His cold stare rebuffed Marlene, who moved on, disconcerted. Behind her, Reynolds laughed and slapped her fanny. Marlene yelped. Susannah joined the general, rather shaky laughter.

The guards stopped them on the mezzanine and one with a rudimentary knowledge of English and a list in his hand grouped them by their floors and room numbers. Susannah kept her back to the dining room. As she moved to stand beside the Weisensteins, she saw that the Russian had risen and was standing at the window. But he was not looking out at the street. He was gazing intently and directly at her.

Chapter 5

SUSANNAH DIDN'T SLEEP THAT NIGHT. It had been three o'clock when she returned to her room. Gray dawn was already in the sky. She spent the remainder of the night perched on her table, watching. There wasn't anything to see except the play of light on the square. The stranger's limousine had gone. The security men went quietly about their duties. They ignored the streams of workers in blue coveralls hurrying to work. Susannah wondered if Novak had ever walked that way.

At nine o'clock three buses drew up and parked in the circle. The drivers were met by armed guards, but after they had identified themselves, the guards ignored them. They stood and talked quietly. Noises in the hotel told of activity. After a while, the Japanese tour group came out and filed smartly onto the first bus. The guards supervised the proceedings, and two of them accompanied the group. The bus drove up the boulevard and swung around the cathedral.

Gradually the hotel was emptied of its guests. Some were taken in cars. The organized tours went in buses.

After two hours, the Japanese returned without the guards and went inside. When they didn't come upstairs, Susannah assumed that they had stopped in the dining room. Enviously, she thought of lunch. The Elberts must be in positive agony.

At twelve-thirty, Olaf called.

"What's happening?" Susannah asked as soon as he had identified himself.

"Bulgarian security police wish to question all members of our party. We are to go at one o'clock."

"What do they want to know?"

"They haven't said. And I have not been able to find out. The other guests are being allowed to return, so I assume it is entirely routine. I was permitted to call our headquarters office. Carter's Worldwide Tours recommends that we answer all questions as honestly as we can. We do not believe that the police are interested in us."

"I see. Are they escorting us again?"

"Yes, indeed. Your guard will knock on your door. I will meet you downstairs."

"Has anyone called the American Embassy?"

"Carter's assured me that the embassy is fully informed and is trying to expedite our questioning. It's unfortunate that we lost our free day, but we won't have to delete any of our planned schedule in Bulgaria."

"That's good." Only a trace of dryness in her voice betrayed Susannah's wish that the group would be expelled from the country and sent to Zurich. There she could get a plane to Washington.

The same guard knocked on her door at exactly one o'clock. He looked rumpled and grumpy, and glared rudely at her. She ignored it.

The party milled uneasily about in front of the hotel while roll was called. Then, peremptorily, they were ordered to get onto the bus. For a moment the group hesitated, uncertain in the unfamiliar situation. Then Miss McMillan turned and, in a commanding voice, said, "Well, come along."

Susannah had to grin. How many times in her forty

years as a second-grade teacher had Miss McMillan
said "Well, come along" in just that tone?

As the group shuffled forward, Susannah and Marlene stepped aside. With the exception of the two
daughters taking graduation trips with their mothers,
they were the youngest members of the party, and it
was their custom to let the older ones go first. As
usual, Marlene was eyeing the men. She was bold, but
so far as Susannah knew, she had scored only once,
in Dubrovnik. Now Marlene edged over to Susannah.

"There he is," she murmured.

"Who?" Susannah asked. But she knew. She had
already seen him come out of the hotel. He stood on
the curb and watched the boarding with open interest.
The commanding officer of the Bulgarian police said
something to him, and he laughed outright. The Bulgarian seemed quietly gratified that his sally had been
a success.

"You know who," Marlene hissed. "The one with
the dog."

"Have you decided on his nationality yet?" Susannah asked.

"The man's or the dog's?"

"The man's. The dog is a German breed."

"Look. They're laughing at us. I bet he said something lewd."

"No doubt."

"Here he comes."

"Then here's your chance," Susannah said.

"Hell, no. Not as long as he has that dog."

"Marlene! I didn't think you were afraid of anything."

"I'm not afraid of anything that walks on two legs,
but do you see how close the dog keeps to him? He
might as well be six-legged."

"He's a beautifully trained animal."

"His master is the beautiful animal."

The man laughed.

"I think he understood you," Susannah said.

"I hope he did. I'll tell him my room number is three fourteen."

"Marlene, come on!" Susannah moved toward the bus.

Marlene laughed and followed. "Shall I tell him yours?"

Susannah didn't answer.

Suddenly, ordering his dog to stay behind, the stranger strode to the bus. He dismissed the driver, who was helping the women climb the steps, and took his place. He held out his hand to Marlene. She took it.

"Interested after all?" she asked challengingly.

He stared at her unblinkingly and handed her quickly up the steps. He turned immediately to Susannah.

Anticipating him, Susannah had already reached for the handrail. His hand closed on her upper arm and he held her back, stepping close to her as he did so. "It is *your* room I would wish to visit," he said softly.

Startled as much by hearing English as by what he said, Susannah looked directly up into his face.

No man should have eyes like that. Almond-shaped, not black but deep blue, with heavy lashes and strong winging brows. Their expression held her. There was no smile. He was not propositioning her. He was serious. The flush that had been climbing her throat faded. For a long moment they looked at each other. Susannah moved first. He let her go, but his hand lingered on her arm as he helped her up the steps.

She walked quickly down the aisle to her seat. The driver and the guards climbed in, and the door swung shut. The man stood directly under her window. Their eyes met. An expression glinted in his and was gone before she could read it.

"Looks like you beat Marlene's time."

"What?"

"You heard me," Weisenstein teased, leaning across the aisle. "What did he say to you?"

"I didn't understand it."

"He *is* Russian, in case you're interested. I heard him speaking it. He also speaks excellent Bulgarian. But keep away from that dog. It's a killer."

"How do you know? All Dobermans aren't killers."

"That one is. I tried to pat him and he nearly chewed my hand off." He stuck out his hand. The scratch was short and rather deep. It had bled.

"Serves you right for patting strange dogs," Aggie spoke up behind them.

"I appreciate the warning," Susannah said to Weisenstein when Aggie didn't comment any further. "Did you find out anything else about the man?"

"I tried to speak to him but he didn't choose to understand my Russian." Susannah smiled sympathetically at the indignant note in Weisenstein's voice. "He's important. He's being treated extremely well. And if you want further proof, he wears a gray suit."

Susannah looked mystified.

"You've never been to Russia. All the important bureaucrats, the apparatchiki, wear gray suits. It's a uniform, but better. In fact, though they would deny it, it really is the mark of the privileged class."

"Then what is he doing here?"

Weisenstein had just had time to shrug when the guards got up. They stood a moment, machine guns cradled in their arms. Then, stolidly, they moved to the front as the bus passed the Balkan Hotel, turned right and stopped before a gray neo-Renaissance building. Beyond the small park gleamed the white headquarters of the Communist Party.

Security police swarmed around the bus, blocking

from view the American Embassy limousine standing at the curb, its fender flags curling in the breeze. Three men waited beside it. Two of them moved through the guards to board the bus. They introduced themselves to Olaf and Dimitri. Then they turned to face the silent group.

"My name is Donald Trapp. And this is Sam Murphy. We are consular officers of the American Embassy. We regret the inconvenience you have suffered. I know you'll be glad to hear it is only temporary. The Foreign Minister has just assured our ambassador that Bulgaria seeks to obtain information leading to the eradication of a narcotics ring."

"Are we to believe that?" Phillips spoke up from the middle of the bus.

"It might be wise to appear to. We believe there is more to this situation than we know. Nevertheless, you'll be asked to present your identification and to describe what you saw of the shooting incident in front of your hotel yesterday afternoon. If there is more, we don't know it. Be careful. Say nothing political and make your answers short. Now, did any of you actually witness the shooting?"

There was a babble of voices. Four hands were raised.

"I see. Thank you. What is your name, sir?"

"Herbert Weisenstein. I'm a physician from Philadelphia."

"Dr. Weisenstein, you and those who were with you must be prepared to be interrogated rather closely. Everyone else can expect routine questioning. The regime certainly doesn't want to endanger its tourism by unfavorable publicity. The police have been courteous to others questioned today. We have no reason to anticipate anything worse. There are enough translators so you shouldn't have to wait long. Now, are there any questions?"

No one spoke.

"All right, then. Let's go."

Chapter 6

THE UGLY LITTLE ROOM with the chipped conference table smelled of faulty plumbing. There were no chairs to sit on and nothing to read. *Dead Souls* was in her purse, but Susannah was afraid to take it out. She leaned against the wall and smoked and timed each individual's interrogation. They were being called alphabetically. She would be sixth and, she hoped, reasonably inconspicuous.

It was almost her turn when Ed Elbert edged closer to her. "Are you nervous?" he asked.

He was a heavyset man with a snout for a nose and a nasty habit of fondling any woman within reach. Susannah didn't like him and had often found it necessary to be rude to him. Now, apprehensive over the coming ordeal, she was in no mood to be patient.

"No," she said coldly.

"I'm not nervous either," he said. When she made no further comment, he added, "But then, I have nothing to hide."

"That's good."

Susannah didn't look at him as she carefully stubbed out her cigarette in the room's only ashtray.

"But you do," he said softly.

She controlled the impulse to jerk upright. "I don't know what you mean," she said coldly. She put the ashtray on the table and was standing at the door when Trapp called her name. Her knees were shaking as she followed him down the hall to a smaller room. There, two men in the two-toned khaki and red shoulder boards of the security police and a woman in drab civilian clothes were seated at a table. Trapp introduced them, but Susannah didn't get their names.

"Your passport, please," the woman said. She was the translator.

Susannah handed it over.

"Is this your first trip to Bulgaria?"

"Yes."

"Sign this, please."

Susannah signed a small card which they compared closely with the signature in her passport. When they were satisfied that there was no forgery, they studied the passport photograph and compared it feature for feature with Susannah's face.

"Stand and turn around, please."

Susannah stood and turned. Trapp watched warily as the two men muttered together in Bulgarian. Finally, they returned the passport to her.

"Where were you at 4:10 P.M. yesterday afternoon?"

"In my room at the hotel."

"Did you see the shooting?"

"No."

"Why not?"

"I was in the bathroom. The window was closed. I did hear something faintly, and when I went to look, it was over."

"Do you recognize this man?"

He handed her a photograph. It was a snapshot of Novak, a younger Novak, dressed in street clothes. He had been photographed in a bookstore, but the picture was too blurred for her to ascertain the shop's nationality. Instinct told her it was neither Bulgarian nor American. She shook her head slowly. "No."

In the second picture, Novak wore a moustache and glasses and looked like a different man. "No," she said.

There was one more, of Novak in his Bulgarian working clothes. It had been taken recently. Suddenly not able to trust her voice, Susannah shook her head and returned it.

"What exactly did you see of the incident?"

To give herself a little time to recover, Susannah lit a cigarette. Then she answered steadily. "Only a body in the street. I didn't see that very well because of the crowd."

"Can anyone confirm that you were in your room?"

"Dr. and Mrs. Weisenstein and the Misses Endicott."

"Very well. May we see your purse?"

"We were searched in Belgrade before boarding the plane."

"Please." It was said politely, but it was an order. Susannah looked at Trapp. When he nodded that she should comply, she handed the purse to the officer.

The contents were dumped on the table. One by one, the items were inspected. They opened her package of cigarettes and examined each one separately. They dismantled and inspected her lipstick and fountain pen and felt the lining of her purse. When they picked up the camera and started to open it, Susannah stopped them.

"Wait! Don't ruin my film."

A little surprised at her boldness, they stopped and looked up.

"There's only one picture left. Let me expose it, so I won't lose the roll."

Her request was translated. The senior officer considered it. Clearly, he didn't like the idea.

"It would be a courtesy," Trapp said quietly. Only then did the officer nod reluctantly and grant permission. With the lens covered, Susannah snapped the last picture, rolled the film and handed the camera back to him. He opened it, took out the film and batteries and deliberately inspected the cavity with a flashlight. Then, gesturing for Susannah to reassemble it, he laid aside the film and took up the paperback book.

Susannah sat quietly, praying that her apprehension didn't show. The officer leafed through it, shook its pages free and put it down.

"You may replace the items in your handbag now," the translator said. "Your film will be returned to you at the airport when you exit the country. That will be all."

Gratefully, Susannah preceded Trapp from the room. "Are all the sessions like that one?" she asked when the door had closed behind them.

"Pretty much. You were lucky they didn't ruin your film. The Japanese were furious with them for that and protested through diplomatic channels. They're getting tired now, and they aren't as thorough as they were this morning. Your group won't have much longer to wait."

"Good," Susannah said dryly. "I was warned about the possible inconvenience of traveling in Eastern Europe, but this has been a bit much."

"Exactly. Thank you for cooperating."

Trapp called for Ed Elbert next, and Susannah stood by the Phillipses.

"How was it?" Frank Phillips asked.

"Irritating, but not bad," Susannah said.

"That seems to be the consensus, then. Have a candy?" He offered her rock candy from a bag he took from his pocket. Susannah recognized the brand they had all purchased in Yugoslavia.

"Yes, thank you."

Her thoughts turned to Elbert. Did he know something, or was he bluffing? Either way, the pest threatened to become a menace. Her cover of inconspicuousness depended upon how well she handled him. She timed his absence with care, and when she was able to conclude that his interrogation was no longer or shorter than any of the others, she relaxed a little. Had he made any startling revelations, his session with the police would have been prolonged. As expected, the Endicott sisters and the Weisensteins were questioned at length. The only surprise of that long afternoon was that the police kept Aggie Taliaferro for an hour.

It was six o'clock when they were dismissed. The guards were no longer interested in them, and Trapp guided them from the building. The tourists gave a ragged little cheer as they stepped into the street and left the clammy odors behind. Miss McMillan led the way directly to the bus. There was no dawdling this time. Everyone was anxious to leave. Only Marlene lingered. She had found someone to talk to.

Curiously, Susannah studied the man with Marlene. He was six feet tall and slender. A Vandyke beard adorned a face that was oddly unformed for a man apparently in his late thirties. But it was his attire that arrested attention. Like an apparition from another era, he wore a black pin-striped double-breasted suit, a white shirt, white tie, red suspenders and a Panama hat with a red band. His black patent leather shoes were partially covered by white spats. The clipboard and pencil in his hand struck an incongruous note as he leaned against the embassy limousine and languidly chatted with Marlene. Occasionally his eyes lifted to the group as if to check on the progress of the loading.

"He's a strange-looking young man," Christine Endicott commented to her sister. "Is he American?"

"Of course he's American. He's on the embassy staff, I should imagine. He was here with those other young men when we went in," Azalea Endicott replied.

"If he's an example of our diplomatic service, I'm going to write my Congressman."

"Now, don't be old-fashioned. That's the style these days."

"It was the style in our day, you mean. Here, give me that tote bag before you spill everything. Why do you insist on carrying it by only one handle?"

Susannah had to smile. The tote bag was voluminous and heavy, and why anyone would want to lug such a thing on a trip she didn't know. The two sisters climbed onto the bus, bantering back and forth as sisters who are close do. Susannah followed them to her own seat. Then she looked out.

She knew several members of the Foreign Service whose admission to that elite corps had always puzzled her, but this man exceeded even their eccentricity. The man now came forward to help Marlene onto the bus, while to one side Trapp talked quietly with Olaf.

"Do you mind giving one of Mr. Trapp's colleagues a lift to the hotel?" Olaf asked the group a moment later. "It's difficult to get a taxi at this hour of the evening."

When a general nod of heads assented, Olaf beckoned to the man in the pin-striped suit to board the bus. Trapp introduced him as Vladimir Voorhies from Washington and slapped him on the back as he passed down the aisle to join Marlene in the rear. Then Trapp thanked everyone for cooperating, and with a cheery wave and a smiling wish for a good trip from here on, he swung off the bus.

As the bus left Sofia's Red Square behind, Susannah glanced backward. Voorhies was lighting a slender cigar with an Italian wax match. Marlene was smiling eagerly up at him. Susannah put her head back and closed her eyes. She was hungry and tired, and tension was making her head ache. But she had passed the first hurdle.

Chapter 7

THE TOUR GATHERED PROMPTLY at seven o'clock on the top floor of the hotel. To compensate for the ruined day, the Balkantourist agency was treating them to an especially elaborate dinner at the hotel's Panorama Restaurant, free of extra charge. To show that they recognized the gesture, the women on the tour had agreed among themselves to bring out their party dresses. Some were a little wrinkled from the suitcases, but everyone looked festive. Susannah lagged behind until the Elberts were seated. Then she slipped into the one remaining chair at the table occupied by the Phillipses, Miss McMillan, Miss Tillie Cary and Aggie Taliaferro. Aggie had been drinking in her room and was sullen and uncommunicative company. Nevertheless, Susannah was satisfied; she had outmaneuvered Ed Elbert, and now she could try to enjoy the dinner.

Unlike the dining room where they ate every day, this restaurant was truly elegant. Arranged and partitioned to create an atmosphere of intimacy, it was decorated with fresh red and pink carnations. Fine crystal and silver shone on damask linen, and bottles of Bulgaria's best wines lay in coolers at each table. The thick red carpet muffled the sounds of cutlery on china. The waiters, while not up to Paris standards, were pleasant and helpful within the limits of the language barrier. Susannah glanced around. Marlene and Vladimir Voorhies occupied a table for two out on the terrace. They could be seen through the filmy curtain, leaning close and whispering. The Elberts were out of sight behind the partition in the rear section of the dining room. *Dead Souls* was hidden in the purse at her feet. Except for the undercurrent of outrage in the murmur of voices, everything was perfect. Then the Russian crossed her line of vision. He was speaking to the headwaiter and gesturing to a table for four by the window. The waiter led the way and with a little bow held his chair. The Doberman settled at his feet. The Russian had placed himself carefully. His back was protected by a solid wall. His view of Susannah was unobstructed.

The party lingered over dinner, indignantly discussing the day's events. Susannah tried to relax and laugh at Frank Phillips' witty account of his interrogation. Her own had been very similar, but she had been too apprehensive to see anything amusing in it.

"It's not funny!" Aggie's rasping voice broke into the general mirth that followed Frank's description of the search of his camera. The venom in her tone stilled the laughter.

"Well, *I* thought it was," Phillips said defensively. "But what did they ask you? Why did they keep you so long?"

"They recognized my name."

"Recognized your name! Have you been to Bulgaria before?"

"During the war."

She had their full attention now. With prodding from Miss McMillan and everyone's interest to encourage her, the story came out.

Agatha Taliaferro's husband had been an airline pilot who had flown to England and joined the RAF the week after Hitler invaded Poland. When he was killed in the Battle of Britain, Aggie forgot the promptness with which he had left her. She was the widow of a war hero, a man decorated posthumously for gallantry by the British Government. She went to London to accept his award and stayed on to help the war effort. On the melodramatic ground that she had nothing left to live for, she volunteered for intelligence work. Tough, smart and insensitive enough to be absolutely ruthless, she was good. She built a reputation for deviousness that no other woman equaled. Even capture by a roving German SS patrol had not daunted her. She flirted, lied and finally machine-gunned her way out of captivity. By war's end, she was a skilled underground agent specializing in operations along Greece's northern border with Bulgaria. After one particularly successful operation, the Nazis placed a price on her head. She had been one of the first employees of General "Wild Bill" Donovan's Office of Strategic Services, which in time became the nucleus of Allan Dulles' CIA. There she spent twenty years in clandestine work, only to be fired six years before retirement age by an upstart whiz kid, a new and younger man whose inexperience made him totally unappreciative of Aggie's knowledge.

The severance had been complete. It angered her that no one sought her advice afterward, and it baffled her that on the rare occasions when she did encounter former colleagues, they refused to discuss the people and activities that had been her life. She was an embittered old woman, and she used abusive language to describe those who had misused her. Her voice rose until it was audible through the dining room. Apprehensively, Susannah glanced around.

The Russian didn't seem to be listening. He was opening an envelope the waiter had brought him. He read the single sheet inside and with a curt little nod indicated that there would be no reply. Then, contemptuously, he wadded the paper in his hand. For an instant, he seemed undecided what to do with it; then he shrugged and stuffed it into his pocket. Quickly, before he could notice that she was watching, Susannah turned her attention back to Aggie. The older woman had drained her wineglass, and the waiter was hovering, waiting to pour more. Aggie held out her glass, but at the last minute put it down again.

"No. That tastes like vinegar. Bring me something substantial. Bring me some Scotch."

The waiter looked blank.

"Scotch. Scotch. Whisky," Aggie ordered impatiently. She pulled a twenty-dollar bill from her wallet and dropped it carelessly onto the table. "Scotch," she repeated loudly.

The waiter finally understood, for he brought an old-fashioned glass filled to the brim with the liquor. It didn't have any ice.

Aggie swore and took a big swallow of the liquid. She dipped ice from the wine cooler at her elbow and dumped it into the glass. Susannah watched her thoughtfully. She knew precisely why Aggie had been retired, and while she sympathized with her disappointment, she agreed entirely with the decision. Alcohol was no keeper of classified information. Aggie Taliaferro had become a security risk.

Aggie's abrasive manner with the waiter had embarrassed the others and dispelled their sympathy. They fidgeted a little, lighting cigarettes and fiddling with their wineglasses, until Mrs. Phillips changed the subject.

"Where's Olaf? Isn't he going to eat tonight?" she asked.

"He was downstairs when we came up," Miss McMillan answered. "He looked upset."

"He was questioned this afternoon," Phillips said. "Do you suppose those bastards gave him a rough time?"

"I can't imagine that he would know anything sinister," Louise Phillips answered. "He's such a nice boy."

"Nice boys can be killers," Aggie said shortly.

"It's another mystery," Miss McMillan said.

"What's the first one?" Phillips asked.

"Marlene, of course. Who *is* that young man?"

"He works for the embassy," Miss Tillie answered.

"Have you talked to him? What does the embassy think about our interrogation?"

"No, I haven't. And I'd like to wait up and ask him, but they are not going to quit anytime soon. I'd better go to bed."

Everyone turned to look out on the terrace. Marlene and her escort were pantomiming kisses. The Russian was quietly amused.

"Marlene can tell you *all* about him tomorrow," Phillips consoled.

"She undoubtedly can, but in her place, *I* wouldn't tell a thing," Miss Tillie retorted. Her nose twitched mischievously.

They all laughed and rose. Susannah was tired. The strain of looking and acting normal was exhausting, and she was anxious to be alone. But the others had risen too, and the party mingled together, discussing once again the meaning of the day. Susannah glimpsed Ed Elbert edging closer. He had already dismissed his wife, and Imogene was walking out of the restaurant with Miss Tillie. Hastily, Susannah excused herself, hoping to get away before Elbert reached her. She moved quickly, but the Russian was watching, and rising swiftly, he stopped her with a hand on her arm.

"Miss Clarke, will you join me?"

Susannah looked up at him. He was smiling a little, his head tilted, his expression attentive. There was a cleft in his chin. She turned her head. Ed Elbert was waiting for her. Trapped, she hesitated, weighing the unpleasant alternatives. The Russian took her arm firmly. "I am not to be refused," he said softly.

"Then I must," she answered.

"Will you be cold if we drink on the terrace?"

She shook her head.

He led her to a table at the end of the terrace and seated her ceremoniously. He kept for himself the place overlooking the square and the cathedral, again with his back to the wall and his chair turned so that he could see Susannah and, through the curtains, the entire dining room. He was a cautious man.

"Two slivovas," he said to the waiter.

The Russian turned then to look at Susannah. Without speaking, he studied her closely. She was small and finely boned, with a mass of black hair worn in a chignon. Her complexion was porcelain pale, her profile delicately chiseled. She wore a short silky black dress with ruffles around a low V neck and at the wrists of the filmy sleeves. Her fine legs were sheathed in dark stockings, sheer and smooth-looking. He found her provocative—quite a treasure to find in drab Sofia. He had noticed that she smiled frequently and that her gray eyes were clear and alert. Like fine bone china, she looked expensive and fragile, but he sensed that she would not break easily. There was no smile now on her pale face. Her eyes were watchful, even guarded. As an unusually handsome man, he was accustomed to flattering female attention. This woman wasn't reacting to him in the usual way. He began to wonder why.

"I don't know your name," she said into the lengthening silence. Her voice was soft, surprisingly deep.

"Aleksei Azarov."

"And how did you learn mine, Aleksei Azarov?"

An enigmatic expression crossed his face. "I asked Dimitri," he said after a moment.

"What else did you ask him?"

Azarov threw back his head and laughed in real appreciation. There were laugh lines around his eyes, and the deep lines around his mouth, severe when he was solemn, now seemed to have been made by laughter. "I asked him to tell me everything. I learned that you are from Fredericksburg, Virginia, that you are thirty-three years old, that you were traveling alone and that you drink coffee instead of tea. And he said one other thing."

"And that was?"

"That you are not a difficult tourist."

"I'm glad he thinks that."

"But there was one thing he did not know."

"What was that?"

"He said that you were neither a Miss nor a Mrs. but a Ms. What is that?"

"It's a new form of feminine address in America, used regardless of marital status. Business and professional women particularly find it quite helpful."

"I think it hides the fact that you are not married."

He was testing her. Susannah smiled faintly. "It does, yes. It also gives a woman protection."

"But it leaves unanswered the question. How is a man to know?"

"He must ask."

"I asked and I did not receive an answer."

"You didn't ask the right person."

He smiled as he grasped her meaning. "You are not married, so I do not need to ask after all."

"How do you know?"

"Your hands."

"I left my rings at home."

"It is not necessary to see the rings to know that they have been worn." He reached and touched her right hand. "You wear rings here and here, but not on your left hand."

"You are very observant," Susannah murmured. Too damned observant. It was unnerving.

The waiter quietly placed their drinks before them. Azarov dismissed him with a nod and raised his glass. "I drink to you," he said with more meaning in his voice than a friendly little toast required.

"Thank you."

They sipped in silence. Susannah didn't help him.

"Dimitri also said you were a dealer in antiques," Azarov said finally.

"Yes."

"Why did you come to Eastern Europe? There is nothing to buy or sell here."

Why indeed? Susannah's eyes clouded. Azarov watched her face closely. He sensed a personal tragedy which he wanted to know about. He let the matter pass. He could ask about it later.

"It is my vacation," Susannah explained. "I have been everywhere else. I wanted to see the Balkans."

Azarov nodded. He knew that could be true.

"I generally combine my buying trips and vacations. It saves the extra air fare across the Atlantic. And you? What brings you to Sofia?"

"A holiday also." Susannah didn't believe that. There were Russian workers vacationing at the hotel, but Azarov was not one of them.

"Where is your business located?" he asked.

"Outside Fredericksburg. Here is my business card."

She took it from her purse and handed it to him. It bore a picture of her shop and, on the back, a map showing how to reach it. Azarov studied the card carefully.

"Clarke House—Antiques and Objets d'Art," he read. "Do you live here, too?"

"Yes."

"Who lives with you?"

"Only Max and Frederica."

"They are relatives?"

Now she smiled a little. "No, they are dogs. Doberman pinschers."

"So that is why Ivan did not disturb you." Hearing
his name, the dog raised his head. Azarov fondled his
ears absently while he studied her card. "It's a big house
for a woman alone." There was a thoughtful tone in his
voice, not quite an envious one, as he looked at the
picture of the big Georgian house with its tall chim-
neys. "Do you own this house?"

"My family does."

"And is the house an antique too?"

"Yes."

"I see." Reluctantly, he handed the card back to
her.

"Would you like to keep it?"

"Yes," he said with a slow smile, and put it in his
wallet.

Seeing that her glass was empty, he signaled the
waiter. To fill the silence, Susannah reached for a
cigarette. Azarov held the match for her. She didn't
cup her hand intimately around the flame as he had seen
her do the evening before. Having watched her now
for two evenings, he felt that she was being abnormally
reserved. He decided to probe.

"You smile for your friends, but not for me," he
said. "Why?"

"I don't feel like smiling now."

She stared into her glass and moved it in little squares
on the table.

"Is it the shooting?" he asked finally.

"Yes."

"It is not important."

"Then why are we held and questioned?"

"He was a narcotics smuggler, guilty of corrupting

young people. Those who helped him must be found. Why should you care about a petty criminal?"

"He was a human being."

"He preyed on society. He had to be punished."

"It was not necessary to shoot him."

"He would have been shot anyway."

"He deserved a trial." Her gray eyes darkened with anger.

"Why are you angry with me? I had nothing to do with it."

"You are a member of the system. You condoned it."

"There are shootings in your country. Criminals, bank robbers, narcotics peddlers, spies, thieves are shot by the police while trying to escape. Do you condone that?"

Susannah suddenly felt she was drowning. That word "spies," spoken softly in a voice as smooth as black velvet, had been slipped into the conversation on purpose. Could he know? She could say nothing.

"Do you?" he insisted.

She managed to shake her head.

"Yet you remain a member of your system. You would not consider changing?"

She nodded again.

"You were questioned today?"

He took her silence for assent.

"Did they accuse you of any knowledge of the criminal? Did they find heroin in your handbag? Did they threaten you in any way?"

He sounded like an interrogator. He even looked like an interrogator—his eyes narrowed, intent on her every reaction. Susannah was numb. She could only shake her head.

"Did they show you photographs?"

This time, he waited for a spoken answer. Susannah

forced her mind to operate. It seemed to take a long time.

"Yes," she said finally. Her voice cracked a little. "Yes," she repeated more steadily.

"How many?"

"Three."

"Did you identify them?"

"No."

"And they dismissed you?"

"Yes."

"They don't wish to see you again?"

"No."

He lifted his hand in a little gesture of finality. His voice relaxed. "Then you have nothing to worry about. We are not butchers, you see. We wish only for a little cooperation in apprehending a parasite on society. You cannot blame us for that."

Susannah said nothing. The silence stretched.

"Would you care for another cigarette?" he asked, offering her his own pack.

Susannah shook her head. Her hands were twined around her glass. He couldn't be allowed to see how badly they were shaking.

He studied her. On the surface she seemed composed, but her face was too pale. He saw the trembling hands and the way she avoided his eyes. He felt her fear.

"Then drink your brandy and we will speak of more pleasant things. Tell me, who is in the family you mentioned?"

Susannah swallowed the brandy down. The fiery sensation helped. When she was able to look into his eyes, she saw that the grimness that had marked his face a moment ago was gone entirely. Now it seemed open, friendly, pleasant, even candid. The straight mouth was humorous. The face of mine enemy, she thought, is entirely too appealing. It made him all the more deadly.

"My parents are retired from the farm and live in Fredericksburg now," she said finally. "I have six brothers."

"Six!" He did not lean forward or otherwise alter his position, but his expression betrayed his interest. "With so many brothers to protect you, why do you need dogs?" he asked.

The dangerous subject was over. Now he was simply a man interested in a woman. Except that the woman could not forget that other Aleksei Azarov.

"My brothers no longer live in Fredericksburg, and I have no neighbors nearby. Living alone and advertising a business there, I just feel safer with the dogs." Relieved that her voice sounded normal, Susannah began to relax a trifle.

"You would be molested?"

"It could happen. It has in the past."

"That would not occur in my country." His tone was positive.

In reaction, her anger flared. "Freedom includes the freedom to be bad," she snapped.

"We are free and we are not bad."

"That depends upon definitions."

At that moment, the dog got up and put a paw on Azarov's knee.

"Now?" Azarov said in Russian. Susannah had to smile.

Azarov rose. "Walk with me, Miss Clarke," he said.

"I'd rather not. Thank you for the brandy. I'll say good night."

The commanding hand stopped her. "I want you to. I must know you."

"Why?"

"What are you afraid of?"

Susannah stopped. Careful. She had survived his inquisition. Her defense still lay in being a tourist, innocent, willing to talk to a handsome stranger.

"Please," he said. "We will not talk of ideologies."

"Tell me one thing first."

"What is that?"

"Are you a Communist?"

"Why is that important?"

"I don't like politicians."

"Is that why you came to Eastern Europe? To escape a politician?"

"That is no concern of yours."

"Did such a man make you unhappy? I want to know. I make your welfare my concern."

"I wish you wouldn't," she said sharply, turning and walking quickly away from him. This man knew far too much. He was dangerous, and she was vulnerable. He couldn't be permitted to guess just how vulnerable.

He caught up with her at the elevator. "But I will. I want to," he said softly. His eyes lingered on her face and caressed the curve of her throat in the ruffles. He reached for her hand and laid it in the crook of his elbow. "Now walk with me," he said.

It was quietly spoken, but it was an order. He held her hand on his arm as they rode the elevator to the lobby. Only two guards remained on duty. They stiffened respectfully and held the doors for them as they walked into the street.

Outside, several members of the tour were sitting over coffee and brandy in the sidewalk café. Ed Elbert was one of them. Azarov led Susannah away from them, around the curve of the square, past the place where Novak had died. The Russian made no sign that he noticed it. Susannah glanced at him. He was looking ahead, up the street, eyeing the cathedral appreciatively. His face was relaxed.

Butcher! She thought fiercely.

Sensing her change in mood, he looked down at her with a quizzical little smile.

Quickly she said, "Your dog doesn't know he is a Russian."

"How can you say that?"

"Look at him."

The dog had been given permission to run. He raced ahead, running and urinating happily and running again. Now he was carefully sniffing a lamppost, trying to decide if it was a suitable place.

"My dogs behave in exactly the same way," she said. "It's a game with them. It's a game with your dog too."

"So you must be living with two Russians." He laughed heartily at her expression. He was genuinely amused, she noticed.

"I purchased Ivan's mother in Berlin a number of years ago," he said when his laughter died. "Ivan was her best pup."

"Do you breed them?"

"No. Only Ivan."

"Dr. Weisenstein believes he's a killer."

"If I order it."

The quietly spoken words were chilling. Susannah said nothing.

"Now you are afraid of me?"

"You are to be feared."

"Do you believe I could order a dog against you?"

"You trained him to kill."

"For my own protection."

"You said that was not necessary in your country."

"You argue well. I like that in a woman."

"Does it make you nervous to have Ivan around your family?"

"I have no family."

"No one?"

"No."

The park smelled of tea roses. They walked quietly, saying nothing.

"You are from Moscow?" Susannah asked after a while.

"I live there."

"And you work for the government?"

"Yes."

"What do you do?"

"I am a planner."

"That isn't very descriptive."

"Planning isn't easy to describe. Isn't that your friend Miss Wells?"

Susannah glanced at the two figures sitting on the bench beside the path. "Yes."

As she looked, the man in the pin-striped suit slipped his hand under Marlene's skirt. Susannah looked quickly away. Her reaction amused Azarov. He laughed softly and clasped her hand more intimately. Susannah wondered if she would be able to get away from him without a scene.

"Who is that man?" Azarov asked.

"His name is Vladimir Voorhies. She met him today."

"Why do you suppose he wears a beard?"

"To hide a weak face."

Azarov smiled. "Beware of men who have something to hide."

"Does that include you?"

"You can trust me completely. Is Miss Wells a good friend of yours?"

"No."

"I'm pleased to hear it. I don't like women with loud voices."

Now Susannah laughed. "Did you ask Dimitri about Marlene too?"

"No. He told me about her first, thinking she was

the one I was interested in. She is not like you. She is a chameleon. Fascinating, but inconstant. Do you like her?"

"She is quite entertaining. She has traveled everywhere in the world."

Azarov led her to a secluded bench. He released her hand but sat close to her, turned so that he faced her. His eyes wandered over her body. He could smell her perfume. "Why have you never married?" he asked.

He sensed immediate withdrawal, even a slight defensiveness.

"I have my reasons," she said.

"Do you want to be?"

"I don't have time."

"Do you have a lover?"

"I am not prying about the women in your life."

"Do you want to know?"

"No."

"I am divorced."

"I'm sorry."

"There is nothing to be sorry for. It was a marriage of convenience. When she met someone she loved, we separated. They live in East Germany. She is quite happy."

"And you?"

"I have my work."

"And Ivan to talk to."

"Tonight I have you."

"And I must go. It's very late and we start early tomorrow."

"Stay with me awhile longer."

She took a heavy gold watch on a chain from her purse, opened the cover and turned it into the moonlight so that he could see its face. "It's after midnight," she said. "I'm tired."

Azarov rose then, whistled for the dog and led

Susannah back through the park. Marlene and Voorhies had gone. They saw no one. The well-lighted streets were deserted. Neither spoke. From time to time, Azarov glanced down at her, savoring the daintiness that contrasted so strongly with the stolid amplitude of Soviet women. She was aware of his gaze and was disturbed that she was.

Only Aggie and Dr. Weisenstein remained on the terrace. Weisenstein grinned knowingly when he saw how closely the Russian held Susannah's arm. Susannah wished them good night in an even tone and they passed into the lobby.

She had hoped to say good-bye to Azarov there, but changed her mind when she saw Olaf and Elbert at the desk. Olaf signaled to her to wait and then crossed the lobby hurriedly to speak to her. Elbert followed.

"Miss Clarke, I must tell you. I will be leaving you in the morning," the guide said.

"But why, Olaf?"

"There has been a death in my family. I have received permission from Carter's Tours to return home. Another guide will be here in time to take you to Plovdiv. His name is Hans Goethe. He's experienced. You will like him."

"We shall be very sorry to lose you, Olaf. You have made it an enjoyable trip for us. The others will be as disappointed as I am. Will you be here to tell them?"

"I must leave before breakfast to catch my plane, but I will speak to those who come down early. I am sorry, very sorry, to leave you."

"And I am distressed that you must go in sad circumstances. Our thoughts and sympathy will be with you."

"Thank you, Miss Clarke. Good night."

Olaf returned to the desk. Susannah looked after him. She liked Olaf. He had been a gracious guide and a considerate traveling companion. He would not have

been able to help her if she needed it, but he was pre-
dictable. Hans would be a new uncertainty.

Elbert's touch on her shoulder interrupted her
thoughts.

"Are you going upstairs?" he asked.

Susannah reached for Azarov's arm. Her gesture, in
contrast to her former reserve, surprised him, but his
hand closed possessively over hers. He looked from
Elbert to Susannah and back to Elbert as she said
coolly, "Yes. Good night, Mr. Elbert." Then she led the
Russian to the elevator.

As soon as the doors closed, she dropped his arm and
slowly took the key from her purse.

Azarov went directly to her room without asking for
its number. He took the key on its heavy bronze holder
from her hand and inserted it into the lock. When he
too had difficulty with it, Susannah smiled a little.
Azarov saw her expression.

"The little things may not work," he said, "but the
big things do."

"I was afraid of that."

"Why should you be afraid? Our intentions are
honorable."

"It wasn't too long ago that one of your leaders
threatened to bury us. Is that honorable?"

"If you are buried, I will spare you."

"You would take the trouble?"

"You have a saying, I believe: finders keepers. I
have found you. I want to keep you . . . alive."

"Do I have anything to say about it?"

"No."

He shook her hand formally, then closed his free
hand over their clasped ones. With a little jolt, Susannah
realized how callused his palms were. They were as
hard, as rough and horny, as a laborer's. It was in-

consistent with the smooth manner and the cultured voice.

"Good-bye, Mr. Azarov."

"Aleksei."

"Aleksei, then. Thank you for the brandy."

"We will drink again together. Good night, Susannah."

Pulling her hand from his, Susannah walked into her room and turned to shut the door. He had not moved. There was a speculative expression in his eyes as he watched her. With a final nod of farewell, she closed and locked the door and leaned against it. The encounter was over. She began trembling violently.

Chapter 8

IT WAS MIDMORNING. The new guide had arrived and the luggage had been loaded. Today Susannah was the first to enter the bus. She sat and watched the others file slowly on board. Suddenly, she felt lonely—lonely and very frightened. Her eyes sought the place where Novak had died and lingered as the bus started up and pulled slowly out of the square. The delicate scent of tea roses along the highway was refreshing, yet the endless lines of flowers to the horizon only depressed her. They seemed to emphasize her helplessness.

With an effort, she finally roused herself from her thoughts. "Miss Tillie wanted to talk to you," she commented to Marlene, who was her seatmate today.

"I know. I sat with her at breakfast. She had more questions than my mother."

"Tell me about Vladimir Voorhies. What is he doing in Sofia?"

"Trying to get a visa into Russia."

"Why does he want to go there?"

"His mother is Russian-born. She's seventy-five and in poor health. Her only other living relative is an older sister in Kiev who wants to emigrate to the United States. Vladimir is waiting for permission to go help her move."

"Will the Soviet Government let her out?"

"He believes so. They have spoken favorably of his petition. It would be one less pension to pay."

"What's he doing here?"

"Just waiting. He's been traveling in Eastern Europe, visiting our embassies."

"Is he with the State Department?"

"He didn't say. I believe he has a classified job. I didn't press it. He's rented a car and is coming to Plovdiv. Is he behind us?"

By leaning forward a little, Susannah could see through the driver's rearview mirror. There was a car just behind the bus. The man at the wheel wore sunglasses. He drove easily, his elbow resting casually on the sill of the open window, his hands toying loosely with the steering wheel. He looked American, but it was not Vladimir Voorhies. Susannah's mouth suddenly went dry as she recognized him.

"Marlene, change places with me," she said hoarsely.

"Don't you want to sit by the window?"

"No."

"Hey, are you OK?"

"Yes. Just change places with me."

They switched, and Marlene looked out. "That's your Russian friend! Is he coming too?"

"I don't know," Susannah said faintly.

"You were getting along famously. Do you like him?"

"No."

"Why not?"

"He's sanctimonious, among other faults."

Marlene laughed. "A physique and a face like that and you worry about a little sanctimony! No wonder you aren't married. You're too particular."

"You aren't married. Are you too particular?"

Marlene wasn't at all offended. She laughed. "Certainly not. My problem is just the opposite. But I've *been* married, And I'm *not* wasting my youth waiting for that mythical right man."

"I didn't know you'd been married."

"I don't tell everything."

"What happened?"

Marlene was willing to talk. Susannah put on her sunglasses, leaned her head back and encouraged her. It was a familiar tale: a high school romance, a June graduation and wedding all in one weekend and then a long, slow awakening to a basic difference in intellects, tastes and interests. The high school football hero grew into a truck-driving bonehead. Marlene endured until she learned how many girls he visited along his route. Then she unloaded him and went to college. Now she was a well-paid computer systems analyst, president and owner of a small software company. And she picked her own escorts.

Susannah listened with only half an ear. The evening before and the long sleepless night that had followed could not be laid aside easily. The ague that had seized her body as she leaned against the door had threatened her very balance. Tears rolled down her cheeks and wouldn't stop. It took a tremendous exercise of will and a minute reexamination of every word and nuance of her conversation with the Russian to convince herself that while he might wonder, he didn't *know*. He couldn't know that Novak had had information to collect at the precise moment of his death. He couldn't know to whom he had entrusted it. Novak had made the final sacrifice to protect Susannah, and it appeared that his gamble had succeeded. Had the Communists suspected her of being Novak's courier, they would have arrested her this afternoon. Finally, weary and still only half convinced, Susannah had made herself undress. When she was ready for bed, she flicked out the lights and went to open the window.

In the sidewalk café below, Azarov sat with Ed Elbert and Aggie Taliaferro. Susannah could see the Russian's face clearly. He seemed to be exerting himself to be charming. He smiled frequently, and once he threw back his head and laughed heartily at one of Elbert's interminable stories. Elbert smirked in appreciation and leaned forward intimately, his manner suggesting that he had some revelation to impart. Hypnotized, Susannah stood in the shadows and watched.

The waiter left at three o'clock. His last service was the delivery of an unopened bottle of Scotch and a bucket of ice. Azarov opened the bottle, his roughened hands moving gracefully on the seals. With a winning smile at Aggie, he put ice cubes into her glass and poured in Scotch until she nodded approval. Aggie was responding well, talking with more animation than Susannah had yet seen. Azarov drank sparingly, smiled often and lit a steady succession of cigarettes. He smoked his own brand, Susannah had noticed.

Aggie was very drunk when the Russian finally upended the bottle into her glass—so drunk that she wasn't able to finish it. When she suddenly lurched upright, the two men rose quickly and helped her into the lobby. Azarov carried her pocketbook. And it flashed into Susannah's mind then what he was doing.

The Russian had second-guessed Novak. If the American had had any information, he would have tried to pass it to another, trustworthy American. The only Americans staying at the hotel were the members of Carter's tour. Azarov had only to find the right one.

Marlene talked on. Susannah was sorry that she had asked to change seats. As she had once probed an aching tooth to see if it still hurt, she wanted to know if Azarov was still there.

"May I have your attention, please?" Hans Goethe had risen and now faced them, microphone in hand. "I have an announcement from Balkantourist, and then I shall explain the day's schedule."

Susannah studied him as he waited for the murmur

of voices to die away. His name was German but he looked Slavic, and his English held no hint of the *v* and *f* sounds that haunted the speech of the Germans she knew. He was unprepossessing-looking.

"My name is Hans Goethe," he began. "I am from West Berlin, and I have been with Carter's Worldwide Tours for eight years. I have several languages, but not Bulgarian, so we shall continue to rely on our friend Dimitri." Everyone smiled politely and waited.

"We are very sorry that a death in his family forced Olaf to return home. We shall continue our trip as he planned it. But first, I will make the announcement. Balkantourist has informed me that the Bulgarian Government is offering a reward of five thousand dollars American currency for any information concerning accomplices of the narcotics criminal. Everyone, Bulgarian or foreigner alike, is eligible to receive the reward provided the information leads to actual arrests. Dope smuggling is a problem familiar to us all. If you have any information you have not already told the authorities, you are urged to notify either Dimitri or myself. We will put you in immediate communication with the proper officials, who will receive your information and disburse your reward. Are there any questions?"

There was a snort from Phillips, sitting behind Susannah, but there were no questions.

"Our first stop today will be at a state rose farm."

Susannah didn't listen to the remainder of Hans's talk. A bribe. Five thousand dollars wasn't a large sum, but the offer was a shrewd gamble. There were several pensioners on fixed incomes with the tour. One of them might welcome such an amount. Particularly, the Elberts didn't look well-to-do and they liked to travel. She wished she knew whether Ed really knew anything.

She couldn't muster interest in the rose farm. When

the bus slowed to turn off, Azarov had swung out and passed it without a glance. The lump of fear Susannah experienced eased somewhat, but the cloying scent of roses, the hot sun and the uncomfortable sensation of waiting for the other shoe to drop gave her a tension headache instead.

"Five thousand dollars is a lot of money," a voice said softly. Elbert's damp hand touched her bare arm.

She shrugged away. "Yes, it is."

"I might tell what I know."

"What *do* you know?"

"Then again, I might bargain."

And he moved off, that exasperating smirk on his face, before Susannah could say anything else. She looked after him, worried and curious.

"He thinks you're a real cute gal," Aggie Taliaferro said on her other side. In spite of the bright sun, Aggie's Henry Higgins sweater was buttoned all the way down. She looked hung over.

"Does he?" Susannah said shakily.

"His opinion is worthless. He's a stupid ass if I ever saw one," Aggie said unkindly.

Susannah couldn't resist the temptation. "I saw you talking to the Russian last night. What is your opinion of him?"

Aggie shrugged. "I travel behind the Iron Curtain a lot, I know, but I don't like Russians. I don't trust them. Azukov drinks too much for my taste."

Susannah glanced sharply at her. There was no double meaning, no trace of humor in the other woman's words. She was walking heavily along the dirt lane, her big feet in golf socks and oxfords clumping heel first in the dust. She didn't look up. So Aggie wasn't very observant, Susannah thought. She didn't even remember his name.

"He had an opinion about you too," Aggie said after a long pause.

"You must have had quite a discussion about me."

Aggie didn't notice the dryness in her tone. "He said you were a pretty bit of fluff who doesn't have enough substance to satisfy a man for long."

"He's used to potato-fed Stakhanovites," Susannah retorted, forcing herself to speak lightly. "Did he say anything else of interest?"

"No. That jackass Elbert did most of the talking. Good lord, he's tedious."

Aggie paused to light a cigarette, and Susannah let the Phillipses catch up with her. Even knowing that Aggie was a security risk, Susannah had toyed with the notion of enlisting her help if necessary. Now she saw the impossibility of that idea. Azarov undoubtedly had pumped her. She hadn't noticed. Unaware that she was being used, she had parroted his comments to Susannah. The hurtful words might reflect his private thoughts, but they seemed more calculated to sting her into some response that would give the Russian the lead he needed. A shrewd man, Aleksei Azarov. Shrewd and dangerous.

Chapter 9

AZAROV'S CAR WAS PARKED before the dreary restaurant where they were to have lunch. With a resurgence of uneasiness, Susannah let the others precede her. She wanted to avoid another confrontation with the Russian.

The group clattered into the dining room. Chairs scraped noisily on the bare floor as they found places. Azarov was already sitting at a table in the rear. A bottle of Vat 69 stood before him, and the glass in his hand held a small amount of the golden liquid. Susannah remembered Aggie's comment and turned to look for her.

Aggie had seen him. Hynotized by the liquor, she crossed the dining room. The Russian rose and courteously held a chair for her. As he straightened, his eyes sought and found Susannah. A little smile of pleasure touched his mouth as he recognized her, but he didn't invite her to join them. Instead, he beckoned to the Weisensteins to take the two remaining seats at his table. Gratefully, Susannah accepted the chair proffered by Vladimir Voorhies and Marlene. Relief was short-lived, however. Elbert came out of the men's room, ostentatiously overlooked the place Imogene was saving for him and took the fourth chair next to Susannah.

"I'm ditching my wife," he said.

"What? Again?" Marlene murmured dryly. She didn't like Elbert any better than Susannah did.

"I think husbands and wives stick too close together

on trips like this. They don't get a chance to know anyone else. And I especially want to know you and Susannah."

"What about me? I drove all this way just to join you for lunch," Voorhies said, looking at Marlene.

"My interest in you is not quite the same as in these lovely young ladies." Elbert's smirk was almost a leer. Marlene and Susannah exchanged glances, but let the men banter. Susannah was silent during most of the meal.

Voorhies had placed her so that she faced Azarov. The Russian plied Aggie with Scotch as assiduously as he had the evening before. Remembering Aggie's comment and her own observation, Susannah noted carefully how much he drank. He sipped often and refilled his glass frequently, but the amount of liquor he actually consumed was minimal. He was taking no chances on inebriation. Aggie was not so inhibited. She drank steadily and rather sullenly while Dr. Weisenstein talked. From his indignant gestures, Susannah guessed that the doctor was discussing the shooting. He too received Azarov's flattering attention. Only once did the Russian lift his eyes to Susannah. He caught her looking at him, and his face became thoughtful.

Susannah dropped her eyes immediately, mortified that he had seen her curiosity. Why was he still paying court to Aggie if he had learned all he needed to know last night? He had had the opportunity to search her room. Did he perhaps believe that Aggie *had* the information? Elbert's knee pressing hers under the table interrupted her speculations. She moved aside and lit a cigarette.

"Did you actually see the shooting?" Voorhies asked Susannah.

"Only after it was all over," she answered.

"He may be a crook, but I feel sorry for the chap,"

Voorhies said. "Where could he have gone? They would have caught him almost immediately."

"I think he must have been more than just a smuggler," Elbert said.

"How do you figure that?"

"The way they're treating us. The interrogations. They held the Japanese too, and Dimitri said they were an official trade delegation. And now the reward. They wouldn't launder their linen in public unless they really wanted something."

"What reward?" Voorhies asked with interest.

"Five thousand dollars. It was announced on the bus this morning that the Bulgarian Government will pay that amount for any information leading to the arrest of the man's accomplices," Elbert explained.

"Ah, very interesting indeed," Voorhies said, lighting one of his long cigars and leaning back comfortably. "Downright capitalistic, as a matter of fact. But what do they hope to learn?"

"I wouldn't know that, but I have figured out one thing," Elbert said.

"What's that?" Voorhies prompted.

"They must think he talked to someone in the hotel."

"I wonder if he did?" Voorhies asked.

"*I* wouldn't know," Elbert replied, his voice softly ominous. "But they're betting a lot of money that someone knows something and will tell them."

"Perhaps the person he met will betray him," Marlene suggested cynically.

"Surely his *friend* wouldn't betray him," Voorhies protested.

"He might be exposed before he had a chance to cover himself," Elbert said slyly. "Or, maybe, it's a she. It wouldn't have to be a man, would it?" He glanced sideways at Susannah.

"*I* wouldn't tell these people anything!" Marlene burst out.

"Do you know anything to tell?" Voorhies asked. His voice was casual, but the sudden intentness in his eyes as he turned to Marlene betrayed a quickening interest.

"Who, me? Certainly not. I was asleep and missed the whole incident. It's the principle of the thing. What would you do, Susannah?"

"I'd say nothing," Susannah replied. "Whoever talks risks being arrested as the accomplice."

"Exactly," Elbert said. "That person will be still as still can be. And if he suspects someone *else* knows, he would be wise to match the five-thousand-dollar offer and throw in additional compensation in return for silence."

"Now, where would a Bulgarian find five thousand dollars?" Susannah asked as the group rose and started to mill about preparatory to departure. "These poor people can't even dig up enough stotinki to buy a steel rake."

"Good question," Vladimir laughed. His eyes lingered thoughtfully on Susannah's face and moved slowly to Elbert. Then they too rose.

Susannah glanced toward Azarov's table. He was hefting the bottle of Scotch, testing its weight to see how much was left. It was more than half full. He capped it and offered it to Aggie.

Halfheartedly, she demurred.

For answer, the Russian picked up her tote bag and, carefully rearranging the items to make room, stuffed the bottle deep inside. It could be seen through the transparent plastic. Azarov patted the bag teasingly and offered it to Aggie. The woman snatched it from him. Dr. Weisenstein watched the byplay with a doubtful expression.

"I don't see how she can drink anything more today,"

Marlene muttered as she walked out with Susannah. "She was falling-down drunk last night."

"She was?" Susannah asked with great interest. "She was all right when she left the dining room."

"This was later," Marlene said.

"Much later," Voorhies added from Marlene's other side. They exchanged significant glances.

"Is there a story?" Susannah asked, intercepting the look.

"Not really. Vlad was leaving my room and here came Aggie with that Russian and Ed Elbert. So I rescued her and put her to bed. Her room was right next to mine."

"We didn't put her to bed." Voorhies corrected. "We lowered her into a horizontal position and covered her up. She's surprisingly heavy for someone who looks so shriveled."

"Elbert ran. Your Russian friend helped. Then we left her."

"Didn't anyone stay with her?"

"Certainly not. She was OK. Snoring loudly and out cold. I'm surprised she was able to get up this morning."

"Poor Aggie," Susannah murmured. So Azarov hadn't had his chance after all. That explained the bottle of Scotch today. She wondered what Soviet Government fund had paid for it. Imported liquor was too expensive for the average Russian's pocketbook. Suddenly curious, she glanced around. Imogene Elbert was hanging on to her husband's arm, a pleading look in her eyes. But Elbert ignored her. He was watching Susannah and now smirked meaningfully at her. Susannah jerked around and followed the others to the bus. Her hands were trembling again. His insinuating conversation had seemed to mean something to Vladimir Voorhies.

Chapter 10

PLOVDIV WAS AN ANCIENT CITY, Bulgaria's second-largest, built on six hills beside a shallow, dirty river. Romans, Greeks and Turks had lived there and left their ruins and their golden treasure. Communism had overlaid the remains with crumbling concrete buildings, but a small Turkish section which had survived the wars had been restored. The tour party walked through narrow lanes blessedly devoid of political advertising, enjoying their first view of an old pre-Communist Bulgaria. Cobblestones underfoot, roses spilling over stone walls, an old workman in blue sweeping the street with a stick broom made for a pleasant interlude. The Russian had not followed her here, and Susannah could be at ease.

The Church of Saints Helena and Constantine was the last stop in the tour of the old section. Although it had been restored and whitewashed on the outside, the interior was shabby. A single bulb on a frayed cord illumined the sanctuary, revealing water stains on the wall and a Franklin stove in the corner. The church, with its golden icons, was decaying, but the priest transcended the squalor. He was as handsome as an ancient Greek. His pure profile, flowing white hair and fine black eyes arrested attention. But it was to the sweetness and serenity of his expression that Susannah was drawn. It gave him a beauty that she had never seen before. Attracted to his quiet strength, she stood close to him while he described the church and its treasures. He spoke no English; Dimitri translated. Straining her Russian to understand his Bulgarian, Susannah comprehended just enough to realize that Dimitri's translation omitted the pride and love the priest expressed in his church.

"Do you like religious art?" Voorhies murmured in her ear.

Susannah nodded without taking her eyes from the priest.

"I don't. It's doleful in here. It reminds me of a friend who died recently. I believe you knew him too."

Susannah looked up at him sharply. "Whom do you mean?"

"We can't discuss it here. When we get to the hotel, meet me in the lobby thirty minutes before you join the group for dinner. We can discuss mutual friends then."

Susannah nodded. Voorhies slipped away.

The group milled about the church, studying the icons, criticizing, admiring, comparing. Susannah wandered with the rest, her concern over Voorhies' meaning interfering with her deep appreciation of the art. Was this another threat? She didn't know. She sighed a little, turned and walked out into the sunlight.

Outside, the priest was graciously permitting the group to photograph him in the doorway of his church. Seeing her emerge, Phillips called out.

"Stand there beside him, Susannah. We want your picture too."

"Jazz up that pose a bit," Elbert called. "I need a little something to show the boys when I get back to Milwaukee."

Susannah's smile stiffened, but she stood while the pictures were taken. Then she turned to the priest and held out her hand.

"Thank you very much," she said in English.

The clasp of his work-worn hand was strangely comforting. "Friends can be found in strange places," he said in slow Russian, "and enemies can pose as friends."

"What do you mean?" Susannah asked in the same language.

"I watched you in my church. You liked the treasures, did you not?"

"Very much."

"I'm glad. I hope you enjoy your visit to Bulgaria."

"Thank you, Father."

Susannah turned away. Then, troubled, she paused at the gate to look back. He lifted his hand in a little wave. She would always remember him thus: the luxuriant white hair, the dark handsome face, the sweet smile of a man who has made his peace with the world and with God.

"What did he say to you?" Elbert asked. His chubby hand closed on her elbow, holding her back to match his pace.

"I don't understand Bulgarian," Susannah said.

"I think you understood him. Did he give you new instructions?"

"I don't know what you're talking about."

"I'll bet you don't."

Susannah made no reply.

"Would you like to hear what I know?"

"You'll tell me whether I want to or not."

"I'll come to your room tonight. I'll tell you then. Will you let me in?"

"Tell me now."

"There isn't time."

Susannah pulled away from him and moved quickly, hoping to get onto the bus before he could help her. But Elbert, for all his size, was nimble. His pudgy hands hovered around her back and arm and then dropped to her fanny as she mounted the steps. She shuddered with fury and distaste and went quickly to her seat.

Across the street, the Russian stood in the shade of a giant beech tree, his hand on the dog's head. When he saw her anger, he smiled a little.

Her face flamed and she looked hastily away, dismayed that he had seen her humiliation. She didn't look up again as the Russian slowly crossed the street to his car. Deliberately, he opened the door and let the dog jump in. The man paused to light a cigarette before he bent into the driver's seat. As he cupped the match in his hands, he glanced briefly at the bus. Unexpectedly, there was a puzzled expression on his face.

Chapter 11

DINNER IN THE TRIMONZIUM HOTEL courtyard
was an unexpected pleasure. Nothing in the travel literature had prepared them for birch trees strung with col-
ored lights and lanterns, a band playing American show
tunes, a dance floor, a festive crowd of Bulgarians. The
air was soft. There was a moon. The group was in a
good mood. There were no new grievances to recount.
It had been a nice day for them, and this was a delight-
ful finale. They were enjoying themselves. Susannah
wished she could be as relaxed.

She had been relieved when the day's sightseeing was
over. Gratefully, she had accepted her key from Hans
and, anxious to be alone, had taken her luggage from
the pile in the crowded lobby, climbed the steps to the
second floor and locked herself into her hotel room.

It was large and airy and smelled faintly of wax.
Turkish carpets lay on the shining parqueted floor.
Big double-glass windows overlooked the hotel square
and, to the left, the thick green of a city park. After a
long, slow bath, a drink from her own flask and a
change of clothes, Susannah was refreshed. Some of her
confidence returned. Only two and a half more days
remained in the trip. Her ordeal was almost over.

It was tempting to stay in the room, where there
were no Russians, no sticky wandering hands, no com-
plaining tourists, but it was impossible. Failure to appear at dinner would bring Dr. Weisenstein with his
bag and too many questions. And Voorhies waited. She

smoked a final cigarette. Her assurance lasted until she reached the lobby. Voorhies wasn't there. And he didn't come.

His failure to keep their appointment nagged at Susannah until he and Marlene finally came late into the courtyard and took a table for two. Voorhies caught Susannah's eye and raised his hands as he gave a little shrug. She smiled and relaxed. If Vladimir and Marlene had found more important things to do, there couldn't be anything sinister in his absence.

They were waiting for dessert to be served when the Russian came out of the hotel and stood on the balcony overlooking the courtyard. A smile lit his face. His dark eyes roamed over the people below until he located Susannah sitting with Mrs. Burton, her daughter, Edie, and Hank and Kitty Reynolds. Then, slowly, he passed around the balcony to a table that permitted observation of the entire courtyard.

The waiters expected him. As before, they jumped to attention at his approach and attended promptly to his wants. Who *was* this man who received wine, a second serving of salad, a slivova and coffee while Americans with the much-desired hard currency were ignored? The others were beginning to notice the preferential treatment he received. A few muttered comments were made, and Edie asked Susannah about him. There would be more questions if he continued to shadow the party.

Susannah glanced up. The Russian was watching Vladimir Voorhies and Marlene Wells whisper together. Marlene was especially sultry tonight, her dark hair a froth on her shoulders, her dress a slither of black knit. She wore no underclothes and was the object of a greater-than-usual number of Bulgarian stares. A little smile touched Susannah's lips as she saw that the Russian disapproved of Marlene.

In that moment, his gaze flicked to Susannah and

caught her amusement. A broad smile crossed his face. He lifted his glass in a rueful little toast to her and drank.

Susannah was suddenly wary. Only a highly trained reflex could have taken such quick advantage of her relaxed guard. Had he succeeded in including her in his laughter at his own Soviet puritanism, it would have been a moment of union, a first step toward friendship that would have dangerously increased her vulnerability. Susannah controlled her spontaneous reaction. Instead, she inclined her head in acknowledgment. It was a queenly little gesture—not cold or forbidding, simply reserved. Once more, she slipped away from intimacy. As she returned to the conversation in progress at her table, she saw a bemused expression replace the smile on the Russian's face. Julius Caesar's words flashed into her mind: "He thinks too much. Such men are dangerous."

Hans Goethe interrupted her thoughts. "Would you care to dance?" he asked.

She smiled, excused herself to the others and rose.

"It's a beautiful night, yes?" he began.

"This is wonderful. The information from Carter's didn't lead us to expect such a treat."

"They don't have dancing here every night. I believe that is why the agency does not include it in its regular publications. Do you like it?"

"Very much."

"And do you like Bulgaria?"

"It intrigues me."

"The government is striving hard to improve itself. It is succeeding, I believe, in a steady way. Everyone has enough to eat and to wear. The amenities will come later."

"I know the people will welcome that."

"They are making impressive progress in controlling crime."

Immediately, Susannah was alert. "Indeed," she said quietly.

"Yes. Its proximity to Turkey makes smuggling a problem."

"I'm surprised."

"Opium is smuggled through Bulgaria to other parts of Eastern Europe and the West."

Traversing Bulgaria sounded unnecessarily risky for the Turkish opium smugglers, but Susannah didn't interrupt Goethe's narrative with argument.

"The police have caught quite a few smugglers," he continued. "They must apprehend them all to prevent corruption of their youth. Their young people are fine, handsome, as you can see here tonight. It is your duty to aid the arrest of that criminal's associates. We must report everything we know. Do you have any information you have not yet revealed to the authorities, Miss Clarke?"

Susannah's pleasure in the evening was gone. There was now a numb feeling in her stomach. "Certainly not. I answered all the questions put to me fully."

"Good. I hope so, Miss Clarke, because . . ."

At that moment, Elbert cut in.

"Because what, Hans?" Susannah asked.

"Just that the government will be very grateful to have any information you or any one else might have." He turned away then, and Elbert claimed her attention.

"You see?" he purred in her ear. "They all believe you know something."

"He's making the rounds. Everyone will hear the same speech."

Elbert held her too tightly. Susannah tried to put him at a greater distance and to stay the hand that wandered too often onto her buttocks, but failed. Remembering the earlier incident, she glanced around. The Russian wasn't paying attention to her. He was dancing with Sara Abbott.

Elbert intercepted her expression. The smirk appeared on his face. "I believe you're afraid of Mr. Azarov," he said in a tone of revelation.

"Certainly not."

"Old Ed's gut intuitions are never wrong. You're afraid of him. And that gives me a new idea. It might be more lucrative to speak to him. He would pay more than the Bulgarians for my information."

"What is your information?"

He pulled her closer and pressed a sweaty cheek against hers. "Ah, ah, now!" he murmured coyly. "You're fishing! I won't be bamboozled so easily. If you want to know, you must let me in tonight when I knock. You know my price. And it's going up every day. You smell good, honey. What perfume are you wearing?"

"Tigress. And if you aren't careful, you'll learn that tigresses have claws."

Elbert suddenly released her and stood aside. Azarov had cut in. Susannah was almost grateful to him.

"You are even lovelier tonight than last night," he said softly. He took her in his arms. At once, Susannah knew he was a superb dancer. He held her just right. She was short, and generally found dancing with tall men awkward. She was comfortable in Azarov's arms. He led her surely, without effort. They danced silently, moving easily in their little corner of the floor. Azarov looked down at her, admiring the fine brows, the smoothness of that incredible complexion. The bright green that she wore suited her exactly. It was the color of new grass, perhaps of new corn. It made her seem as fresh, as miraculous as the growing things it brought to his mind. He wanted to touch her cheek, but the averted gaze, the hand placed so precisely on his shoulder deterred him. It wasn't enough that he had made her aware of him. He wanted to penetrate her reserve and learn the reason for it. He drew her infinitesimally closer. Her hair smelled good. Their silence was increasingly friendly.

He felt the tap on his shoulder. Vladimir Voorhies waited to dance with her. Azarov took his time. He released her slowly, and smiled warmly as he thanked her with a formal little bow. Then, reluctantly, he gave her hand to Voorhies.

"Thank you, Aleksei."

"It was my pleasure," he said. And meant it.

"If I had known how popular you were going to be tonight, I wouldn't have dared stand you up," Voorhies began. "I was waylaid. I'm sorry."

"So I suspected," Susannah said dryly. Her nose wrinkled. Voorhies' after-shave lotion was pungent, but it didn't quite cover the garlic on his breath. It was an odd combination of scents.

He laughed. "It was not what you are thinking. But no matter. Shall we ease out for a few minutes? Marlene is busy with that Bulgarian athlete and won't miss us."

"If you wish. Where shall we go?"

"The park by the hotel is quite nice if you haven't seen it yet."

The park was heavily wooded and dark under the lush foliage. They wandered on sand paths for a few minutes before Voorhies said, "No one is around. Let's sit here and talk." He sat close beside her on the bench and lit a cigar. The fumes mixed poorly with his other smells.

"You said you knew a friend of mine," she began.

"I said I knew a friend of yours who is dead," he corrected. "John Novak."

Susannah suddenly went cold. "John Novak! Are you sure? When did he die? What happened?" It wasn't difficult to make her voice distraught.

"Come on, Susannah. He was shot in front of your hotel two days ago. You knew that."

"No. No, I didn't. You don't mean to tell me that was John Novak! They said he was a Bulgarian narcotics smuggler."

"It was Novak, all right. He was due to receive information that afternoon. He transferred it to you for safekeeping. I've come to take it back to Washington."

"Vladimir, I don't know anything about this."

"I think you do. I think he talked to you. Then, later, in trying to escape from the hotel, he was murdered. The authorities were really close on his tail. Had been for some time. The poor bastard didn't know it."

"Why not?"

"So you admit you knew who it was?"

"I admit nothing of the sort. You just told me. Why *wouldn't* he have known it?"

"He was getting shaky and too damned independent. He knew you well. He knew you were no dummy. He would have gone straight to you. What is it? Don't you trust me?"

"That's an irrelevant question."

"For Chrissake! Look. You entered on duty with the CIA in June 1961—June 17, if you want to be precise. You resigned effective 31 August 1968. Your last badge number was AB-758. Your service began with training at the Virginia farm. You managed 'Clarke House—Antiques' on the corner of Independence Avenue and Fifth Street, S.E., as cover for a safe house. Boris Rasnikov blew your cover in 1965 and you joined the agency's Soviet desk. You speak and read fluent Russian and you became a damned good analyst, especially on the subject of Soviet missile-range construction. What more do I need to tell you?"

"I know all that."

"Do you want to know my credentials? If I tell you, will you give me the information? It can't wait until you carry it to Washington in person."

"In that case, I will have to forgo the pleasure of knowing more about you. I don't have any information. I haven't seen John Novak for years."

"Then what the hell was all that about at lunch?"

"At lunch? I don't really remember."

"Elbert. He knows something."

"Maybe *he* has the information you want."

"That's not what I meant. Novak wouldn't give it to a loser."

"Then what does Elbert have to do with the matter?"

"I don't know, but that was the point of that conversation at lunch. He knows something about you and John Novak and he's blackmailing you into bed over it."

"Ed Elbert talks that way to any woman over the age of ten! He's constantly on the make."

Voorhies smiled a little. "That's true. He nearly raped Marlene. She refused him."

"Good for her!"

"But you won't be able to. You're afraid of him. You'll have to sacrifice yourself to buy his silence, but he's such a stupid sonofabitch, he'll give you away by mistake. How long can you expect to go undetected then? That Russian is watching you. And he's so sure of himself he doesn't care who knows it! One misstep on your part and he'll pounce. And he won't treat us kindly. He could even order our execution. Be sensible, Susannah. Let me have it. I can leave now, be at the embassy in Sofia by midnight, have it encoded and on its way within an hour. Please. For your sake. For the country's sake."

It was tempting. How easy it would be. But Susannah's hesitation was brief. Novak's tired face, the urgent whisper, the blood pouring onto yellow bricks were too overpowering. He had made the sacrifice. And she had made a promise.

"Aleksei Azarov?" she said lightly. "He's not watching me. He's courting me, to use an old-fashioned phrase. I'm sorry, Vladimir. I don't know what you're talking about. But if that was John Novak, then I'm very sorry. I was very . . . fond of him."

Voorhies smiled tightly. "He's KGB—one of their very best," he said. "You should at least be aware of that. He made colonel at an unusually early age."

"How do you know that? He told me he was a planner."

"The CIA's biographic files have a little on him. Not much. He doesn't leave any traces. He's a killer. He could murder you with a snap of the wrist. You'd never know what happened."

"I don't believe that. He gives such a different impression."

"He does. It's part of his effectiveness. He's a spider. And you're a most succulent fly."

Susannah forced a little laugh and was gratified that it sounded almost natural. "And we'd better fly back, Vladimir. Marlene will wonder what happened to you." Susannah rose and turned to go.

"To hell with Marlene. I had to use a little bitch in heat as an entrée to the group."

"Then I'm glad it wasn't entirely a disappointment for you."

"What wasn't a disappointment?" asked a voice from the darkness. Marlene and the Russian emerged from the shadows. The dog came directly to Susannah and delicately sniffed the hem of her skirt. She stood quietly and in a moment laid her hand on his head. He moved away.

"There you are!" Voorhies exclaimed in a jovial tone. "We were just coming to find you."

"You answer my question, Vladimir Voorhies. What wasn't a disappointment?"

"Being trapped in Bulgaria. Had I not been stuck in Sofia, I wouldn't have met you."

Marlene laughed. "Liar," she said without rancor. "But it's nice to hear anyway. Aleksei is a real angel. He rescued me from the assault of the dark foreigners and we came out to look for you."

Azarov laughed softly. "Rescuing you is a pleasure, Miss Wells."

"You must do it again," Marlene trilled. Her voice was dropping rapidly, growing more sultry as they bantered. "When can we arrange it?"

"I think your friend Vladimir will not permit me such gratification again," Azarov said, and started to disengage his arm from hers.

"Not so fast. I have not thanked you properly, Aleksei." Marlene reached up and kissed the Russian on the mouth. "As I said," she purred, "you are an angel."

"I have been called many things," Azarov answered, "but never an angel." Marlene laughed and released him. She linked arms with Voorhies and they wandered away in the general direction of the hotel.

Azarov turned to Susannah with a welcoming intimate little smile. "Shall we walk?" he asked. "Or must you run from me?"

Susannah regarded him in silence. KGB. One of the best. An elite opponent. She had no illusions about her ability to beat him at his own profession. Now more than ever, her defense lay in being the innocent, ignorant tourist. She wanted to run, but she must stay.

"If you would like to, I can for a little while."

As before, he took her hand and placed it on his arm. He led her deeper into the park, to a small circle where a fountain dripped water. There were benches around the edges. Trees grew thickly overhead. Azarov picked the bench with the most clear space around it and they sat down. He offered her a cigarette.

"Is this a Russian cigarette?" she asked.

"Yes. Try one. You will like it."

"You've been listening to American radio and television."

"I? Certainly not!" The denial was too quick. Susannah had read that many Russians, even the leaders, listened to Western news broadcasts.

"Then you have a capitalist's mind."

"Why do you say such things?"

"What you just said. About trying one. There's a commercial on American television that goes something like that."

He laughed. "Pure coincidence!"

"Perhaps." She had won that round. It was a meaningless victory. They smoked in silence. Susannah didn't like his cigarette. It was hard to smoke.

"Voorhies is an ass," he said suddenly.

Susannah laughed. She had to agree with that, at least insofar as his attire went.

"He knows friends of yours," Azarov said.

Susannah looked at him sharply. "When did he say that?"

"Tonight. We talked."

So *that* was the reason Voorhies had been delayed. To talk to Azarov. Had they spoken of John Novak? "What did he say?" Susannah asked, taking pains to keep her voice from trembling.

"Something about mutual friends and meeting you at a party in Washington several years ago. Did you remember him?"

"No."

"He did not think you had. What kind of man do you remember?"

"One like you."

"Why?"

"You are unforgettable." There was a little fervor in her tone. Or a tremor. He couldn't be exactly certain which.

"I'm not sure that is a compliment. Did you discover that you had mutual friends?"

"No."

"Then what did you talk about?"

"Nothing much."

"Did he make love to you?"

Nettled, she replied sharply, "That's no concern of yours! But no, no, he didn't."

"Then what?"

"Why are you so curious about him?"

"He is a caricature. Maybe even an anomaly. I want to know what such a man would want with a woman like you."

"He tried to meddle."

"In what? Your life?"

"Precisely."

"What did he say?"

Susannah looked over at him. A little smile was lurking on his lips. But he was serious. He really wanted to know. He would probe until he got some kind of answer. "If you must know," she said, "he was warning me that you are too interested in me for my own good. Or for your own." She prayed that her voice held the proper blend of lightness, rueful confession and annoyed amusement.

"So," he said softly. His smile widened, but his eyes remained unscrutable. "So," he repeated. "He's right, you know."

He didn't move, but Susannah felt suddenly as if he had touched her. She reached for another cigarette, one of her own this time. Azarov lit it for her, his fingers brushing hers as she shielded the match in his hands.

"Nevertheless, I am sorry to learn that that is what he told you," he said, extinguishing the match. "It explains why I didn't like his face. He is a spoiler. The rotten potato that looks sound until you turn to its other side. What gives him the privilege of selecting your friends?"

"He doesn't select them."

"What did he say about me?"

"Just that associating with a Westerner could endanger your position. Would it?"

"Any Westerner? Or just you?"

"Any Westerner. Why should I be a particular threat to you?"

"Why indeed?" He was silent a moment, staring thoughtfully into the fountain. Then, in a new tone, he said, "There is another rotten potato in your group."

"Who is that?"

"Edward Elbert."

"He's a nuisance," she said scornfully.

"You don't have to tell me what *he* wants."

Susannah suddenly was still.

"Yes, I know what he wants of you," he continued without waiting for her to comment. "But what I don't know is why you permit such a man to be free with your body."

"I don't like scenes."

"Are you afraid of him for any reason?"

"No. But thank you for cutting in tonight. He would

have been difficult." Her voice was light, but this time the tremor was noticeable.

"I am glad to have been of service to you. Perhaps you will not think so unkindly of Russians hereafter."

"That depends on whether you are the exception or the rule in Russia."

"I think you have just skewered me on the horns of the dilemma. No matter how I answer, I cannot win all I want from you."

Susannah was silent. Her face was turned away from him.

"Don't you want to know what I want?" he prompted.

"No."

"Why not?"

"It may be more than I want to give."

"What is the least that you can give me?"

"I won't answer that either. It may not satisfy you."

"And do you want to satisfy me, Susannah Clarke?" he asked softly.

Suddenly, he seemed to be terribly close. He leaned nearer and she was in too deep. The light banter couldn't conceal the significance in his tone, the tension between them. He was fishing—fishing delicately, but fishing nonetheless. Perhaps all he wanted was a rendezvous, but things were never that simple. Susannah was afraid of him, and she wanted to go—to escape that smooth, insinuating voice, the handsome face smiling in the dimness, the arm that lay across the back of the bench and brushed her shoulders.

"I make it a policy never to satisfy any man," she answered.

"That is a tragedy for me. You have so much to give. Before you leave Bulgaria, I will change your mind." The undercurrent, the second meaning behind the bland words, was unmistakable.

"Do you think you can?" she asked. Her tongue was dry.

"Yes."

"Time will tell," she said. "And now, it's late. I must go. We have another long day tomorrow."

He rose without protest. She let him take her hand, lay his arm against the length of hers and clasp it to him. She started to walk quickly, but he held her pace to his. They strolled slowly through the shadows, their bodies touching closely, saying nothing. A bird rustled overhead and fell silent. The only other sounds were the splash of water in the pool behind them and, faintly, the music of the band still playing. It was a beautiful night—the kind of night that always made Susannah want someone to love and be with. Her dread of Azarov's dark bulk beside her ruined it.

"Will I see you tomorrow?" he asked.

"I don't know. We are going to the Rila Monastery. It's a long drive over the mountains, I believe."

"Not so long. You will enjoy it."

The brightness of the square before the hotel was unpleasant after the soft darkness, but Azarov did not alter his pace until he saw Ed Elbert rise from a table on the terrace. Sharply, the Russian glanced at Susannah. Once more she avoided his gaze. His hand tightened on her arm, his step quickened and he led her past Elbert, into the hotel and up the stairs to her room. There, he unlocked the door for her, then laid the key in her hand and closed her fingers over it. He clasped her fist tightly, his callused hands gripping hard. Wordlessly, she looked up into his face.

"I'm sleeping in the room next to yours," he said. "I hear every sound you make."

"I shall be careful not to awaken you."

"I should like being awakened by you, Susannah Clarke. Good night. Sleep well."

He released her and walked away. As she watched him go, Susannah suddenly realized anew how striking he looked. He gave the stiff gray suit a distinction the Soviet clothing ministry had never intended.

Chapter 12

HER FEAR FELL AWAY when the door closed behind her, and she knew a terrible fatigue. She had had little rest for two nights, and now shuddering yawns betrayed her need. Sleep came instantly.

Susannah awoke abruptly. Next door, Azarov's impatient steps sounded clearly as he paced the room. Her clock read 12:30. She had slept just thirty-five minutes. Now she was wide awake, her thoughts as restless as Azarov's steps.

Whom *did* Vladimir Voorhies work for? He had implied that it was the State Department and had insinuated that he held a classified position. Yet when he needed to gain Susannah's trust, he had not revealed any substantial identification. She wondered if he had it to give.

At that, Susannah sat upright. She suddenly realized that he seemed to know no more than Azarov. If he were genuine, he would have spoken of the operation in such a way that his authenticity would have been unmistakable. Instead, he merely repeated her own biography, general information that could be obtained from the KGB's voluminous files on American intelligence personnel. She knew that thanks to Rasnikov, a card for Susannah Pence Clarke lay within the KGB's archives deep under Dzerzhinsky Square in Moscow. She had no doubt that it was complete, even to the picture. Voorhies' recital of her biography had had a stilted tone, as though he had memorized it from an index card.

Colonel Azarov would have access to those files. He had probably obtained a list of the Americans staying at the Grand Hotel in Sofia and run it through the KGB's computers and card sorters before he left Moscow. That would explain why he had focused so quickly on Susannah and Aggie Taliaferro. It was coincidence that two ex-CIA agents were on the same tour, but it was unusual enough that the Russians wouldn't believe it. They would think it was intentional, that Novak had planned all along to pass the information to a CIA agent posing as a tourist. Stranger contacts than that had been used in the intelligence business.

Then who else on the tour would be apt to have a KGB index card? Other candidates might be Dr. Weisenstein, a professional man and physician, president of his state medical society; Frank Phillips, an executive whose company traded with the Soviet Union; perhaps Mr. Reynolds, who had served a term in the Texas legislature. And these were the very ones Azarov was interested in. He or Voorhies had talked to them all at one time or another. They had gone further, talking and dancing with several of the women on the tour. There they were merely probing, touching bases, listening for any signs of abnormal nervousness or fear. It was doubtful that they had learned anything of interest from any of them. So they were concentrating on the two ex-agents. . . .

Her thoughts were shattered by a gentle tap on her door. In the next room, the pacing stopped abruptly. The rap came again. Quietly, the Russian crossed the room to his door, the wooden floor creaking audibly as he moved. Susannah could imagine him bending forward, listening, perhaps leaning his weight against

the door and easing it open just enough to hear, even
to see who knocked.

A voice called softly, "Susannah?"

It was Elbert.

Susannah was frozen. The third knock was louder.
"Susannah? I know you're in there. Let me in."

She made no response.

"Susannah!"

When there still was no answer, Elbert became angry. "All right, Miss High and Mighty. If you won't talk
to me, that Russian will."

For an interminable moment there was silence outside her door. Then Susannah heard Elbert's plodding
tread retreating down the hall.

In the next room, the pacing resumed. Azarov made
several turns before he snapped his fingers for the dog
and went out, locking the door noisily behind him. He
was whistling as he passed her door.

Panic-stricken, Susannah leaped to her feet and
rushed to the window. She had opened it a little and was
standing quietly in the shadows when Azarov came out
on the terrace below. The dog was permitted to go and
relieve himself, but was immediately recalled to lie
beside Azarov's table. The Russian sat quietly, smoking.
A glass of slivova on a saucer had been placed before
him, but he didn't touch it. Once, he looked at his
watch. He seemed to be waiting.

It was Hans Goethe who finally sidled forward.
Azarov didn't rise. A jerk of his head instructed the
German to sit. During their five-minute talk, Azarov
asked the questions and Hans answered with repeated
shakes of his head. Then, angrily, he was dismissed.
The Russian's scowl told that he wasn't pleased with
Goethe. Remembering her first uneasiness about the
guide, Susannah now wondered what his political loyal-
ties really were.

Hans must have been instructed to bring the desk clerk, because in a moment he reemerged from the hotel with the girl at his side. Hesitantly, she approached the Russian. His manner with her was only slightly less curt than it had been with Hans.

The girl was torn between Azarov's looks and her apprehension of him. She sat tensely, knees tightly together, her eyes never leaving his face as she answered his questions. A stack of passports was in her hand. The girl leafed through them, picked out three and handed them to Azarov. He opened and studied each one carefully, turning the pages slowly. Then he stacked them, lining up their edges neatly and tapping his fingers thoughtfully on the pile. Susannah could see his indecision as once more he spread open the documents and reviewed each page. Finally, he handed one and then another to the girl. The third one he put in his pocket. The girl seemed uneasy at that, but he killed her protest with a word. Slowly she returned to the hotel, pausing first to look back over her shoulder. The Russian was not looking at her and did not turn his head. Only the dog watched.

More minutes passed before a Bulgarian dressed in the uniform of an officer in the security police crossed the square and mounted the steps to the terrace. Stars of rank decorated his shoulder boards, and Azarov rose to greet him. But this was a gesture of extreme courtesy. It was obvious from the Bulgarian's manner that Colonel Azarov was the ranking officer.

Taking the passport he had retained from his pocket, Azarov handed it to him. The officer studied it closely, turning it into the light to see the photograph more clearly. They discussed the document for a moment and Azarov seemed to be making a suggestion, for the Bulgarian demurred, diffidently and a little fearfully. Then,

encouraged by the Russian, he shook his head more
vigorously and spoke intently for several minutes, leaning forward and gesticulating to illustrate his points.
Azarov listened closely, nodded agreement and rose
to terminate the interview. Once more they shook hands.
Azarov remained standing as the man strode across the
square. Susannah studied him with equal intentness. He
was stocky, dark, Slavic-looking, just like hundreds of
other Bulgarians she had seen. She had not been able
to see his face clearly, and she knew she wouldn't
recognize him again.

Once more Azarov resumed his seat and waited.
Slowly he took out his cigarettes. Susannah had to smile
as the light shone on the package. He had switched to
an American brand. He lit one meditatively. The match
illumined his face briefly. He looked tired.

Suddenly, Susannah caught her breath. Voorhies
came forward, stepping quietly, almost sliding across
the terrace to Azarov's table. The Panama hat sat rak-
ishly on the back of his head. His coat hung open. He
hooked his thumbs over his suspenders and leaned his
chair back, teetering on the two rear legs. Something
Azarov said brought the chair crashing down and made
Voorhies sit upright and look nervously around before
he could bring his eyes back to the Russian's face. The
expression of self-satisfaction had disappeared entirely.

Azarov spoke sharply. Voorhies tried to reply with
an air of bravado, but Azarov would have none of
that. He suddenly leaned forward, his eyes narrowed,
his mouth drawn into a thin line. He looked hard, and
after a long stare into his face, Voorhies gave in and
nodded reluctantly. Slowly, the Russian sat back in
satisfaction. His dismissal was wintry. Voorhies slunk
away.

Contemptuously, Azarov stubbed out his cigarette in

the ashtray. He drained his glass and snapped his fingers
for more. When it was brought to him, he made the
waiter stand while he drank the liquid in a single swallow and returned the glass to the tray. Then, wearily,
he rose. He stood, flexing the fatigue from his shoulders
while his eyes traveled around the windows and found
Susannah's. His hand strayed into his pocket for the
passport. Thoughtfully, he studied it again. Once more
he glanced upward, toward Susannah standing back in
the dark, hardly breathing. Then his eyes dropped to
the dog. He smiled broadly. The dog leaped up, his
stub of a tail wagging eagerly, and bounded down the
steps to the street. At the curb, Azarov paused to light
another cigarette. Susannah's eyes followed him until
he and the dog disappeared into the park. Unexpectedly,
he didn't look menacing or dangerous. He looked like
a man one might like to know, walking his dog before
bedtime.

Anxious not to miss anything, Susannah lingered by
the window. Voorhies was not what he seemed, and
the discovery shook her badly. The priest had warned
her.

The priest! How had he known to speak to her in
Russian? At the time, forgetting he didn't understand
English, she had assumed he was responding to Elbert's
boorishness. Voorhies knew she spoke Russian. Had he
asked the priest to speak to her? She had seen them
talking together—Vladimir's Russian fluent, the priest's
slow and halting. She had thought nothing of it. Tourists always questioned the guides. Now she wondered.
Voorhies would not call attention to the fact that he
was working for the Russians. But if he was pretending
to be a double agent, he would want a hint of his true
loyalty to reach Susannah without the risk of revealing
it himself. If that was true, he would be feeding Azarov

false information to steer him away from Susannah. She might have an easier time from now on.

Still, Susannah wasn't very hopeful. Voorhies might have tried, but she doubted if he had succeeded. Azarov had studied the American travel documents and selected the passport of his primary suspect *before* he talked to Voorhies. And the Russian's final perusal of that passport had been more thoughtful than doubtful. What was more, his plan was already in effect. His meetings, in full view of the Carter's tour members occupying the choice rooms overlooking the terrace, were carefully staged to stampede Novak's courier into the open. Ironically, it was thanks to Elbert and not to Azarov's own effort that Susannah had been pinpointed as the courier. At the very least, she could now expect a search of her belongings. *Dead Souls* looked like any other well-thumbed paperback, but a colonel in the KGB would know all the tricks of concealing messages. *Dead Souls* was no longer safe in Susannah's possession.

Her alternatives were limited. If Elbert managed to talk to the Russian, he would look for the message before she had time to dispose of it. She had already selected a suitable place. Azarov had paid no attention whatsoever to the Endicott sisters, and Azalea's canvas tote bag was a wild conglomeration of travel literature, whodunits, plastic rain gear, film, flashbulbs, cameras and knitting. *Dead Souls* could safely finish the trip there.

Below, a black car drew up to the curb and a man with a briefcase climbed out of the rear seat and hurried into the hotel. He soon returned and reentered the car. Rather ominously, it waited, its windows shrouded in curtains and darkness. The last guests left the dancing and straggled across the square, followed in a few minutes by the musicians, carrying their instruments. Then it was quiet.

Much later, the Russian and his dog returned. As they approached the hotel, the man in the car got out and waited for them. Light glinted, and Susannah realized that the briefcase was chained to his wrist.

Her interest quickened. The courier seemed to want to go inside, but Azarov took the same table he had occupied previously. A little grudgingly, the man sat on the edge of a chair and, unlocking the briefcase, handed Azarov an envelope. It resembled the envelope Susannah had seen delivered to him at the restaurant in Sofia. This time, however, the letter was several pages long, and Azarov went into the lobby to read it. The messenger rose to follow, but Azarov coldly ordered him back into his seat.

Almost fifteen minutes passed before Azarov returned, folding the letter into the envelope as he walked. The courier rose. Azarov shook his head. When the other man replied rather forcefully and pointedly, Azarov regarded him steadily for a moment. Then with a little shrug, he sat down and wrote a single line in reply. Once more the courier protested. Azarov's face stilled. His lips barely moving, he said something that froze the man into obedience. Quickly snatching the paper from Azarov, he locked it into the briefcase and hurried to the car. He did not look back.

When the car had gone, Azarov and the dog entered the hotel. Susannah waited, her breath shallow and fast as she strained to hear them come down the hall. Their steps passed her door without pause and went into the adjoining room. When her knees started shaking suddenly, Susannah realized just how afraid of them she was. Fearfully, she leaned against the window frame, finding no comfort in its rough support. The jar of his bed against her wall told when Azarov lay down. She heard his deep sigh. Then, silence. Carefully, shakily, Susannah crept to the chair. She sat in the dark, staring at the red glow of her cigarettes, while early dawn brightened the room.

Chapter 13

IT WAS SEVEN FIFTEEN. Briskly, Susannah crossed the cavernous dining room. Her eyes were gritty and dry. Her mouth tasted sour from too many cigarettes. Tension knotted her stomach. But her face wore a cheerful smile as she found the Endicotts and sat down at their table. They greeted her happily.

The sisters had never married. They had grown up in rural Georgia on a farm large enough to be a plantation, and while they had been modest about its main house, they had let slip that only their grandmother's beauty had persuaded Sherman not to burn it to the ground. Somewhat isolated from the world, they lived for each other and for "Brother," who was five years older than Azalea and ten years older than Christine. Brother had had a heart attack, and this was the first time in twenty-two years that he had not accompanied them on their annual vacation trip to the Continent. Avidly, they had collected information, taken pictures and questioned their fellow tourists in order to take back to Brother everything, absolutely everything, that they had experienced. Their role as eyewitnesses to the assassination of a smuggler was so tantalizing that they repeatedly told the story to each other and to the other members of the party. Undoubtedly, they would tell Brother so often he would rue the day he had stayed home. They were mannerly, flutter-headed women who were pleasant in small doses. Susannah had not been able to decide which was the more "girlish" of the two.

Today, she listened to their flowing chatter and anxiously watched Hans handing out passports. He was nearing the end of the stack. Hers was the last. With a relieved smile, she accepted it from him, and as soon as his back was turned she leafed through it. It had not been altered or disturbed in any way, and thankfully she slipped it into her purse and zipped the compartment closed. When she looked up, her eye fell on Voorhies, sitting with Elbert. Their heads were close as they murmured together. They were entirely too clubby. It made her uneasy.

The Endicotts had finished. Graciously, they waited while Susannah forced down her bitter coffee and the last of the watery fruit juice. Then they walked out of the dining room together. The sisters did not have the tote bag with them, and glancing over the luggage stacked in the lobby, Susannah did not see its distinctive red plaid. Optimistically, she rode the creaking elevator with them, only to learn that they were not on her floor. Her hopes for concealing *Dead Souls* faded. She would have to create another opportunity. Her mind worried with the problem as she unlocked the door to her room and shut it firmly behind her. She turned.

Azarov stood by her suitcase, her travel diary in his hand.

"What are you doing?" she demanded.

"Reading." He turned a page.

She glanced at her luggage. The suitcase and the flight bag had been searched.

"What are you looking for?" she asked coldly.

"I want to know what you wrote about me in your diary."

"Had you asked, I would have told you. There's noth-thing about you there. How did you get in?"

"I opened the door."

Susannah knew she had locked it. She had put her weight against it to make sure.

"If you don't mind." She crossed the room, plucked the diary from his hand and clutched it to her chest. "Can you get out the same way, or shall I help you this time?"

He smiled a little, touched her arm as he passed and walked out without speaking. He shut the door very, very quietly behind him.

Susannah stood for a long moment, the book clenched in both hands, her eyes on the door. His touch burned her arm, and tears of fury and helplessness scalded her eyes. She bit her lip to still the quivering agitation. Then she turned to examine her luggage.

He had been neat and thorough. And he had taken one of her silk scarves.

Mystified, Susannah took up her bags and left the room. She hurried a little, hoping to find the Endicotts' tote bag with the other luggage in the lobby. But the delay had been too long. The baggage had already been loaded, and the last passenger was finding his seat on the bus.

Suddenly conscious that she was holding up their departure, Susannah quickened her step. Eyes intent on the driver waiting to receive her bags, she didn't see the loose flagstone on the terrace. Her foot caught, and with a little cry, she fell heavily. Her purse burst open, and its contents spilled over the terrace and down the steps. *Dead Souls* landed in full view, fifteen feet away.

The feeling of hopelessness that surged over her was almost overwhelming. They were all there: Voorhies starting forward. Hans caught off guard. Dimitri frozen in horror. And Aleksei Azarov, running to her.

"Susannah! Did you injure yourself? Let me help you." The concern in his eyes was genuine as he lifted her to her feet and held her against him until she was steady.

"Are you all right? You haven't sprained your ankle or damaged any muscles, have you?" His hands slid gently down her bare arms as he bent to feel her ankles.

She was breathing hard. She had struck her hip on the stone step, and it hurt. The ache was welcome. It concealed her fright and provided the excuse for the moisture in her eyes. Voorhies and Dimitri had jumped to pick up the things that had fallen from her purse.

"I must—" Susannah began.

"No. Stand right here until you are recovered. Here, Vladimir, put it in here. Do we have it all? Is that a lipstick there in the gutter?" He held the empty purse while the others dumped the items they had collected inside. A pleased little smile touched his lips when he saw *Dead Souls*.

"So," he said softly, looking down at her over the book in his hand. His glance numbed Susannah. Cornered, she stared back at him. His voice seemed very far away.

"So," he repeated. "I'm glad to see that you don't hate all things Russian after all. Good. Are you feeling better now? You have ruined your stockings, and that is a nasty scrape on your knee. Is there any pain?"

By now, Weisenstein had bustled off the bus with his medical kit and was hurrying forward to render first aid.

"Oh, please, Herb. It's nothing," Susannah protested. "I've had worse playing football with my brothers. Just lend me your merthiolate and give me some Band-Aids and I'll go fix myself up."

"Shall we come with you?" Azarov asked. "Are you sure you're all right? You don't feel faint?"

Susannah looked at him. There was no undercurrent in his voice now. But there wouldn't be. He was smooth.

"Thank you, no, Aleksei. I simply must learn not to hurry. I appreciate your help."

She excused herself and, taking her flight bag, went back into the hotel to find the ladies' room. She had gotten everything back, including *Dead Souls,* but now Azarov knew where it was. She hadn't missed the speculative look in his eyes as he held the thin paperback.

The ladies' room off the main lobby was dark and clammy, but she cleaned her scratches and was taping a gauze pad to the scraped knee when there was a sound outside. Hardly breathing, she waited as the heavy door swung slowly inward.

It was Azalea Endicott. And the tote bag. Susannah's grin held a trace of nearly hysterical relief.

But Azalea wanted to commiserate. Patiently, Susannah answered her questions as the minutes slipped away and she finished bandaging her knee and put on fresh stockings. At last satisfied that Susannah didn't need assistance, Azalea went into the toilet cubicle and closed the door.

Quickly, Susannah took *Dead Souls* from her purse and slid it into the narrow crack between two guidebooks. It was so slender it did not disturb the appearance of the tote bag at all. Now, if she could make it appear that she and Azalea had not been together, the gamble might work.

"I'm going on, Azalea," she called. "I want to take an aspirin."

"You go right ahead, dear. I'll see you at the bus."

Several of the other tour members had gotten off. They loitered on the terrace, enjoying the sun while they waited. Susannah fell into step with Edie Burton, and the young girl stayed at her side to be introduced to the Russian.

Azarov acknowledged the introduction courteously, but his smile was for Susannah. "Vladimir has persuaded Marlene to drive with him today," he said. "I want you to come with me, Susannah. You will be more comfortable, and we can have luncheon together."

"What a nice idea," Edie said hopefully. Susannah found his invitation ominous.

"Thank you, Aleksei. It would be pleasant, but I have a bad headache. I want to stay by Dr. Weisenstein, just in case."

"You didn't tell me! Did you hit your head when you fell? Please let me take care of you." He put his arm around her and started urging her to his car.

"That won't be necessary!" Susannah said firmly. "Dr. Weisenstein can take care of me."

"Of course, of course," Weisenstein agreed heartily. He held her elbow now, and Susannah edged away from Azarov.

He let her go. "Be careful, Susannah," he pleaded. "Please, be very careful."

Smiling a shaky farewell, Susannah hurried onto the bus before he could help her. She let Herb fuss over her a little. Her pulse was irregular, and she was cold to his touch. He feared shock.

They were ready to leave. Susannah looked out. Azarov had disengaged himself from Edie and now was having difficulty with his car. He had lifted the hood to peer inside. When he emerged, Susannah saw that he was not just angry or annoyed. He was explosively furious. In that moment, Voorhies, with Marlene beside him, passed the bus with a toot of his horn and rounded the corner. As the bus slowly fell in behind Vladimir's car, Susannah looked back once more. A little smile touched her lips. There was a frantic cast on Colonel Azarov's face. Perhaps it would be easier from now on after all.

Chapter 14

SUSANNAH SAT ALONE, moodily staring out at the mountains, narrow cobblestone roads and towering trees. Her head ached and her knee hurt, but the tension had faded. No one was following her now, so she could sleep a little. She was very tired.

Susannah slept until the bus braked to a stop before the resort hotel where they would lunch. Once a summer holiday place for the nobility, the resort was now a workers' retreat. Its hotel was new, but like those of other resort hotels they had visited, its empty lobbies and echoing reception rooms were already becoming seedy. The curtains were crooked. All the curtains in Bulgaria were crooked, Susannah thought as she sat down in the dining room and unfolded her napkin. The food was good, however, and she enjoyed the meal even while dreading the coming hour. There would be free time for a stroll in the woods. The party would scatter, leaving her dangerously vulnerable. She glanced around. Azarov had not followed, but on the far side of the dining room Vladimir Voorhies kept watch in his place. Ed Elbert and Hans were other sources of unease.

Oddly, the woods reminded her of the Kentucky River cliffs where she and her brothers had spent summers with their grandparents. She found the same trees, the same little wild flowers—Queen Anne's lace, red and white clover, and even bluegrass, with each tiny seed tipped in bluish purple. The rock formations and the smells too were nostalgic. She wandered along with the

Burtons and Miss McMillan, chatting idly, a little bouquet of bluegrass and clover in her hand. It was restful until they met the Elberts. Maneuvering adroitly, Ed Elbert fell into step beside Susannah. The others went ahead.

"Why didn't you let me in last night?" he began.

"Did you knock?"

"You know I did."

"I didn't hear anything."

"I don't believe that."

"Believe what you like."

"The time has come for me to speak to the Russian. He'll be interested in what I have to say."

"I think you had better tell me what you know. We have time today."

"But I'll—"

"Tell me now, or I'll think you're only bluffing."

"Very well. I saw him."

"Who?"

"The smuggler. He was leaving your room. He talked to you."

"Where were you?"

"Just coming down the stairs. He didn't see me. He opened the door to a back exit and disappeared. I didn't think anything of it at the time, but when he was shot and they detained us, I put two and two together. Old Ed served his term in the military. I know a little about intelligence work. That's what he was doing. I think he gave you something."

"That's quite a story, Ed. Have you told anyone else?"

"Well . . ."

"Have you?"

"I did mention a little of it to Vladimir Voorhies." At her expression, he went on hastily, a little defensively. "It's all right. He's working on the same operation."

"Did he tell you that specifically?"

"Well . . . not exactly. He couldn't. Its classified, you see. But he might be interested in buying the information. He's consulting his superiors."

"Oh, brother!"

"You'll have your opportunity to bid. Vladimir mentioned two thousand dollars. The Bulgarian Government will pay five thousand dollars. So what will *you* pay for silence?"

"I should think Vladimir *would* be happy to pay two thousand dollars if he thinks he can use your information to collect five thousand dollars from the Bulgarians. But you'd better get your two thousand first or you'll wind up with nothing."

"How's that?"

"There's no truth in it. There was no Bulgarian smuggler in my room. And I don't have anything from such a person. If I recall correctly, the police will only pay for leads that result in actual arrests. You have made a mistake, and if I were you I wouldn't mention it further to anyone. This is a Communist country, you know. The Bulgarians won't like being sent on a wild-goose chase. If you annoyed them, this whole tour party could disappear and there wouldn't be anything Washington could do but protest."

"You're a slick one, honey, but you can't diddle old Ed out of what's due him. I think you'll ante up. And for you, baby, it won't cost more than a night of your time. It will save you from the Russian *and* the Bulgarians."

"We won't see the Russian again."

At that moment, a wild scream shattered the quiet. It was repeated, shuddering screech after shuddering screech. The tourists all looked at one another and broke into a run.

At the top of the hill, the group clustered around

Aggie Taliaferro, huddling on a low stone wall. Her
Henry Higgins sweater was torn and raveled, her hair
burst from its knot. There was a puffiness around one
eye that threatened to close it entirely.

"What happened?" My goodness!" Are your hurt?"
The exclamations came from everyone. Weisenstein was
applying first aid.

"Hell, Herb. Cut that out," Aggie commanded un-
graciously. "Give me a drink. That's the only medicine
I need."

At Weisenstein's nod, Aggie's satchel was brought
from the bus and the flask was handed to her. She
ignored the nicety of pouring the liquor into the cap and
drank straight from the flask.

"Now what happened?" Weisenstein asked.

"What does it look like? I was attacked!"

"What?" "Who?" The exclamations rose again.

"They were dressed like farmers. You know, in those
jean outfits. But they weren't farmers!"

"How do you know? What were they?"

"They wore city shoes. I grew up on a farm. I know
what farmers wear in plowing season. These were no
farmers."

"Then who? Thieves?"

"Oh, they took my Bulgarian leva, but they left everything else. I had American cash and they didn't even
look at it."

"How many were there?"

"Three. One was definitely in command. He did all
the talking."

"What did he say?"

"I don't know! I couldn't understand the gabble."

"Did you recognize the men who attacked you? What
did they look like?" Susannah asked when there was a
break in the general questioning.

"Hell, no. These Turks all look alike." Susannah saw

Dimitri wince a little. "But it wasn't all one-sided," Aggie concluded in satisfaction. "I got one of them. I may recognize *him* again."

She held out her right hand to show two heavy diamond-cluster rings covered with blood. Her knuckles, too, were cracked and bleeding. They all looked, mouths agape a little. Some of the women exclaimed at her presence of mind. Aggie's laugh was a raucous, unpleasant sound. A spasm crossed Susannah's face.

Bit by bit, the story came out. Aggie had been walking by herself on a deserted trail just out of sight of the hotel. Two men jumped her from behind and held her down while the third searched her body and her purse. When she resisted, the biggest one slugged her across the face, knocking her out momentarily. When she came to, they were gone and she began screaming.

Susannah edged backward out of the crowd and sat farther down on the stone wall by herself. Meditatively, she lit a cigarette. Had Azarov picked Aggie Taliaferro and arranged the assault? She had noticed the shoes the security police wore. There was no uniformity; each man apparently wore his own. But they would all fit the description of "city" shoes. Aggie wasn't so unobservant after all.

Thoughtfully, she spun a weed in her fingers. Would they be attacked and searched one by one? Or would the authorities detain and examine them en masse? Either way, the Communists were closing in, threatening the Endicotts and the security of *Dead Souls*. A new hiding place would be needed. Could an adequate one even be found?

She leaned over for another sprig of grass, and her watch suddenly swung free from her neck on its chain. Her hand closed over it. The big gold hunting case watch had belonged to her great-great-grandfather. He had carried a miniature oil portrait of his wife in the back. It had never been removed. Folded tightly and carefully, page 51 of *Dead Souls* would fit there. Should she get back the book and put it there now? Instinct said no. It was logical for Azarov to assume that Novak had sought out the wily old pro, honed by years of underground work, for the task of transporting the information back to Washington. Susannah Clarke was young and inexperienced, definitely second choice for a man in Novak's jam. She should wait. The information should not be in her possession at all when she next confronted Colonel Azarov.

Chapter 15

IT WAS IN YET ANOTHER grim dining room that
the group gathered that night. They were disgruntled.
Aggie's encounter had frightened them. The virulent
nausea that subsequently attacked the Weisensteins and
the Endicotts had delayed them. They had arrived at
the Rila Monastery too late for an afternoon tour. Although an evening tour in the moonlight had been
scheduled in its place, the opportunity for the usual pic-
ture-taking had been lost. Then, when the hotel staff
failed to deliver their luggage to their rooms, it was the
last straw. Now the low murmur of complaint around
the tables betokened a vague sense of unease, a feeling
that something, they weren't quite sure what, was the
matter.

Susannah's own feelings were mixed. She had seen
an ashen-faced Azalea Endicott carrying her own tote
bag upstairs. Thus, the whereabouts of *Dead Souls* was
ensured for the night. On the other hand, Vladimir had
quarreled with Marlene. The abruptness of it seemed
contrived, and certainly Marlene herself seemed be-
wildered by his sudden change of mood. To Susannah,
the explanation was obvious. Vladimir had said he used
Marlene. Clearly, he no longer needed her. The situation suggested that he suddenly had other plans. The
fact that he had driven away in a scatter of gravel and
dirt and that Azarov had not arrived gave Susannah no
relief. An odd sense of disappointment, uncertainty, the
feeling of waiting was almost oppressive.

"You look glum," Phillips said to her as the group gathered in the hotel foyer for the tour. "Are you ailing too, or are you coming with us?"

Suddenly, Susannah remembered Azarov's quiet words that morning. "I opened the door." Cowering in her room would not ensure her safety.

"I'm coming. I wouldn't miss it," she answered.

"The question is, are you missing that big Russian?" Louise Phillips asked.

"No pain on that score."

"You must have a heart of stone, then. I saw you dancing last night. How can you be immune to someone who looks at you like that?"

Louise had caught her off guard. "I must prefer the homely type" was the best Susannah could manage.

"Seriously, though," Phillips asked, "what is he like? Is he a Communist?"

"Yes, he's a Communist, but other than that, I really don't know. He asked all the questions and I did most of the talking. He's smart. Certainly trusted, since they let him out of the country. That's all I learned."

"Is he likable?"

Susannah hesitated. "I suppose he could be, if the subjects of politics and political philosophy are avoided. He believes in his government and its policies. That makes him part of the problem."

"I've met several of their chaps on my visits to the Soviet Union for the company," Phillips said. "He's unlike the rest of them in one thing: when he smiles, he doesn't look like his face will crack. They're a grim bunch. When they did smile, I found myself wondering why. It actually made me nervous. It's hard to know the Russians. I've spent hours with some of them, both in meetings and socially. They rarely mention their personal lives and never invite you into their homes. In negotiations, I always had the feeling they were holding out on me. I'll tell you this much: détente is all very exciting, but I'll wager you anything you want it's illusory."

"You're a pessimist," Louise said. "Surely it's to their advantage to trade with the West. And once they get consumer products, they'll want to cooperate to get more."

"They'll take," her husband said. "I'm not sure they'll give anything but trouble in return."

They were strolling down the road as they chatted. Others straggled around them, some ahead, some behind. The slow dusk, the tranquillity of the monastery nestling deep in the shelter of looming mountains did not soothe the group very much. There were complaints about the chill in the air, the lateness of the hour, the poor light.

Pictures and descriptions had prepared Susannah for the austerity of the monastery's exterior walls, but not for the magnificence of its interior courtyard. White walls, black wood, striped Moorish designs outlined in deep coral glowed in the pearly light. In the center of the courtyard, the walls of the cathedral glowed in medieval richness. Life-sized saints clustered about the entrance to the sanctuary, their golden robes shimmering in the twilight. Above the rooms on all sides the mountains towered, steep, green, dense. Entranced, Susannah wandered with the others, her ears attuned to Dimitri's patter, her eyes acutely aware of the play of light. They climbed wooden stairs and their steps echoed and creaked along dark galleries past silent cells. Pines whispered softly. A priest in the black robe and long beard of a Greek Orthodox patriarch padded across the court below, his stature strangely foreshortened by their elevation. Here, on the top floor of the monastery, they were above the cathedral domes. Even from here the glint of golden figures could be seen, gathered closely around the cathedral door. It was spectacular. And a little eerie. The others felt it too. The litany of complaints died away and they walked and looked in silence, their faces stiffened in awe.

"And that concludes the organized tour," Dimitri said briskly. "If you are careful with your shutter speed, there's still enough light for photography. You should taste the water, too. It comes from mountain springs and is pure."

The group scattered. Susannah stayed by Louise and Frank Phillips while he took innumerable time exposures. When they finally joined the others at the fountain, they were all thirsty. Water poured from brass faucets into a basin at their feet. Hans and Hank Reynolds were drinking from the two brass cups chained to the fountain.

"It's really good," Reynolds said. "Who would like some?"

"I'll taste," Phillips said, stepping forward. He drank deeply. "Oh, my, yes," he exclaimed when he had finished. "That's better even than the well on the farm where I grew up."

Someone handed Susannah a cup. Thinking only of Phillips' pleasure, she took it and drank.

Immediately she knew her error. The light breeze in the pines became a roar. The mountains tilted in on her. The cup fell, spilling water over her feet.

"Are you all right?" someone asked anxiously.

She tried to shake her head, but it was too late. She was falling.

"I'll help her," Hans said quickly, almost too quickly.

Susannah wasn't entirely unconscious. She could hear voices and distinguish who was speaking. But she couldn't move. Her limbs would not obey. Her vision was distorted. The mountains, the monastery, the crowding faces were terribly, grotesquely distended, like things seen in a horror house.

Hans's voice, that odd, accentless voice, reassured the others. "It must be the same virus that sickens the others. I'll take her to her room. Dr. Weisenstein can attend to her. Don't bother yourselves. She should sleep." He was edging out of the crowd with Susannah held firmly in his arms.

She tried to call to Phillips. Her voice came out a croak. Or a groan. He didn't understand. No one did.

"It's a good thing Hans was here," Edie Burton said.

"Isn't it lucky we have a doctor in the group!" Miss McMillan added fervently.

Susannah tried to protest. That was false. Dr. Weisenstein was sick. He couldn't see anyone. But no one paid any attention to her. Solicitously, the other tour members watched Hans carry her away while they muttered darkly against sanitary conditions in the Balkans.

Once on the other side of the cathedral, out of sight of the party, Hans turned down a dark gallery.

"No," Susannah tried to say again. "Where are you taking me?"

"To a doctor," Hans said. "You need a doctor."

She tried to struggle. A door opened. Hans went in, past Ed Elbert, who held it open for them.

"Where are we? What do you want with me?"

"To make you talk." That was Voorhies looming out of the dimness. When the needle pricked her arm, Susannah knew that he could.

How long was it? Someone was pinching her feet. Her feet were bare, and it hurt. Rough hands slapped her face. Her body shuddered heavily, although not with cold. She tried feebly to escape the irritation of those bruising hands. Then, blessedly, they let her alone.

The door was opened, bringing a gust of air from out-side, and a voice spoke heartily.

"Come in now, Ed. She's all yours. Don't waste too much time. She'll be conscious and full of fight."

"I like my women awake," Elbert's truculent voice said.

Dimly, Susannah saw Vladimir Voorhies in the shad-ows. He laughed harshly. She hadn't realized before what an evil-looking man he was.

"You've earned your pleasure," he said. "The little bitch will probably like it. Her kind always does. Well, you have your money and you have your woman. I'll leave you to enjoy yourself." And Voorhies laughed again.

Desperately, Susannah tried to clear her head, to understand what had happened and where she was. Her facility for coming out of an anesthetic with clear facul-ties didn't help her now. She felt befuddled, uncertain. Her body was leaden and unresponsive. Groggily, she moved. She wasn't bound.

The old metal latch clicked. Startled, the two men looked up. The door swung inward. Susannah's vision was clearing a little, and she saw Colonel Azarov stand-ing on the threshold.

"Voorhies, if you are done here, I want a word with you," he said. His tone was authoritative.

"Here at last?" Voorhies replied. "I had given you up for lost. Did you get your car repaired?" He went out with the Russian, and the door closed behind them with an ominous little click.

Slowly Susannah rose to a sitting position and swung her legs over the edge of the table where she had been lying. The room heaved and tilted.

"Not so fast, little girl. It's old Ed's turn now."

Susannah tried to stand, but her legs crumpled and she fell. Dizziness assailed her and she almost passed

out a second time. Elbert's touch galvanized her clumsily to her feet.

"You leave me alone," she muttered thickly.

He lunged, the force of his rush slamming her back
against the wall. He pushed his face into hers. Susannah
twisted her head away, but undaunted, he buried his
mouth in her neck, chewing and snuffling. His thick
body suffocated her as he pressed her into the wall. But
her head was clearing. She endured and waited for the
dizziness to pass.

He tried to kiss her. Holding her wrists immobile, he
shoved his face into hers, reaching for her lips as she
strained away. His breath was offensive. Susannah
shifted a little. When Elbert moved in response, she
rammed her knee upward. She missed his groin, but
he had had to sidestep. It gave her a little freedom of
movement. It was difficult to do without shoes, but she
tried to trip him nevertheless. When he lurched and
released her hand, she slammed her open palm against
his ear and leaped for the door.

Elbert cut her off, his body blocking her only escape
route. Slowly he advanced, head down a little, eyes glit-
tering. The struggle was only exciting him. Susannah
could see his trousers bulging.

Frantically she looked for her shoes, for a weapon,
for anything to use against him. There was nothing.
She backed toward the room's only window and darted
a glance over her shoulder. There was a twenty-foot
drop straight down onto rock. In that moment, Elbert
lunged again.

Susannah stepped aside, but he grabbed her blouse
and dragged her down with him. The thin fabric ripped
as her head grazed the wall. A button clicked on the
floor and rolled. Susannah was inert.

The suffocating pressure of his weight roused her.
She twisted and fought, trying to get a hand free to

deliver a resounding blow. He lifted his head to kiss her once more.

Susannah's teeth clamped on his lip. Blood poured from the wound. He howled and dabbed at the injury.

Instantly, Susannah rammed her fist into his solar plexus. He grunted and moved a little, and she shoved him off and struggled to her feet. Her blouse hung from one shoulder and hampered her, but she didn't stop. Elbert rolled. As she leaped for the door, his big hand grasped her ankle and brought her down. She fell hard, full length, face down, on the floor. The breath rushed away and she fought to retain consciousness. Elbert was on top of her now, his trousers open, tearing at her clothes.

Silently, desperately, Susannah clawed to get away, but he was bulldog strong. He hung on, trying to get positioned. Her nails raked his cheek from eye to jaw-bone, raising still more blood. It only infuriated him. He struck her hard across the face and knocked her head against the floor. Her teeth rattled and jolted against her tongue. More blood poured down her chin. Her vision suddenly blurred. Now it was a matter of blind, dogged determination. Not to give up. Not to give in. Fight a little longer. No woman determined enough can be raped. She had heard that many times. But Elbert was so big. So heavy. So strong.

He was on top of her again. Now. Now. Oh, dear God.

Susannah made a final effort and heaved.

He fell away so easily she lost her balance and rolled. Azarov yanked Elbert to his feet. There was an expression of extreme distaste on his face. Contemptuously, he slapped him twice across the mouth with the flat of his hand. Then, hauling the man by the collar like a recalcitrant truant, he dragged him to the door.

"Mrs. Elbert, here he is," he said courteously. The calmness of his tone seemed incongruous.

Mrs. Elbert said nothing in reply. Her eyes—big, brown, bitter—rested on Azarov a moment. Then she turned away. She didn't look at her husband. Whipped, he trailed after her, adjusting his clothes as he went. Azarov shut the door quietly and turned.

Susannah was in a heap on the floor. Instinctively, she had curled into a fetal position and was sobbing in great racking spasms. Her hands were knotted into tight fists and hid her face from him. There was a lot of blood.

For a long moment he looked down at her. Then slowly he crossed the little room and knelt beside her.

"Susannah."

She cringed. "No."

"I won't hurt you, Susannah."

"No. Go away. Dear God, leave me alone!"

He took his hand away from her shoulder. A moment more he knelt there on the floor, trying to see the injuries through the torn blouse. It was too dark. Silently, he rose and left the room.

The sound of the latch falling penetrated Susannah's consciousness. Slowly she stumbled to her feet, saw her shoes in the far corner and with trembling steps went to put them on. Standing on one foot, she almost fell, but when her shoes were on, she groped to the door. It opened easily. The dog lay across the threshold. He raised his head and looked inquiringly at her. Susannah stepped around him.

He rose immediately and blocked her way. Her eyes on the animal's face, Susannah tried to evade him. He lowered his head. His ears flattened. He looked murderous, although he had not growled. Tentatively, she tried once more. This time he did growl—a soft rumble that was more a warning than a threat. He had his orders. Azarov didn't mean for her to leave. The nightmare wasn't over yet. Despairingly, she turned back into the room. With a thump and a sigh, the dog lay down again.

The barren little room offered no place to hide. A small animal rustled in the silence and she jumped, heart pounding heavily. Then it was quiet. Her ears strained for the sound of Azarov's footsteps. Stealthily, she hid herself in the darkest shadows behind the door, a shoe gripped determinedly in one hand.

Susannah didn't have to wait long for Azarov's return. The Russian was carrying a metal box and two candles. He left the dog outside and, shutting the door firmly behind him, crossed to the table. The moment his back was turned, Susannah stepped forward, the shoe raised to strike. A match flared. Glancing around, the Russian saw her. Susannah stopped, her movement arrested by his expression. Then, deliberately, he lit the candles and stuck them into wax that he melted on the tabletop. When he turned to face her, Susannah backed away, shrinking against the wall. He took no notice of the shoe clutched in her hand. This time there was no expression in his face at all.

"Let me see what he did to you," he said.

Susannah regarded him fearfully. She didn't move.

"You are bleeding. And this floor is filthy. You must avoid infection." He had opened the box and was laying out cotton and gauze, putting them neatly on a clean cloth.

Susannah looked around. In the candlelight, animal droppings were visible on the floor, and now the smell came to her. Mustiness, decay, a dead animal someplace in the walls. Blood was on her hands. Her nails were torn. She came forward slowly into the light of the candles. Her eyes were dark with pain and fear. She seemed to be in shock.

Azarov examined her critically, his face intent, concerned. He turned her chin into the light.

"Is all that blood yours, or is some of it his?" He began swabbing it away with gauze, preventing her answer. His hands were gentle, knowledgeable.

"His," she whispered finally.

"I should have guessed. Take off your blouse and let me see your back."

Susannah hesitated. But he had turned away and was looking through the box. Slowly, she slipped it from her shoulders. It was in shreds. Dismayed, she looked down at herself. Her skirt was ripped, the hem hanging loose, the zipper destroyed. Wide ladders marred her stockings. The straps of her underclothes had broken. There were long scratches on her shoulders running down her breasts and over her arms.

Azarov took the ruined blouse away from her and dropped it on the floor. When he turned back, his breath caught and he stopped abruptly.

Her lingerie was lace, of a deep pink that matched the blouse she had worn. He had forgotten, or maybe he had never realized, just how seductive lace can be. She had a neat little figure, and the angry scratches across the swell of breast only accentuated it. His fingers shook suddenly, and he dropped the cap to the antiseptic bottle.

She looked questioningly over her shoulder and saw the sudden tightening of his mouth, the darkening of his eyes. Her hand went protectively to the torn slip.

"Will it burn?" she asked matter-of-factly.

"What?"

"That Communist brew you have in your hand."

She had broken the mood. He laughed. "Like hell," he said. "And don't tell me we Communists don't believe in it. You don't know what we believe."

She smiled faintly and let him clean the wounds. Several of them were oozing blood.

"You'll heal without scars, I should think," Azarov said.

"Thank you." She reached for her blouse.

He stopped her. "Better wear this instead. Your shirt-waist has been on the floor and it isn't clean." He took off his suit coat and held it for her. The fabric was rough and hard under her fingers, but it covered her, restoring a little of her confidence.

"Now let me examine your head."

Turning her to face him, he inspected her skull with sensitive fingers, probing for any sign of concussion. His hands were oddly comforting, even a little mesmerizing. She sensed the exact second when his manner lost its professional tone and became personal, intimate. Subtly, his touch became a caress rather than a medical measure of injury. He glanced down at her. His expression warmed. She backed away.

His hands fell to his sides at once. "You have had a severe shock to the head," he said evenly. "You should not be alone for a while."

"I don't feel like walking." Her voice was rebellious, a little ungracious. She was afraid of him and was uncertain how to respond to his present kindness.

"I didn't invite you to walk," he said with some acerbity. "You should not move around at all. There's a bench outside. It's a beautiful night, and this is a mystical place. You may never return here. Regardless of what has happened, you should not miss it."

He sounded pedantic, like a guide pointing out the sights. With someone else, the offer would be attractive. But Susannah wanted only to be alone, to escape this man who had gathered the things that had fallen from her purse and who now stood holding it out to her. He dropped her watch into her other hand.

"The chain is broken," he said.

Silently, she took it from him. His clasp on her arm caused pain, and she remembered the needle, clumsily injected. Sodium pentothal rarely failed. Was Voorhies even now slipping into the Endicotts' room while they slept, or was he already waiting to hand the book to Azarov? Would they be satisfied with that? Or were the Endicott sisters in physical danger as well?

Suddenly, she was trembling. Azarov put his arm around her and led her out, down the gallery stairs to a bench under the pines. Ivan followed and lay down beside them, his nose only inches from Susannah's foot.

Azarov took a small cup from his first-aid kit, filled it with water from the fountain and brought it to her. Susannah shook her head.

"I may be a Communist, but I'm not a poisoner. Drink it."

Susannah obeyed. It was clear, fresh, bitingly cold. Someone—Hans?—had put something in that other cup. The medicinal taste was still in her mouth.

Azarov sat down beside her, his shoulder touching hers. He lit two cigarettes and handed her one. They smoked silently. The monastery was deserted now. The moon had risen above the roofs. The air was soft.

"Do you want to tell me what happened?" Azarov asked after a while.

"Wasn't it obvious? I wish you had taken him with you the first time."

"There was something I had to do just then. I gambled that you could take care of yourself for a few minutes."

"*You* gambled! You *knew* what would happen?"

Azarov smiled a little at the bitterness in her voice. "No. I knew only that he wanted you." He paused, inhaling deeply. "I think you won't have any more trouble with Elbert. Neither will anyone else for quite some some time."

Susannah made no answer. The silence lengthened. "Were you looking for Voorhies," she prompted finally, "or did you just happen by?"

"I was looking for you."

"How did you know where I was?"

"I didn't. Mrs. Elbert had followed her husband. She told me."

"Why didn't she interrupt?"

"Her husband beats her."

There was another long silence. Did Imogene know about Novak too? There were so many who did. "What did Vladimir Voorhies say?" she asked.

"That you had fainted."

"That's all?"

"Yes."

"And what did you say to him?"

"I ordered him to stay away from you."

"And will he?"

"I expect so."

"Where is he now?"

"I don't know." He stubbed out his cigarette and reached slowly for another.

"You said you were looking for me. What for?"

"To see you. To be with you. But you make it very difficult."

Susannah was silent. The match flared and went out. He inhaled deeply.

"Has that ever happened to you before?" he asked.

She shuddered suddenly. He reached for her hand, slid back the sleeve, found her pulse. His fingers were rough on the bare skin of her wrist.

"Once. Years ago," she answered.

"That is why you keep the Dobermans?"

"Yes."

"What happened?"

She made no response. He released her. "Does it hurt that much?"

The silence was so long he didn't think she would answer. When she spoke, her voice was just a wisp of sound. "It shouldn't. But it does. He was a . . . a friend of my father's. Tonight . . . it was . . . a . . ." Her voice faded away. She suddenly thought of all those women in the war, and a terrible spasm passed over her body.

Once more his fingers found her wrist. His hand lingered, giving her the opportunity to reach out. She didn't.

"You deserve to be loved carefully," he said softly.

When she made no response, his voice changed, became a little brisker. "Elbert is a coward. And Vladimir Voorhies is sniveling scum. You are rid of them both. We can concern ourselves with more pleasant things now. Have you seen all the monastery here?"

"Yes."

"Do you like it?"

"Very much."

Azarov's eyes were roving around the quiet galleries. One side of the building was gleaming white in the moonlight, the other still in shadow. "It's restful," he said. There was another long pause. "There's something about these old religious structures. They always seem to be waiting."

"Perhaps they are."

"I don't believe that."

"Perhaps they've never been abandoned."

"I don't believe they're haunted."

"Not haunted. Just inhabited."

"Come, now. You don't really think so?"

"You noticed the difference. What do you believe?

"Just that it's calming to visit them. And disturbing too, sometimes. Lonely. But Ivan doesn't seem to mind." The dog's ears twitched, but he didn't move. "If there are spirits, they must be kindly."

Susannah suddenly remembered the priest in Plovdiv. His words *had* been a warning.

"Do you visit such places often?" she asked.

"Not often. Sometimes on a holiday."

"What do you generally do on a holiday?"

"I don't have many."

"But when you do have one."

"I used to go mushroom-picking with friends in the woods. Or skiing. Or skating. Depending on the season."

"And now?"

"Now we find a big field and Ivan runs."

"We?"

"Ivan and I."

A lonely man. An outcast, probably. No one would like an officer of the KGB.

"Tell me of your life."

"I want to hear of yours."

"Not now. I don't want to talk." Her voice weakened.

"Do you feel faint?" The instant anxiety in his voice as he sat up and looked closely at her was unexpected.

"No. Just very tired."

He settled back. His fingers sought her wrist again, then in a moment fell away. "What shall I tell you?" he asked.

"How you live. What you want from life. Your childhood. Whatever you wish."

None of that was exactly appropriate to tell this woman. "You have never been to Russia, have you?" he said instead. "Shall I tell you about it?"

"Begin with your favorite place."

"That's easy. There's a glen in the woods about twenty miles outside of Moscow. Spring flowers are there long before they bloom in town. They are thick, fragrant—an ethereal fragance—and the clearing has just the right amount of light. To the west there is an old village—a small one, very rural. You can see the domes of the church. It is crumbling now. The roof is almost gone. But from a distance, it looks whole."

He talked on, painting a vivid picture of the great cities of Czarist Russia and of the ramshackle villages close to the land. His voice was deep, softly resonant, the words enunciated clearly and without accent. There was the slightest lilt to his sentences that made his speech seem musical.

Susannah listened more to the sound of his voice than to what he said until she realized that he spoke of Russia's past and not of its present or future. Then, more interested, she heeded his words and discovered that he had a sensitive eye for beauty. He found it even in the disintegrating villages and the ordinariness of the countryside. He seemed to be yearning for the culture of a more romantic age. In America he might have been a collector and preservationist. In Russia he was a looker, spending his leisure time in museums and wandering empty lanes to forgotten villages. If he had any friends, he didn't mention them.

Suddenly, Susannah felt herself slipping. She rose abruptly, an uncertain hand to her head.

"If you don't mind," she said shakily. "I don't feel well."

He caught her as she swayed and lifted her easily. "The reaction is delayed. Don't worry. I will stay with you."

Dimly, she knew he carried her from the monastery to his car and drove her to the hotel. There he lifted her out again and, with a porter running ahead with the key, took her to her room. Once flat on the bed, she let go and slid into unconsciousness.

She didn't know how long she slept. Once she drifted

awake and heard voices speaking Russian. Only Azarov's was clear.

"You tell them that if they interfere in my operation again, I will personally see that they regret it."

The reply was inaudible.

"When I know, I will cable at once. As always. Meanwhile, repeated requests for reports threaten the security of my procedures. Emphasize that in your cable to Moscow."

There was further exchange that Susannah didn't hear. When she awoke again, it was dawn. Azarov sat in a chair beside the bed, his face in profile. He was reading.

Susannah stirred restlessly. He looked up immediately.

"Good. You are awake. I was beginning to worry." He put the book down, reached for her wrist and carefully, a plain pocket watch in his hand, counted her pulse. Then he felt her forehead and cheek with the back of his hand. "You will be all right, I think. Do you feel ill?"

"I don't believe so," she whispered. She shoved the blanket aside, realized she wasn't wearing his coat anymore and pulled it over her shoulders again.

"Then I'll leave you now. It is still very early. You should sleep. Shall I set your clock for you?"

"We must leave at nine."

The clock was wound and set. Then there was silence. She opened her eyes. Azarov was looking down at her, a little smile playing around his lips. "Good night," he said.

"Good night."

He turned away then and snapped his fingers for the dog. It rose reluctantly and padded mournfully to the door. Azarov followed.

"Aleksei?"

"Yes?"

"Thank you."

He smiled in genuine pleasure. "I am pleased to have been of service. Good night." The door closed quietly after him.

Susannah lay without moving—drifting. Suddenly remembering, she propped herself up on her elbow and reached for the book he had left face down on the table beside the bed. It was all right. It wasn't *Dead Souls*. With a sigh, she fell back on the pillow and was instantly asleep.

Chapter 16

THE ALARM AWAKENED HER. Susannah drifted
for a moment, thinking of Azarov's last smile rather
than the traumatic events of the previous evening. She
was afraid of him, and yet he had not harmed her. But
then why should he—if he had what he wanted? Vladimir Voorhies! That bastard!

Worried now, she rose to dress. Sometime during her
absence, her suitcase had been placed on the luggage
rack. One glance inside told her that it had been
searched again, this time so clumsily that it was incon-
ceivable that Azarov could have done it. Instead, she
blamed the hotel staff, working hastily and amateurishly,
and probably on Azarov's orders. Nothing had been
stolen this time, however, and trying to control her
irritation, she began repacking. It was a good opportunity to consolidate her packages and to make room
for her trench coat. She didn't want to have to carry
it any longer.

As she worked, she went through everything, discard-
ing ticket stubs and timetables, emptying the pockets of
matchbooks and forgotten change. At last she took up
the trench coat and dug deep into the first pocket. Her
fingers touched something unfamiliar, and as she pulled
her hand out, a paper fell to the floor at her feet. It was
folded into quarters and seemed curiously pure there on
the dark carpet. With a sense of foreboding, she bent
slowly to pick it up. The letter read:

My dearest Susannah:

How I miss you! I never knew how much! Our last night together was so perfect that I ache from the memory. It has grown worse day by day, until now I feel that I am only half a man. My customary haunts will surely smother me to death. My duties intrude upon my thoughts of you. My feelings have grown until they can no longer be contained indoors, and so I prowl the streets and byways of this city, hoping for enough weariness to sleep. I long for the freedom of your wide Virginia acres and the peace of loving you quietly in the evening when the fire burns low and the day is over. Only then will I feel whole again. Dearest heart, I cannot endure alone much longer. Hurry.

Absalom

Susannah was stunned. How long had it been there? It was impossible to guess. She hadn't worn the coat for days. She had guarded *Dead Souls* until it was no longer expedient to do so, but she had been careless with her coat. It had been left on the bus, lain over the backs of chairs, hung in restaurant coatrooms. Dozens of people had had access to it. Any one of them could have put the letter there. But she felt that it was Novak. The coat had been in the closet of her room while he waited for her return. Seeing that he couldn't stay, he had left this last urgent warning of Absalom's increasing danger.

And yet—was it possible? Novak had been too long in Bulgaria. Where would he have obtained the heavy cream paper, so readily available in any American stationery store but so rare in Eastern Europe? She had never seen Novak's handwriting and couldn't say whether the flowing print was his or not. The letter appeared to be a simple love letter, written by a man waiting in America to a young woman vacationing alone. How innocent. And how very dangerous. For the double meaning was clear to anyone who knew of Absalom. The sudden yearning for the freedom of Virginia, the urgency he expressed could mean only one thing: Absalom was in great danger and wanted refuge. Did that mean that Absalom was a man and not just an intelligence operation with a colorful code name?

Susannah hesitated for a long time with the letter in her hand. It could be a trap. It fingered her as an American agent. And yet she didn't dare burn it. It might be treated paper, carefully kept by Novak for just such an emergency. It might contain a microdot or a special ink. Slowly she returned it to the pocket and folded the trench coat over her arm. The letter had been safe there for several days. For the moment, that was as good a place as any for it. Only this time, she would guard the coat.

Azarov had gone. Susannah noticed, as she crossed the lobby to the dining room, that his car was no longer parked before the hotel. She shouldn't be surprised. If he had the information he wanted, there would be no reason to linger.

Susannah had dressed carefully, taking pains to hide the evidence of her struggle with Elbert. But she need not have feared that anyone would notice. The group was preoccupied with a new outrage: the luggage had been searched as clumsily as Susannah's. They threatened to complain to the State Department. They looked for Hans to register a more immediate protest, but neither Hans nor Dimitri had come down yet. That too irritated them. They were afraid now, and wanted very much to go home.

Susannah said little. She too wanted desperately to leave. Even without *Dead Souls,* she must still try to obtain an interview with the President and give him an accounting. How long could Absalom wait? How long would it take the KGB to unmask each layer of the operation until they had Absalom himself? Could she expect the KGB to fumble, just long enough for her to get home and for the President to act? No, that was pointless. It might take her several days to arrange an appointment with the President. And then it could be too late. Colonel Azarov was not a man who fumbled.

There was a sudden commotion in the lobby just outside, and then Christine Endicott stumbled, screaming and sobbing, into the dining room. Exclaiming in dismay, the others in the tour party all jumped up and rushed to her. More slowly, Susannah joined them.

Gentle, ladylike Christine was completely incoherent. Tears poured down her wrinkled cheeks; her face was chalky white, her eyes wide and staring. She was hysterical, and Dr. Weisenstein struck her smartly across the face and then gathered her comfortingly into his arms. Only then did they learn what she had seen.

Vladimir Voorhies. Dead. In the stream by the monastery.

Susannah went with the others, pelting down the hill after Dr. Weisenstein, around the grim walls of the monastery to the far side, well removed from any but the most determined hiker. Voorhies lay face down, half-submerged in the stream that rushed close beside the monastery's wall. He might have fallen from a window above and drowned.

And yet?

Susannah knelt beside Dr. Weisenstein. "What are those bruises?" she asked, pointing to a broad discoloration at the back of the neck.

"That's probably what killed him. Obviously, he didn't have enough consciousness left to crawl away from the water. It would require an autopsy to know whether he died from the fall or from drowning."

"Did he suffer?" Marlene asked faintly.

"Probably not for long. Here, let me help you!" he exclaimed.

But it was too late. Marlene let out a shivering moan and fainted. Dr. Weisenstein jumped to catch her. The others too hurried to Marlene's side.

Susannah gulped. Vladimir was not a pretty sight. The injuries to his head were bloody and gruesome. But she had to know.

Quickly, she searched his pockets. Passport; a fountain pen; aspirin; keys; a wallet full of credit cards, club cards, money, a picture of a girl aged about ten. She opened the pen. Black ink. The same color as in Absalom's letter. Could Valdimir have written it? The signature on the passport was in cursive scrip and it was hard to say, but she thought it was possible.

She rose then. Dr. Weisenstein had turned and was watching her with an odd expression. Susannah handed Vladimir's possessions to him. "You'll be our spokesman, I'm sure," she said. "The embassy should have these."

Weisenstein's face relaxed. "You're right. I'd forgotten. We should go for help right now."

Pocketing the items, he turned back to the group and gave orders—arranging for someone to stay by the body while the others went for Hans and the authorities. Susannah went with the rest and helped Marlene, who was sobbing bitterly.

"How did Christine happen to find him?" Reynolds asked of the group in general. "That's quite off the beaten track."

"Bird walking. How could you have missed that?" Phillips answered, referring to Christine's habit of early-morning walks with her camera. They had all teased her from time to time, accusing her of taking more pictures of birds for her hometown Audubon meetings than of the monuments she had traveled half a world to see. Christine had never minded their kidding. But she had been obviously disappointed that the surveillance of their movements in Bulgaria had often prevented her from taking pictures.

Susannah's fingers slid into the coat pocket and touched the letter. Vladimir? If he had written the letter, it meant that he was only pretending to be Azarov's agent, that he was her ally after all. Had he gone to Azalea's room and taken *Dead Souls* to encode for transmittal to Washington? Had he had time?

The police were waiting for them. They were herded into the dining room, and once more armed guards kept them under observation. They watched out the window as Voorhies' body was brought on a stretcher. No one had thought to cover him.

The police questioned Dr. Weisenstein and Christine Endicott at length, then ushered them into the dining room with the others. They waited, trying to see what was happening. Aggie, helpful Aggie, knew a true story of a tour group in Hungary that had been arrested and sent to slave-labor camps. As the morning passed and they were not freed, it began to seem that they could expect as much.

Finally, they were ordered into line. They would load their own luggage, board the bus and be taken under guard to Sofia. They would be questioned in detail there.

"Where's Hans?" Mrs. Burton asked querulously. "Can't he do something? Why isn't he helping us?"

"Hans was called to Sofia early this morning," Dimitri told her rather shortly. He was pale, and a beading of sweat moistened his upper lip.

"What's the matter?"

Dimitri tried to ignore her, but the woman persisted. "Why? Why was he called to Sofia? We ought to know if it concerns us."

Exasperated, the guide revealed the reason. "I didn't want to worry you, but there are difficulties with the reservations for your flight from Sofia to Zurich tomorrow. One of the guests here was driving to Sofia. Hans went with him early this morning to try to resolve the problem."

"What time did he leave?" Susannah asked quietly, wondering if Azarov and Hans had joined forces openly. The guide's answer revealed that it was possible.

"Early. About six o'clock," he answered. "Now we must get on the bus. Quickly. Quickly."

Susannah maneuvered herself into place behind the Endicotts. She had to see if *Dead Souls* was still in the tote bag.

"That's terribly heavy," she told Azalea. "Let me carry it for you this time so you can help Christine."

"Would you? I know it's tour policy for everyone to carry their own, but she's so upset, poor dear."

Susannah took the bag. It was heavy and awkward to carry, but it was easy to see inside. The book was there. The thin edge of its worn blue cover was visible between the two guidebooks. And page 51—was it, too, intact?

As they waited in line under the vigilant gaze of the guards, Susannah was tempted to look. But that was foolish. If the book was there, so was page 51. Clearly, Voorhies had not had time to obtain the book. It also meant that he had not told Azarov of its existence. If Azarov had believed in Voorhies' loyalty, he would have been unforgiving when he discovered the American's treachery. For Susannah had been too close, had seen too clearly the nature of the bruise on Voorhies' neck. A blunt instrument—more probably, a karate chop— had killed him. He had not been in quite the right location to have fallen from the monastery window. He had been murdered for his loyalty to the United States.

Susannah helped Azalea stow the tote bag and then

took her own place across the aisle from the sisters. The coat, folded carefully, lay on the seat beside her. Her hand lingered protectively. Novak had been gunned down in the open by police gunfire. Voorhies had been killed in the dark, in secret. Vladimir had predicted it. How had he said it? "He could murder you with a snap of the wrist." Susannah thought of Azarov's granite hands, the velvety voice saying, "There was something I had to do just then." Shuddering heavily, she wrapped herself in the coat. She was shivering with cold.

Chapter 17

SEVERAL HOURS LATER, the bus stopped before the same building in Sofia where they had been questioned before. Now, as then, the two American Embassy officials were waiting and entered the bus to instruct them before going into the building.

"I believe one of you found the body of Mr. Voorhies?" Trapp asked.

"I did," Christine Endicott answered, and burst into tears. At Trapp's request, Dr. Weisenstein described the event.

"Does anyone have anything to add to that account?" Trapp asked. There was a muffled sob from Marlene in the back, but no one had anything to add.

"Well, I will say you've certainly had a memorable stay in Bulgaria," Trapp said. The response to his attempt at humor was feeble. Apprehensively, they rose to follow him into the building, to the same conference room as before. This time, there were chairs.

"Just answer the questions," Trapp advised Susannah when her turn came. "Don't make any suggestions or political comments and it won't take long." She nodded slightly as he opened the door and ushered her into the interrogation room.

The man who sat at the peeling table in the center of the room didn't rise or acknowledge her presence. He was so wooden any greeting or pleasantry was unthinkable. A second man sat behind him and to one side. He stared at Susannah and then belched audibly.

142

"Your passport," the official at the table ordered in English.

Susannah already had it in her hand. She passed it to Trapp, who rose and gave it to him. The official studied it deliberately. Light glinted unpleasantly on his green eyeglasses as he compared the photograph with Susannah's own face.

"You knew the deceased?" he asked.

"Yes."

"For how long?"

"Three days."

"Where did you meet him?"

"Here in Sofia."

"When did you first talk to him?"

"At lunch day before yesterday."

"And the last time?"

"In Plovdiv we walked in the park."

"Did you speak to him at any other time?"

"No."

"Do you know if he had enemies?"

"No."

"Do you know any of his friends other than those in your party?"

"No."

"Did he at any time indicate any fear of death or accident?"

"No."

"Do you know anyone who might have desired his death?"

Susannah suddenly knew real fear. "No," she said. Ironically, she couldn't implicate Azarov without incriminating herself.

The second man suddenly cleared his throat significantly. As he spoke to the interrogator in Russian, Susannah suddenly thought how slovenly they were.

Slovenly and dirty. But the Bulgarian was nodding and translating his question.

"Did you know the deceased in America?" he asked.

"He said he had met me at a party. I didn't recall it."

"When did you last see him alive?"

"He followed our bus in his car from Plovdiv to the Rila Monastery."

"Did you see him arrive?"

"Yes."

"Did you speak to him?"

"No."

"What happened next?"

"He drove away again."

"And was that the last time you saw him?"

"Yes."

The Bulgarian turned to the Russian beside him. "Do you wish to ask anything else?"

Susannah waited anxiously until the Russian finished picking his nose and shook his head.

"That will be all," the interrogator said. "You may go."

"Pro forma," Trapp said cheerfully, returning her passport to her.

"Do they actually suspect any of us?" Susannah asked as they walked back to the conference room.

"I don't believe so. They are questioning hotel and monastery staff as well as security guards responsible for policing the area. They haven't learned anything."

"Could Voorhies have fallen?"

"Possibly. But they don't think so."

"Who was the second man?"

"Soviet security—a friendly adviser to an allied government. There are two of them here. We have no reason to believe that their presence means anything except curiosity."

"What was Voorhies doing in Bulgaria?"

"Waiting for a visa into Russia. Now, don't worry. You won't be delayed long today, and tomorrow you'll be on your way home."

There was no more time for questions. They had reached the conference room and the Elberts were waiting their turn. Susannah was uneasy. Her nails had made three distinct vertical scratches in Elbert's cheek. How would he explain that?

Restlessly, she waited. Azarov, Hans, Ed and Imogene Elbert all knew she had talked to Voorhies last night. Any one of them could implicate her. The minutes passed. Ed and then Imogene returned. Neither had been kept longer than the others. Even Marlene Wells's interrogation was handled with dispatch, and at five o'clock the group was shepherded into the street to board the bus.

"Did Ed Elbert say how he scratched his face?" Susannah asked Hank Reynolds. It was taking a chance to ask such a question, but it was important to know the excuse he was giving.

Reynolds made a vulgar gesture.

"Hank!" his wife exclaimed, shocked at his crudeness before Susannah.

"She's a liberated woman," he defended himself. "She asked a question; she shouldn't be afraid of getting an answer. Ed was philosophical about it. He said this was his last trip behind the Iron Curtain. In the future, he'll go where the women are more obliging."

"I wonder what Imogene will say to that?" Kitty Reynolds asked. "That's just why she picked this tour."

"My advice to her would be if you can't beat 'em, join 'em."

"Hank!"

Husband and wife teasingly bantered, forgetting Susannah, who was no longer listening. Colonel Azarov had come into the street, accompanied by the Russian who had attended her interrogation. They stood together on the steps, openly discussing the tourists waiting to board the bus. Susannah wasn't close enough to hear, but she knew by his gestures when the second man asked about her. Azarov, his eyes on Susannah, explained. The second man nodded and asked another question.

"Nyet," Azarov answered positively. Only that much was clear before their attention turned to Sara Abbott, waiting behind her.

Susannah put on her dark glasses and from her seat studied the second man. He was a stocky-looking peasant with porcine eyes and a mean pinch to his mouth. He stood on the step above Azarov and looked self-importantly down at him. Their manner subtly conveyed tension, almost hostility, although it was probably only competitiveness. Suddenly, the shorter man became angry. Rudely waving a finger in Azarov's face, he delivered the severest dressing-down that Susannah had ever witnessed. When Azarov attempted to object, the gesturing finger ordered him into the building. Clamping his jaw on his protests, Azarov went. As he opened the door, he glanced over his shoulder. Susannah saw his expression plainly. He wasn't humiliated. The dark eyes snapped and the mouth was drawn with an anger barely in control. He was a man driven, and his piercing gaze told her that they had seen the last of any kindness from Colonel Aleksei Azarov.

Chapter 18

THE TOURIST LITERATURE had billed the farewell party at the Boyanna Inn as a "gala dinner," but it wasn't much fun. Dancers in native costume, superb food, a quaint inn on a hill overlooking Sofia could not compensate for the ruined trip. Even the presence of the Japanese delegation, whose enthusiasm was always infectious, could not restore the sense of well-being that the group had enjoyed before entering Bulgaria. Voorhies' bloody head, the omnipresent guards, the second interrogation were too vivid. Even now, swarms of uniformed soldiers were massed before the inn, attending a National Independence Day rally in the square just out front. Colonel Azarov stood to one side, quietly observant. The dog at his side didn't flinch during the amplified speeches, the flaring of searchlights, the rasp of marching feet. The sharp *dat-a-dat-dat* of machine guns fired over the city emphasized forcefully that this was a Communist country where exit depended upon the whim of a dictator. Susannah's nerves were raw. Others too were tense until the rally outside ended and the soldiers drifted quietly away. Azarov also left, pausing first, dark head bent, to light a last cigarette. The match illumined his face and then burned out, leaving man and dog silhouetted against the silver sky. Only when they had driven away could Susannah relax and try to enjoy the dancing.

Bit by bit, the mood of the party improved. The Japanese were having a good time and the Americans gradually joined in, clapping to encourage the performers and then participating in the last wild snake dance through the restaurant. Finally, a tiny Japanese stood on a chair and delicately led the crowd in singing "Auld Lang Syne." It was a nostalgic finish to any trip. Everyone shook hands. The Japanese gave the Americans tiny wooden dolls as souvenirs. Then they all spilled out of the inn to mingle quietly and admire the lights of Sofia flung along the horizon. It was not quite dark, and the lavender sky held the faintest trace of light in the west.

They lingered while the light faded. Slowly, a little reluctantly, the members of the tour party boarded the bus. Three of the dancers rode into town with them. They were fresh-faced, smiling young people who clearly had enjoyed themselves tonight. But they were soon let off. Then, almost furtively, the bus hurried through the silent city. The mellow mood on board quickly faded.

Drab in daylight, Sofia was ghostly at night. The dark concrete buildings, the empty boulevards, the cars huddling gloomily under gray shrouds reiterated that this was a Communist capital. Only in the Soviet Union could a more depressing atmosphere be found. Even the luxury hotel was dismaying. Its red interior was decaying after three years' use.

Once again, official cars blocked the way and guards swarmed around the square. Forming lines on either side of the bus, they marched the Americans between them into the lobby. When Susannah appeared in the doorway, two of them stepped forward and took her arms firmly. Quickly, before there could be protest or interference, they compelled her into the back seat of the nearest car. The motorcade was under way and out of sight before the Americans realized what had happened.

Susannah's hands were clammy. "Where are you taking me?" she managed to ask evenly.

There was no response.

"Do you speak English?"

No one answered. Escape was impossible. The two men on either side still gripped her arms. Panic threatened her. The cars drove fast and reached their destination quickly. The men did not intend to give Susannah time to calm herself.

The building was within the central government complex. Although rather new, it was dingy and smelled of damp plaster and bad plumbing. Susannah was forced down steep concrete steps to a dim basement, low-ceilinged and claustrophobic. A heavy steel door swung open. A broad hand between her shoulder blades propelled Susannah inside. She stumbled as the door clanged shut behind her.

Floodlights blinded her. She raised a hand to shield her eyes, to try to distinguish the faces beyond the glare.

"Your name?" She recognized Azarov's voice.

"What is this?" Susannah demanded.

"Why do you not answer the question?"

"Why am I detained?"

"Susannah Pence Clarke, you are a spy in this country."

"Rubbish!" But cold moved down her body. Her passport read only Susannah P. Clarke. Carter's Worldwide Tours listed her as Susannah Clarke. He had indeed obtained additional information about her.

"Disrespect will gain you nothing. We have little time. We want you to tell us of your meeting with the American spy Novak."

"I have not met with any spies," she said steadily. Her fingers pressed against the door at her back. It was cold to her touch.

"We will give you an hour. Then, we will force you to talk."

There was nothing to reply to that.

"You are a beautiful woman, Susannah Pence Clarke. Your face will be marred."

Susannah waited.

"Your body tormented . . . your hands broken into old age. Do you know that you have dainty hands?"

"Why are you cataloguing horrors?" Susannah asked.

"We prefer that you tell us voluntarily of your relationship with the American spy ring. The crime against our fraternal ally Bulgaria is heinous."

"What *is* the crime against Bulgaria?" Susannah asked. Her eyes hurt in the strong light.

"You have no right to ask questions."

"I thought Bulgaria took pride in permitting its citizens justice." That was nonsense, but it was worth a try.

"You are not a citizen. You are a spy. You came to Bulgaria with orders from your imperialist government to overthrow its glorious leader, Comrade Todor Zhivkov."

Susannah laughed.

"The rules must change now," a second voice said in Russian. "Time is valuable and she is uncooperative. Be more forceful." Susannah recognized the voice of the Russian who had attended her interrogation that afternoon.

"That is not the way to manage her," Azarov said, also in Russian.

"Has she weakened you?" the voice demanded. "We know the wiles of female spies."

"No, she has not, Colonel Melinsky."

"Then force her to tell what we want to know."

"In the end, I shall have to use my own way."

"Perhaps. But try the approved method first."

Someone stirred. Susannah realized there were yet others in the room.

Azarov resumed the questioning in English. "Tell us of your relationship with the American spy John Novak, executed before your hotel four days ago."

"That poor man was an American?" she asked in an astonished tone.

A figure moved swiftly. A broad hand cut her across the face. She cried out indignantly.

"You were warned," Azarov said, standing before her. "Speak the truth."

"You promised an hour without this sort of thing."

He slapped her again. Susannah forced back the tears and kept her hands behind her back. Her handbag still hung on her wrist.

"One moment," Colonel Melinsky ordered in Russian. "Use this, Comrade. It's more effective." A leather whip with shredded ends was handed to Azarov.

"He was an American spy," Azarov told her.

"I didn't know that. No one told me."

"You spoke to him moments before he died."

"Impossible."

"Not impossible. He sent you to meet his contact."

"I have met no Bulgarians. Except our guide, of course. Do you mean him?"

The whip danced tauntingly before her eyes. "Do you see this? It is very similar to a cat-o'-nine-tails. Must I use it?"

"I'm sorry. I know nothing."

The whip quivered slightly. Its waving ends were mesmerizing. "Perhaps," Azarov said softly, his s's hissing sibilantly, "this will refresh your memory."

He nodded to a third man, who turned out the floodlights. A single bulb in the ceiling socket illuminated the room. Her eyes adjusting slowly, Susannah saw Azarov's fingers playing gently with the whip.

A door on the opposite wall opened and a figure stumbled inside. She recognized the man who had given her the book. He stood uncertainly; then slowly, almost in slow motion, he crumpled to the floor and was still. He had been horribly beaten and still bled from wounds around the mouth. Susannah glanced at Azarov. His expression was cold.

She backed away. "Is he dead?" she whispered.

"I expect so," he answered.

She said nothing. Fear gripped her.

"What did he give you?" Azarov asked.

"Nothing."

"Use the whip," Melinsky's voice ordered. "I believe you've turned squeamish."

Azarov ignored him. His voice hardened. "I ask you again. What did he give you?"

"Nothing. If he told you that, he lied."

The whip sang in the air. It stung her cheek. She gasped.

"You are the one who lies. What did he give you?"

"Nothing. I told you."

Once more the whip scattered its pain across her face. Tears of fear and hurt rushed from her eyes and she stumbled, her hand raised defensively.

"Then what did he tell you?"

"Nothing. I speak no Bulgarian."

"Have you ever seen him before?"

She shook her head No.

With a rough hand on her dress, Azarov hauled her upright and held her steady. For a long moment he looked down at her.

"Shall we have to use electricity?" he asked finally. The softly worded question was more terrifying than his violence.

When Susannah made no response, he repeated the

question more distinctly, as though she were deaf. "Shall we have to use electricity?"

Susannah said nothing. The question seemed unreal.

"You have never known the meaning of pain. It can break a man in a single minute. We know you are a trained spy. We know you have been taught how to lie. How long can you suffer extreme pain? Even agony? Two minutes? Can you endure that long before you die of pain? Even your CIA doesn't expect that of you."

It went on and on. The beautiful voice poisoned her mind with the horror of the images it created. Susannah fought to shut it out, to use the interval to recover clarity of mind. She wondered if anyone on the tour would be permitted to call the American Embassy.

"Now are you ready to tell us?" Azarov asked finally.

"Nothing. Nothing. Leave me alone. I call tell you nothing."

"As you will, then." He pulled her up. Then deliberately, dispassionately, he knocked her down again. Susannah's teeth were clenched. Apparently, the contact hadn't told of giving her *Dead Souls*. Could she be as stubborn?

He bent and lifted her up once again. This time, he braced her in a standing position. "Be reasonable, Miss Clarke. Tell us. Avoid the crippling."

"There's nothing to tell," she whispered. She was thirsty.

Azarov regarded her levelly. Then, still maintaining his grip on her arm, he turned to one of the Bulgarian guards. "Is there a lie-detector machine in Sofia?" he asked in Russian.

"Of course; we have several. We bought American ones from the North Vietnamese."

"You should have reported their availability sooner and saved the loss of time," Azarov said sharply. "I shall remember that when I make my reports to your superiors. Where are these machines?"

"In Party headquarters. One can be brought here at once."

"Then see to it."

"I shall need permission."

Releasing Susannah, Azarov took a small pad from his pocket and wrote on it. He gave the single sheet to the man, who took it and hurried out. Susannah leaned wearily against the wall.

"This woman should be searched immediately," Azarov said. "Is there a matron here?"

"No, Comrade Azarov," the remaining Bulgarian guard answered. "The matron is off duty."

"You do it, Azarov," Melinsky sneered. "You've never hesitated before."

Azarov ignored him. "Call the matron to duty. We will wait."

"We don't have time," Melinsky said shortly. "You're being too considerate of her feelings."

"We should not give Comrade Kissinger something to tax the Kremlin with when next he visits," Azarov answered sharply. "You know what he said the last time a tourist was unduly mistreated."

"I don't know. But then, I don't have your sources. What will you do with her in the meantime?"

"A black cell should prove instructive."

"Now you are being sensible."

Azarov turned to the guard. "Do you have such a place?"

"Certainly. It is this way."

Azarov's hand tightened on Susannah's arm. He looked neither at her nor at Melinsky as he propelled her from the room. She flinched away from his touch and walked free of him. He saw how painful an effort it was.

The cell was small, low-ceilinged and hot. The floor was wet. Taking the purse from her arm, Azarov pushed her in. Before he locked the door, he handed her a cup of water. It was brackish, but it quenched her thirst.

"Thank you," she said, handing the cup back to him.

He made no response, but slammed the door. He looked at her through the barred window before he turned out the light and covered the peephole. His expression was grim.

The cell was totally black. Susannah groped to the sleeping ledge and lay down. Almost instantly, she lost consciousness.

Harsh light and rough hands forced her into wakefulness. Rudely, the matron undressed her and, with metal probes, searched all the private places of her body. The indignity of it infuriated her. Susannah swore and lashed out, but the woman only stepped aside and signaled that she could dress again. Then, wordlessly, she led her back to the same room.

"You know what this is?" Azarov asked quietly from the center of the room where a chair had been set for the polygraph machine. "You have experienced it at the CIA. Perhaps it is even the same model. Sit here, please."

His hand guided Susannah to the chair and lowered her into it. Sleep had cleared her mind a little, but her head ached and her neck was stiff. Azarov put the electrodes in her hands, the blood-pressure cuff around her arm. Just once, as he locked the rubber tube around her chest, their eyes met. Susannah was quietly, devastatingly furious. The depth of hatred in her eyes shocked him. His gaze flickered aside to the polygraph.

"You are quite comfortable? You must relax."

Susannah glared at him as he sat down. Unlike the CIA's polygraph operators, he didn't sit directly behind her, but to one side. She had only to turn her head to see his face. Melinsky stood at his shoulder. Azarov turned on the polygraph. She could hear the faint scratch of the needles, tracing her emotion on the moving graph paper.

"Answer each question with a simple Yes or No, please," he instructed. His voice was a tone deeper than usual and held the slightest undercurrent. Susannah turned to look into his face, but found no quarter there. Azarov was a determined man.

"Is your name Susannah Pence Clarke?"

"Yes."

"Are you thirty-three years old?"

"Yes."

"Have you ever performed fellatio?"

The polygraph needles jumped. Although she herself had never encountered it at the agency, she knew that some operators used this method of questioning to gauge the truthfulness of answers to other queries. Susannah glanced over at Azarov. His clasped hands hid his face as he watched the polygraph chart. Colonel Melinsky's eyes glittered. She wondered suddenly if he understood any English.

"No," she said slowly.

"Do you have six brothers?"

"Yes."

"Have you had intercourse with many men?"

A needle scratched sharply on the graph paper. Another guideline had been established. Susannah didn't reply.

"Answer the question," Azarov instructed. "Have you had intercourse with many men?"

Susannah took a deep breath. "A baker's dozen," she said clearly. The needle rasped, recording the lie.

"Did you know the man you saw earlier this evening?"

"No."

"Do you know anyone in Bulgaria?"

"No."

"Did you come to Bulgaria to spy?"

"No."

"Do you spy for the CIA?"

"No."

"But you've worked for the CIA in the past?"

"Yes."

"Did you ever spy on the Soviet Union?"

"I've never been there."

"Have you ever been to Bulgaria before?"

"No."

"Did you come to spy this time?"

"No."

"Have you photographed military installations as you've toured?"

"No."

"Or plotted to overthrow the leaders of Bulgaria?"

"No."

"Have you ever been raped?"

The needles jumped. Susannah merely nodded.

"Can you identify this man?" He showed her one of the photographs of Novak that she had seen before.

"No," she said.

"Did you see the man who was shot in the street before your hotel?"

"From a distance."

"Could you recognize him?"

"No."

"Were you raped by a stranger?"

Susannah's nerves were jagged. The needles registered her agitation, her sweating palms. "An acquaintance," she said faintly.

"Did this man give you any government documents

to remove from the country?" he asked, showing her a second snapshot of Novak.

"No."

"Do you know the name he uses?"

"No."

"Do you know where this picture was taken?" he asked, handing her the photo of the disguised Novak.

"No."

"Were you an adult when you were raped?"

"No."

"Have you been given any official Bulgarian documents to remove from the country?"

"No."

"Or from any Communist country?"

"No."

"Have you been told orally any secrets from this or any Communist country?"

"No."

"Do you know any CIA agents living today under deep cover?"

"No."

"Why not? You worked for the agency."

"It was too long ago."

"Once an agent, always an agent."

"Not necessarily."

"How old were you when you were raped?"

"Twelve."

"Have you ever seen this man in the halls or offices of the CIA?" He indicated the third photograph of Novak which he still held in his hand.

"No."

"Have you been given anything by Bulgarians to remove from the country?" The needles wavered and steadied.

"Yes."

"What?"

"Souvenirs from the Balkantourist agency."

"Did any Balkantourist employee give you state security information?"

"No."

"Ask about the contents of her handbag," Melinsky ordered in Russian. He was watching every nuance of her expression, his eyes constantly flicking from her face to the graph paper.

"Wait a moment," Azarov said, rising and loosening the cuff around her arm. "Let her rest."

"The pain will make her talk."

"It could make her lie, too."

They waited while the circulation slowly returned to Susannah's arm. She kept her head down, her eyes closed. Once she opened them to see Melinsky cleaning his nails with a letter opener. The silence was oppressive.

Azarov smoked. When he had finished his cigarette, they resumed.

"Are any of the items in your purse spy equipment?" he asked.

"No."

"Do the papers, passport, address book contain CIA codes to use in spying against Communist countries?"

"No."

"Are you carrying letters from spies?"

"No."

"What about the one from Absalom that begins, 'My dearest Susannah'?"

In fascinated horror Susannah watched as Azarov scanned the single sheet. The needles had gone wild on the polygraph paper behind her. When he finished, he glanced up and noted the paper.

"Tell us about this man Absalom. Does he mean a great deal to you?" he asked.

It was impossible to avoid an answer. "Yes," she

whispered, looking down to avoid Melinsky's probing gaze.

"Are you intimate with him?"

"No."

"But you spent the night with him. Will you do it again?"

"If he wishes it."

"Is she lying about this man?" Melinsky suddenly asked. "Look at the chart."

Azarov nodded to indicate he understood, but didn't turn around. Melinsky still watched Susannah closely. His face glistened with sweat.

"There will be severe consequences if you lie," Azarov said somberly. "Have you lied about this man?"

"No."

"Then why does the mention of his name agitate you?"

"I . . . think of him."

"Is he a sweetheart?"

"I suppose so . . . yes."

"She's evading the truth," Melinsky interjected sharply. Azarov waved him to silence. Susannah was trapped. He too knew she was lying.

"Is he an American spy?"

"Not that I know of."

"Have you ever seen him at the CIA?"

"No."

"Has he ever told you that he works for the CIA?"

"No."

"Once again, did the American spy give you anything to remove from this country?"

"No."

"Very well. Are you satisfied now, Colonel Melinsky?"

"Ask her again about the Bulgarian traitor," Melinsky ordered.

Azarov translated the question. "Had you ever seen the Bulgarian traitor before tonight?"

"No."

The needle wavered out of its pattern, recording the lie.

"She's lying!" Melinsky said triumphantly.

"He was . . . horrible . . . that poor man . . ." Her voice cracked and she covered her face with her hands. The needles jumped.

"Do you know his name?" Azarov prompted.

She shook her head.

"Did you converse or correspond with him?"

"No." The needles were slowly easing back into their regular pattern.

"Have you ever seen a man beaten to death?"

"No."

"If I find you have lied to me, you will share his fate."

Susannah said nothing.

"Have you ever known anyone to outwit a polygraph?"

"No."

"Not even in the CIA?"

"No."

"If I said there was a Soviet agent inside the CIA, would you believe me?"

"No."

"Why?"

"Polygraph tests prevent infiltration."

"You don't think an agent could be trained to avoid detection?"

"Not altogether."

"Very well. Do you have anything else, Comrade?"

Melinsky chewed a hangnail. Clearly, he wasn't happy with the results. "*Nyet,*" he said, finally.

"Then you may go, Miss Clarke."

Azarov rose and unhooked the electrodes. His hands,

usually warm in their touch, were cold on her arm. He stood back and let her go past. Without another glance at any of them, Susannah took her purse from the desk and followed the guard from the room, down the long corridor, up the stairs to the front door. He unlocked it for her and she went swiftly through to the street. She walked steadily down the street and around the corner. Then she ran.

Chapter 19

WHEN SUSANNAH'S FRANTIC PACE SLOWED, unfamiliar surroundings confronted her. There are no street signs in Sofia, and there were no familiar landmarks to guide her. A single car passed, its noise echoing eerily in the empty boulevard. Footsteps strode rhythmically behind her. A block. Two blocks. Their pace matched hers. Through the shadows, she discerned the figure of a man in uniform, following her. It was the guard who had unlocked the door. In terror, she ran again, glancing desperately over her shoulder. The man's stride didn't break. He turned into an apartment building and disappeared.

Her nerves were playing her false. He was only going home. No need for alarm. She had been dismissed. The ordeal was over. But Azarov's voice saying, "If I find you have lied to me, you will share his fate" was too vivid. She walked swiftly in the general direction of the cathedral. Just beyond it would be the hotel.

She had just sighted the glow from the cathedral's floodlights when a car approached from behind. Hopefully, she glanced around, but it wasn't a taxi. It moved slowly, hesitantly. A searchlight stabbed across the pavement, probing doors and alleyways, seeking . . . seeking her. It was Azarov's car. His face was indistinct, but she knew. Now he had seen her. The light went out and the car gathered speed.

Whirling, Susannah raced toward him, drew level and

sprinted on. Her action forced him to slow and look for a place to turn.

She rounded a corner, pounded down a short street and turned again. Hiding places presented themselves immediately. Cars, each one shrouded in its canvas dust cover, clustered together in a small square. Azarov was not in sight. She picked one and, stretching out, rolled underneath and lay still. Heavy tremors attacked her body, and the brick pavement, cold under her cheek, made her shiver uncontrollably. He had penetrated her lies and half-truths and was coming to arrest her. The same fate . . .

Cautiously, the car approached and stopped at the entrance to the small cul-de-sac where Susannah hid. The engine ticked, its distinctive rattle clearly audible, before it was cut off. Now there was no sound. In a moment, a man's footsteps moved slowly, ringing a little as he paced around his car and entered the cul-de-sac.

Then silence. Oh, dear God, she prayed. She didn't move. Time stopped.

Toenails clicked briskly. A cold nose touched her hand. The dog. How could she have forgotten him! Susannah edged away, but the animal followed her under the car and nudged with his nose. When she didn't respond, his teeth closed on her wrist and he backed out, tugging her with him. His jaws gripped firmly, but he did not bite.

"Go," Susannah whispered fiercely in Russian.

But it was useless. The footsteps drew nearer.

"Come out, Susannah," Azarov called softly.

Susannah suddenly remembered his caution. He was exposed here in this little square with its ring of dark buildings and tiers of windows. She could scream, but this was Bulgaria. No one would help her.

She edged stiffly out, ignoring his outstretched hand.

He was on his knees, bending over to help her. The dog stood at his shoulder, his jaws open in a wolfish grin. As Azarov straightened, Susannah bolted.

He caught her in three steps, whirled her around and backed her roughly against the door of his car. She realized he was armed; the outline of the shoulder holster was visible under his coat.

"What do you want now?" she demanded. Her voice shook, belying her bravado.

"I won't hurt you. You can leave in a minute," he murmured. He was holding her scarf, and now he folded it neatly. He had used it to give the dog her scent, and Susannah wondered if he had taken it for just that purpose. He didn't offer to return it, but slid it carefully into his inside breast pocket.

"What do you want?" Susannah repeated, more steadily this time.

"Your itinerary for tomorrow. You're scheduled on Swissair Flight 100 from Zurich to New York at eleven o'clock, aren't you?"

"Yes. Why?"

"Don't take that flight."

"Of course I'll take that flight. The reservation was confirmed today." She tried to inch away, but his hands were on her arms.

"Susannah, trust me this one time. Take any flight but that one." He was leaning very close in the intensity of his plea. "Please, Susannah."

"Why?"

"It's not safe for you. Don't ask me any more. Just give me your promise."

Reluctantly, knowing refusal was impossible, she nodded. "All right."

"I must have your word. Promise it."

"All right. I promise."

He didn't release her, but stood gazing down at her,

seeing her ordeal, her fear, in her face. There was a line of white around her lips, a tiny spot of dried blood on her cheek where the whip had broken the skin. The strength he had sensed was there too. He was pleased. He liked being right about people. She stirred restlessly under his scrutiny, then stilled as he reached up and very softly touched the cut on her face. A new expression deepened his eyes. A smile touched his mouth.

"Susannah," he murmured huskily, stepping closer and bending toward her.

She shied away.

"Susannah!" He froze, but didn't move aside. "I had hoped . . ."

When she didn't help him, his hands dropped to his sides and he straightened. "I won't see you again," he said in a more normal tone. "I leave Sofia before you."

She made no response. A little of her tension eased, and her face revealed her relief.

"Do you fear me so much?"

"How can you blame me?"

"I can't. Still, I hoped that when we parted you would think better of me. I should learn not to want such things. They never become reality."

Startled at the bitterness in his tone, she searched his face. The simple words, the unexpected insight into his life affected her deeply. His intimate questions, following so swiftly on the humiliating search of her body, had aroused depths of fury she hadn't known she possessed. But it was harder to be so angry now that she realized how those probing queries had diverted attention from the questions most dangerous to her. He had resisted Melinsky's urgings for physical abuse. What was more important, not once had he asked her outright, "Did you know John Novak? Did you speak with him on the day of his death?" A diabolical purpose might be governing his action, yet she felt he had chosen to let her go. A moment's search of his face provided a simple reason why. If he had defied his Party for her, the sacrifice deserved recognition.

Hesitantly, she reached out and touched his sleeve. "God keep you," she whispered.

His hand closed hard on hers, trying to hold her a little longer. Her fingers slipped away.

"Susannah!"

She almost stopped. Then, shaking her head a little, she walked rapidly away from him. At the corner, she paused to look back.

He still stood beside the car, head up, looking after her. At his feet, the dog whimpered and reached with his paw to comfort his master. But Azarov's gaze was on Susannah. Their eyes met and held. Slowly, the Russian's hand opened. He reached out and brought the dog's head to his side and held it close.

Chapter 20

THE GROUP WAITED, milling restlessly in the ugly airport. It was past time for their departure, but still the customs officials pawed their luggage and thumbed their passports. Even when their travel documents were returned, they were not permitted to board the waiting plane. Instead, they had to line up before the customs window. Once more their visas were checked. Once more their faces were compared with their passport photographs. Everyone fidgeted nervously as the minutes slipped away. Even the dark-complexioned customs official was jittery. Repeatedly, he licked his lips and looked all around. He worked so slowly it began to appear that he was waiting for something to happen. To Susannah's heightened senses, it seemed that he spent the longest time on her, peering first at her face and then at her passport before finally reaching slowly for the stamp and affixing the precious exit mark on a clean page. She had waited with taut patience for him to make up his mind. Now she snatched the slender booklet from him and fled through the foreigners' lounge to the plane.

Designed for military rather than civil use, the Russian-built plane was hot and uncomfortable, but Susannah didn't care. Movements behind the curtain just ahead signaled that the crew was ready. She latched her seat belt and prayed to leave—but instead, they waited. The air grew stale as one by one the Americans were passed through customs to join their colleagues on board. Outside, the ground crew had disappeared and the airport seemed deserted. A single guard patrolled, a machine gun on his back. Thirty paces down. Pivot. Thirty paces back. Susannah counted as he marched. On his fifteenth return, he suddenly snapped to attention. Anxiously, Susannah sought the reason for his respectful attitude and saw a motorcade approaching swiftly. Its brakes squealing, it stopped at the ramp and discharged armed guards. Weapons poised for use, they rushed up the steps into the plane. Moving more sedately, Colonel Melinsky got down and waited by the lead jeep. Today he wore a uniform and an officer's cap. Last night's stubble still darkened his cheeks.

Frightened, Susannah sat far back in her seat. Azarov had gone. She had watched for him to make sure. Now, as the soldiers ranged up and down the aisle and Colonel Melinsky paced outside, she realized that she feared Melinsky even more than Azarov. Colonel Azarov had become a familiar enemy.

The soldiers were questioning the women, forcing them to look up so that they could compare their faces with the photographs they held in their hands. There was no place to hide. Miss McMillan, Kitty Reynolds, Louise Phillips, the Abbotts, the Endicotts, Miss Tillie Cary were finally passed by.

"You, there!"

Slowly Susannah looked up and faced the guard. It was a shock to see how young he was. Too young to be so cold and grim. He looked from the photograph to Susannah's face and back again while others stood at his shoulder and waited for his verdict.

"That is all," he said. And passed on.

Tears of relief were stinging her eyes when commotion broke out just ahead. It was not Susannah but Aggie Taliaferro that they wanted. She was hauled from her seat and hustled roughly down the steps to face Melinsky. With a curt nod he confirmed that she was the one he was looking for.

The plane lumbered into motion then and pulled away from the parking ramp. Susannah craned to see what was happening on the ground. Aggie had jabbed the young guard in the stomach. When he buckled, she slammed him over the head with her purse. But there were too many of them. They overpowered her and heaved her clumsily into the truck.

Susannah smiled bitterly to herself. Melinsky had met his match in Aggie Taliaferro. Her opinion of the woman rose. And her distress mounted. Aggie knew nothing to tell and consequently, could die in agony and torment, knowing only the injustice of it. Susannah's hand closed more tightly on her purse. Azalea had found *Dead Souls* with Susannah's name penciled lightly on the flyleaf and had returned it. Dread of that moment had haunted Susannah. She felt an overwhelming relief when she realized that Azalea expected no explanations.

Now, as the plane gained altitude, Susannah reviewed her plans once more. Leaving Communist Bulgaria in no way reduced her danger. A fatal accident, and Absalom and his information both would be lost. If she mailed page 51 and Absalom's letter to Maryanne Knowles, the operation at least could still succeed. She recited the letter to herself once more. Assuming she was successful in her effort to gain entry to the Oval Office, she would have to repeat it to the President.

In Belgrade, the group transferred from Balkan Airlines to TWA. The sight of fresh American faces, the mixture of familiar American accents, the first cup of American coffee in six weeks of travel renewed Susannah's confidence. By the time the tour dispersed in Zurich, she felt better.

Once free of the group, Susannah went immediately

through the air terminal and down the stairs to the ladies' powder room. There, in the relative security of a locked cubicle, she wrote her note to Maryanne, tore page 51 from *Dead Souls* and enclosed them with Absalom's letter in an envelope. Except for a stamp, they were ready to be mailed.

Her thoughts turned then to Azarov's urgent plea, the expression in his eyes, and slowly she took the Swissair ticket from her purse. She could see no threat in doing as he asked. In fact, she should do more. His warning must be passed on.

Taking out her last sheet of paper, she wrote in urgent letters: SWISSAIR FLIGHT 100—DANGER—BOMBS/HI-JACKERS ON BOARD. Then, after tucking the paper into another envelope, she licked the seal and wrote SWISS-AIR—MOST URGENT in large block letters on the front.

She left the ladies' room. No one seemed annoyed at her lengthy stay in the cubicle. Briskly climbing the steps, she went directly to the Swissair desk, reached around the shoulders of two passengers and dropped the envelope over the counter face up in front of a uniformed official. He took it up immediately and glanced hastily around to see who had delivered it. Susannah was already hurrying across the terminal. By the flight board, she paused to look back. The man had given up trying to locate her in the crowd and was now ripping open the envelope. His expression told that her message had been understood.

Relieved, she crossed to the postal window and purchased her stamp. For a moment she stood counting her remaining Swiss money while her eyes ranged over the crowds. No one was interested in her movements. It seemed that her plan would work.

Then something caught her attention. An American by his face and dress, the man lounged twenty-five feet away, watching her with bemused, crinkled eyes. Damn him, she thought, and went to stand in line for a new reservation.

It took an endless time. Swissair's difficulties with Fight 100 had lapped over onto other airlines. Security tightened. The number of guards and uniformed officials on duty increased by the minute, making the additional bustle and tension in the big lobby obvious even to the uninformed eye.

TWA Fight 430 through London to Washington left shortly after Swissair 100 and would reach its destination within twelve hours. Satisfied that it was the best she could do, Susannah booked her reservation and paid the difference in air fares. Turning away from the counter, her wallet still in her hand, she saw him again. He was a blond giant, wearing a summer suit of tan polyester and carrying a trench coat slung casually over his shoulder. He was almost too openly interested in her to be conducting surveillance, yet no movement, no expression of hers escaped his notice.

For an hour she wandered through the crowded duty-free shops of the terminal. The American was always within sight, but it was difficult to determine whether he was an agent stalking a quarry or a man flirting with a pretty young woman. Certainly, he didn't care whether she saw him.

He followed her with single-minded determination, flashing a grin whenever he thought she might notice it. Only once did his attention wander. Briefly, he talked with a young woman dressed in the blue uniform of an airline official. A premonition chilled Susannah and she watched them closely. The American gestered to the flight board and checked his wristwatch. Nodding in confirmation, the woman hurried away and did not reappear.

Time dragged. The terminal was jammed with travelers, restive now under the scrutiny of guards and the threat of violence. There was no place to sit. Susannah continued her wandering, hoping for a chance to slip the letter unobtrusively into the mailbox. The man was always there, a discreet hundred paces behind. By the time information on her flight appeared on the board, Susannah had to conclude that he *was* following her. Wearily, she went back down the stairs to the ladies' room and used her last coin for the toilet cubicle.

In angry gestures, she tore open the envelope, ripped the letter to Maryanne into minute pieces and flushed it down the commode. Using a nail file, she pried her grandmother's portrait from the back of the hunting case watch and crammed page 51 inside. She had to kneel on the watch to force the catch to close. It snapped, reluctantly but firmly. Once more she inspected the chain. Her repair was crude, but if the watch didn't swing free, it should hold for another twelve hours. She put it around her neck and tucked it down inside her bra, next to Absalom's letter.

Ready at last, she hurried upstairs. Emerging onto the first floor, she paused long enough to determine that the American was not in sight. Then she moved quickly into line for the security check. The examination was exhaustive, but she endured it patiently. This time there was cause.

Chapter 21

FROM HER PLACE on the aisle of the rear cabin, Susannah could see the orderly bustle down the enormous length of the Boeing 747. Stewards in front and rear communicated with each other by telephone. It was too far to walk. It was almost too far to distinguish faces. In the cabin just ahead, Mrs. Abbott was stowing coats in the overhead compartment. As usual, Sara was letting her mother cope. As far as Susannah could see, they were the only members from the tour on this flight. Four rows ahead and to the right, the American was claiming his seat. He glanced around, found Susannah and smiled ruefully as he sat down. Susannah made no response. Her sigh was not quite inaudible.

"Not scared, are you?" asked the man beside her in English.

Susannah glanced at him. Not American. Good-looking in an intensely masculine way. He radiated strength and vigor, and the brown eyes regarded her with warmth and intelligence. It was hard to guess his age. The expensive suit, the briefcase at his feet, his air of assurance suggested a man of maturity and experience. Yet there was no gray in the black hair, there were no lines around the eyes. He might be forty.

"No," she answered slowly. "I've flown many times."

"Are you reluctant to be separated from your friend?"

"My friend?"

"Isn't he? The one who smiled at you just now?"

"No, I don't know him."

"But he would *like* to know you."

"Perhaps." Her smile was brief.

"And I would like to know you too. May I introduce myself?" His grin was engaging. It made him seem younger. Susannah smiled back.

"Please do. I'm Susannah Clarke."

"Caleb Sharon. Tel Aviv." He held out his right hand. It was at an awkward angle, but they shook hands anyway. Another hard palm. This one had a good friendly grip.

"Are you going to Washington?" Susannah asked.

"Yes."

"Then we'll be seatmates all the way. Is Tel Aviv your birthplace?"

A shadow crossed the bronzed face. "No. My family was Serbian. We emigrated, as did so many others."

"We admire Israel. We like your successes."

"You are kind to say so."

Their conversation ended then as the stewardesses hurried down the aisles for a last seat-belt check. The doors were locked into place. Sharon leaned over the passenger on his left, introducing himself as he did so, and tried to look out the window. There wasn't much he could see. The engines started their faint hum. Easily, the plane pivoted and began its buoyant progress to the runway.

It was an enormous object, yet it did not lumber. The aircraft moved gracefully, regally, its noises muffled. When it lifted off, it rose so steeply Susannah couldn't see over the seat in front of her. "It's like a house taking off," she heard someone say, but that didn't adequately describe the sensation of bulk in motion. It was more like a city block. But there was power to spare. The takeoff was incredibly smooth and effortless.

Suddenly, an uproar erupted in the section just ahead. A strange bellow, almost an animal sound, was followed by rushing feet and terrified screams. Susannah started up in alarm.

"Can you see anything?" Sharon asked tensely.

"No. What is it?"

"A hijacking, I imagine." When there were more screams, people tried to stand up and look. A sharp voice barked in English, "Seat belts," and another took up the cry in other languages. The passengers subsided, but leaned into the aisles to stare toward the forward sections.

There was nothing to see. If there was any scuffle, it was occurring in the first-class cabin. Then, without warning, the plane lurched and plunged. It was hurtling down, out of control.

"Hold on," Sharon said quietly. He was gripping her wrist to the arm of the seat.

A gun cracked.

The man on Sharon's left swore.

Someone's shoes were tumbling down the aisle. The plane pitched again and gradually righted itself. It seemed to slow in midair, as if to catch its breath, before resuming a more normal speed.

"Ladies and gentlemen, may I have your attention, please. This flight is being diverted. We shall land for refueling at Nicosia. No harm will come to you if you remain in your seat with the seat belt fastened."

It was a woman's voice, lightly accented. She repeated the announcement in French, German, Arabic and Spanish. Susannah glanced at Sharon. His expression was grim. He was listening carefully, his head cocked a little, grimacing at the groans that interrupted his concentration.

"What nationality is she?" he asked Susannah when the announcements were finished.

Susannah thought back. "I don't know any Arabic," she admitted, "but I would guess Spanish-speaking."

"I would, too."

"Is that good, relatively speaking?"

"Relatively speaking, no, it isn't. It suggests a carefully planned operation."

Susannah suddenly thought of Azarov. And of her premonition in the airport. "What will happen to us?" she asked. A tremor afflicted her voice.

"Probably nothing except an inconvenient delay."

"And to you?"

"Again, probably nothing. But there may be an attempt to negotiate separately for passengers carrying Israeli passports."

"Bastards," said the man on Sharon's left. He was in his fifties, with grizzled gray hair and liquid brown eyes. The woman across the aisle on Susannah's right was having hysterics, whooping and shrieking. Her husband finally slapped her smartly across the cheek, and the woman collapsed sobbing into his arms. He looked frightened.

"Did you see who they were?" the man behind Susannah asked in her ear. She shook her head.

They didn't have to wait long. The grapevine sprang into instant being, vigorous and full-grown. Within three minutes, the news they wanted reached the rear cabin. There were two men and a woman, all armed. A steward had been shot trying to disarm them. The woman was said to be beautiful.

Once more, screams and cries broke out ahead.

"I hate not knowing," Sharon said.

"You're out of the line of fire. Just lie low," Susannah advised dryly.

He grinned suddenly. "You act like you were born to this kind of crisis."

"Hardly."

"Ladies and gentlemen." Again the loudspeaker. "It is necessary to warn you that opposition will cause injury and death. We have found it necessary to take hostages. Ten adults and two children are at gunpoint in the front cabin. If there is further opposition or interference with our management of the aircraft, they will be shot."

This time, Susannah listened as carefully as Sharon. The woman's English was good, but it had the long *e* sound she associated with English spoken by Spaniards.

"Spanish-speaking?" she murmured to Sharon. He nodded. Around them, the passengers were quieter, more apprehensive.

"This is your pilot, Captain Grant."

Silence fell. Everyone listened tensely.

"The aircraft is in the control of a group of Palestinian freedom fighters. They are seeking the release of Palestinians who are in prison. They have guaranteed safe passage provided we cooperate. I recommend most urgently that you do so. Secondly, if there are any physicians or nurses on board, please identify yourselves to the freedom fighter known as The Lieutenant. He will take you among the passengers to render essential first aid."

There was a slight pause, and then the pilot continued. "We shall be landing in Nicosia to take on fuel. Additional freedom fighters will join us there. To the extent that I am able, I will keep you informed of new developments as they occur. In the meantime, the stewards will instruct you in the aircraft's emergency procedures. I urge you to listen carefully. Although we do not anticipate any difficulty, you nevertheless should be fully informed in case we have to use emergency exits. That will be all for now. Please give your attention to the stewards."

"Keep your eye on The Lieutenant," Sharon whispered. "I want to know what kind of man he is."

"He's black," Susannah whispered in a few minutes.

"Negro?"

"I can't really tell. How could he be if he's an Arab?"

"You'd be surprised at the membership of some of these extremist groups. Where is he now?"

"Going toward the front. There's a man preceding him. He must be a doctor." She remembered Weisenstein. He would have loved being the only physician on board in a crisis.

"How is he armed?"

"Pistol."

"What kind?"

"I can't see. A small one."

"What does he look like?"

"Hungry-looking. Rather dirty. He's wearing Castro fatigues. Wait a minute. He just took off his cap. There's a good deal of hair—Arab hair, not African."

"Hurrumph. Anything else?"

"He's gone now into the front."

"How long will we be delayed, do you think?" the man on Sharon's left asked. Susannah leaned forward to see him more clearly.

"Now your guess will be as valid as anyone's," Sharon said, grinning. "Jacques Armand, may I present Miss Susannah Clarke." Susannah acknowledged the introduction with a smile.

"How can you gossip in an emergency?" the woman ahead of them demanded petulantly through the crack between the seats.

"You'll find it's therapeutic," Sharon told her with a little smile.

They didn't hear the woman's retort. The lecture on emergency landing procedures had begun.

Chapter 22

THE BIG PLANE CIRCLED Nicosia at a dangerously low altitude. The passengers were prepared, pillows clasped in their arms, their shoes off. The precau-
tion was unnecessary. The landing was normal. The
plane rolled to an easy stop at the end of the runway
and cut the jets. Then there was silence.

Across the field a tank truck could be seen, approaching cautiously. It was permitted to refuel the plane.
When it drove away, it departed far more rapidly than
it had come. Then they waited, Armand kept his face
to the window, reporting developments to Sharon and
Susannah in a soft monotone.

"Here comes The Lieutenant," Susannah murmured
after a while.

The guerrilla was moving down the aisle, nodding
and speaking politely to the passengers. He juggled a
grenade in his hand as casually as though it were a
piece of chalk or a worry bead.

"Everyone comfortable back here?" he asked the passengers when he reached the rear cabin. His smile was
pleasant and displayed a flash of teeth. He conversed
easily in French and English, answering questions
thrown at him by various passengers.

"When can we eat?"

"I am afraid that won't be possible for a while."

"How long will we be here?"

"I don't know. Not long."

"Where are we going?"

"Freedom Field."

"Where is that?"

"Beulah Land."

There were more questions. Susannah and Sharon watched bemusedly. The Lieutenant was of medium height, thin, with narrow feet and slender features.

"Is he a Negro?" Susannah asked when he had left. "He certainly doesn't resemble our American ones."

"He's an exotic mixture of dark-skinned Caucasian groups. You know, I suspect that if we want a chance at the facilities, we should go now. One bunch of hijackers didn't let the passengers out of their seats for twenty-four hours."

At her expression of horror, Sharon laughed outright. Susannah smiled weakly and rose. He followed. Others had the same idea, and there was a line. No one stopped them.

"Hi, there," said a voice behind her. Susannah turned. The American had crossed the aisle to stand behind her.

"Aren't you going to say anything?" he persisted. "After all, we are hijacked together."

Susannah nodded but made no further response.

"What's the matter? Frigid or something?"

The remark annoyed Susannah. "Just not very interested," she retorted.

"Well! Pardon me! I thought you might welcome a friendly face from home. I can be very helpful."

"You'll have plenty of opportunity before this flight is over."

"To be helpful to you in particular, I meant." Hidden meaning was strong in his voice. "Did you get your letter mailed?"

A pang of fear suddenly stabbed Susannah's stomach. "Of course," she said shortly, and shut the lavatory

door in his face. When she came out, he had returned
to his seat. He grinned and waved to her over the heads
of the other passengers.

"He's definitely interested in you," Sharon observed
with a smile. "Shall I offer him my seat?"

"Don't you dare!" The vehemence in her tone startled
them both.

"All right. All right. I just wanted to please."

"Here come some jeeps," Armand reported softly.
Sharon leaned over his shoulder to look out. Three
jeeps, each with a driver and four guerrillas armed with
Czech machine guns, were halting by the ramp. They
waited while steps were rolled into position and the
forwardmost door of the aircraft was opened. Then
the men leaped out. Several rushed into the plane.
Others unloaded three crates and, moving with great
caution, carried them on board. The last man waited
until all the guerrillas had boarded. Then, deliberately,
he got out and walked to the first vehicle and talked
for a moment to the man behind the wheel. His gestures indicated that he was giving instructions.

A smothered expletive suddenly interrupted Armand's
running description of events outside the plane.

"What's the matter?" Sharon asked tensely.

"They just tossed the body of a steward out the front
door."

"The hell they did!"

Susannah felt sick. Somewhere up ahead, a woman
screamed.

"What are they doing now?"

"Two of the drivers have picked him up. They are
putting him in the first jeep. They don't have a tarpaulin
or anything to cover him." Armand paused.

"Now what?" Sharon prompted.

"Nothing. The man just dismissed the vehicles. Now

he's boarding." Another pause. "The steps are being moved away." Armand sat back. The engines started their muted hum.

The takeoff was routine.

Chapter 23

ONCE IN THE AIR, the guerrillas spread out through the aircraft. Two stood at the head of the aisles to the rear cabin, their machine guns menacingly leveled. These men looked tough and vicious. Their ages and nationalities were indeterminate. One of the passengers tried to speak to the guerrilla standing directly beside him, but the man snarled and prodded him into silence with the gun. Sharon's hand came up and covered Susannah's. The warning in his eyes was unnecessary.

"Ladies and gentlemen, this is Captain Grant speaking." He did not need to wait for silence. He had instant attention.

"We will be landing at a place in the Middle Eastern desert called Freedom Field. I am told that there is an earth runway, but no ground facilities to assist our landing. We must depend entirely upon the instruments on board. I anticipate that our landing will be routine in every way, but as an added safety measure, we shall observe emergency landing procedures. Please give your attention again to the stewards. We shall review once more what you need to know."

As the lecture resumed, a man passed slowly down the length of the plane and back up the other side. He was dark and stocky, broad-shouldered almost to deformity, with huge biceps and a barrel chest. His gimlet eyes flicked coldly over each passenger. A drooping bandido moustache hid his mouth. He was unarmed.

"He's the one," Armand murmured, his lips barely moving.

"The leader, do you think?" Sharon asked.

Armand nodded.

"Definitely, he's the leader," Susannah murmured, her eyes focused down the aisle on the section just ahead.

"What makes you so sure?" Sharon prompted.

"Because The Lieutenant just accepted an order from him. Accepted it with respect, I might add."

"Silence, there . . . you." They had been heard. The guerrilla's scowl was fearsome.

The lecture continued.

It was almost dark when the plane lost altitude. Below them was the desert. Cautiously, the engines throttled down carefully, the pilot overflew the landing strip, regained altitude and circled again. The wheels were down.

"See anything?" Sharon whispered.

"Sand" was Armand's terse reply.

Once more the giant plane approached the flat patch of desert. At the last moment, the pilot changed his mind, climbed and circled for a third attempt. The woman across the aisle was sobbing into her pillow. This time the 747 approached with even more trepidation, sinking slowly, its wheels just inches above the surface. Gingerly they touched ground and rolled. The engines reversed with a roar. There was one jolt, the nose tilted forward ever so slightly and the plane came to a halt.

"Beautiful," Sharon said fervently. A relieved babble spread through the cabin. The passengers straightened, fumbled for their shoes, shook out their pillows, but the plane was in motion again. It taxied off the strip of packed ground and settled deep into loose sand and gravel. Then it was quiet. No one moved to open any of the exits. The guerrillas kept their places, guns on the alert. Outside, the last of the twilight faded.

After a long wait, a crackle on the loudspeaker presaged another announcement.

"Captain Grant again, ladies and gentlemen. It is our understanding that there are customs requirements here at Freedom Field." There was the smallest trace of dryness in his tone. "The Palestinians have asked that you hand in your passports, wallets, traveler's checks, letters of credit and any other documents of travel, identification or introduction that you may have so that proper examinations can be made."

Susannah glanced at Sharon. "The old game of Arabs and Jews," he said under his breath. His face was composed, but tension knotted a muscle in his cheek. After a while, a guerrilla came down their aisle carrying a plastic garbage bag. It was heavy with travel documents.

Then again nothing happened. The guerrillas patrolled. The lights had been dimmed and it was late enough to sleep, but no one did. The people sat quietly, eyes following their captors up and down the long aisles.

It was long after midnight when a light glanced unexpectedly off the window. Armand sat up tensely and peered out. The light disappeared and they heard the roar of engines, passing very close.

"Another plane?" Sharon asked.

Armand nodded.

"What airline?" Susannah murmured.

Armand gestured a pause.

That plane too circled twice before attempting its landing. Each time its lights raked the ground, glancing off their windows, bringing an eerie sense of otherworldliness to the passengers on the TWA liner. Those with window seats peered out as anxiously as Armand.

Finally, with a scream of brakes and a sharp spray of sand dashed against their Plexiglas windows, it too landed.

"Swissair," Armand said as he sat back.

Swissair Flight 100? Had her warning not been enough?

Susannah closed her eyes wearily and let her head sink back on the seat. Had Azarov not known that a second plane would be hijacked? Or was TWA 430 selected after she had booked passage on it? Oh, but surely that was farfetched. But was it? They could have learned very quickly that Aggie knew nothing and that it was Susannah who was the courier after all.

The loudspeaker interrupted her thoughts. "Ladies and gentlemen. Captain Grant again. We have been notified to evacuate the aircraft. Use all emergency exits, and hurry. Do not wait to collect any belongings. There are explosives on board." His voice was even and quiet, but urgent.

"This way, please." Their stewardess was opening the emergency exit just ahead of them. People were already standing up, moving quickly.

"When you hit the ground," Sharon said in Susannah's ear, "run! Get as far away from the plane as possible."

Susannah nodded tersely. They all realized the danger. She slid down the chute and raced for the open desert. Never had she run so desperately or felt so clumsy. Finally, exhausted by the sand impeding her steps, she collapsed behind a wide dune. Sharon tumbled down beside her. His arms pushed her shoulders into the sand; his body covered hers. There was sandy grit in her mouth.

They waited. Around them, the desert rang with cries and grunts. There was no hysteria. The drilling in emergency procedures had paid off.

Then, just as Susannah hoped it wouldn't happen, the sky thundered into red fire. Rubbery smoke engulfed them. Sharon pressed her more closely into the earth and buried his head in her shoulder.

Explosion after explosion ripped the air, hurling debris and sand over a wide radius. The cries of the injured were drowned in the roar of burning jet fuel. Bits of metal showered down. Heavy smoke filled the air, and the crackle of flames was audible. Finally, the danger of explosions passed. Sharon's body relaxed and he rolled to one side.

"Are you all right?" he asked.

"I think so. Can we look?"

Cautiously, they peered around the dune. The Swissair liner had broken in the middle and was already reduced to smoldering debris. The TWA plane was listing crazily, its proud tail scorched. In the fiery light, two guerrillas staggered under the weight of heavily padlocked bags. A third stood guard, his machine gun cocked. The two lifted the bags into the rear of a waiting truck and laid the garbage bags of travel documents beside them. Carefully, they spread a tarpaulin over the load and tied it down. When they were done, a man stepped forward to inspect the knots.

Susannah's senses stilled. There was no mistaking that blocky figure, the hand raised to pick at the snub nose. Colonel Melinsky paced slowly around the truck, testing the knots, inspecting the fit of the tarpaulin. When he was satisfied, he nodded. The guerrillas saluted him and, hefting their weapons, climbed briskly into the truck. With a little jerk it started and turned to the south. In a moment it vanished behind more dunes.

"What do you suppose is in the bags?" Susannah asked, her eyes following Melinsky until he too disappeared from her view.

"Diplomatic pouches. They always try to get them. Let's hope they had nothing of strategic importance in them this time."

Susannah's sigh was deep and profound. Sharon misinterpreted her despair.

"Tired?" he asked.

"Yes."

"We might as well settle down here for the night. We have our own private sand dune, and you are welcome to my shoulder." His voice was cheerful. He rolled over and propped his back comfortably against the sand.

Susannah's eyes turned to the open desert.

"Couldn't we get away?" she asked urgently.

Sharon shook his head. "It's too risky. I don't know where we are. And we don't have any supplies."

Still she gazed into the darkness. "But couldn't we try?" she persisted. "The guerrillas aren't watching us now."

"No. We flew over too much sand."

"Then I'll try it alone."

"Don't be foolish, Susannah. It's certain death. The guerrillas picked this place for that very reason. That's why they aren't bothering with us tonight."

She turned to look at him then. He wouldn't help her. And she knew she couldn't do it alone. The hopelessness that enveloped her showed in her face.

"There's no need to be afraid," he said softly. "They aren't interested in a pretty little Gentile from Washington. Now, come and rest."

He held out his arm. His smile was relaxed, friendly, comforting. With a little sigh she curled up close to him, her head on his chest. He held her quietly, his arm strong across her shoulders. She closed her eyes. She didn't sleep and neither did he, but after a while they were grateful for each other's warmth.

Chapter 24

"GET UP, YOU."

Startled, Susannah lifted her head. She had slept after all. The sun had risen. Already it was warm.

"Get up."

The guerrilla's rifle was pointing straight down at them.

Stiffly, Susannah and Sharon stood up.

"This way. Quickly."

The Arab followed them, his gun at the small of Sharon's back. Sharon's hand on her elbow guided Susannah through the loose sand.

The guerrillas had herded the passengers into one giant clump of humanity. Hundreds clustered restlessly together under the blazing sun. Some were standing. Most were sitting. A few were lying down. The Palestinians stood in a wide circle around them, the submachine guns aimed into the crowd. Susannah and Caleb Sharon were among the last to be located in the desert and forced to join the captives. It was with a sense of unreality that they did so.

"I believe our friends the Palestinians have received reinforcements," Sharon commented dryly.

"How many are there now?"

"I counted twenty-five. There may be others out in the desert picking up stragglers. As long as they're disorganized, we can move about a little. I want to find out what happened in the night. You should protect your complexion. As fair as you are, an hour will give you a bad burn. Button your shirt up to the neck. Keep your sleeves rolled down. Sit down here with your knees drawn up. I'll cover you with your jacket."

"I'll suffocate."

"You'll have third-degree burns if you don't. And our jailers won't hand out suntan lotion. Quickly, now; you've already had at least thirty minutes."

Susannah complied. The position Sharon had advised was not uncomfortable. With her head on her knees, the jacket casting her lap in shade, she sat calmly, listening to the complaints of people around her. Sharon excused himself. From under the edge of the jacket Susannah watched as he moved among the people, pausing now and again to listen to a conversation or to ask questions. After a while she lost sight of him, and then she watched Colonel Melinsky instead.

The Russian stood beside an unmarked army truck. Guerrillas clustered about him, listening carefully to what he said. He seemed to be in a position of authority, certainly in one of respect.

So the Soviets were behind the hijackings. His presence, the unmarked vehicles, the Czech and Soviet weapons made it almost certain. It was a disquieting discovery. And an important one. As far as she could remember, the Western news media had never revealed Soviet involvement in the hijackings. Yet if the Israelis were aware of Communist interest in the diplomatic pouches, the Americans must know of it too. Was the Russian involvement confirmed? Or was Susannah's ability to identify Melinsky to be the first proof of something heretofore only suspected? If she had the opportunity, she wanted to include the discovery in her report to the President.

Eyes narrowed against the sun, she watched Melinsky. The guerrillas sought his advice frequently, yet he himself stayed in the shadow of the trucks, somewhat removed from the passengers' observation. Clearly, the Russians did not intend to reveal their presence at Freedom Field openly. Susannah felt for the chain around her neck. Would her knowledge of their presence place her in danger?

There were no answers to those questions, and finally she fell into an exhausted doze. Sharon's hand on her shoulder woke her up. She came out from under the jacket.

"I found Jacques," he announced cheerfully. The Swiss was just behind him.

"Good. Come join us. How did you fare?"

"Not so well as you," Armand answered. "I spent the night with the rest of the animals right here."

"Was it gruesome?"

"Almost."

"Did anything happen?"

"No. Two armored cars brought more guerrillas, but nothing else occurred."

"Then they have government support. But which government?"

"There were no markings on any of the cars. I can't tell where we are. And they haven't said. They are a pretty unfriendly group."

"Even The Lieutenant?"

"Especially The Lieutenant. Now that the chief is here, he's quite subdued."

"The chief is the one we thought he was?"

"Yes. He's called Mahoud."

"Arab?"

"Oh, yes."

"And the woman?"

"Her name is Asha."

"What are they going to do with us?"

"Negotiate for our release. But I haven't heard their demands."

"They want the release of two hundred fifty Palestinian rebels jailed in half a dozen countries," Sharon told him. "Or so I learned a few minutes ago."

"Then it will take a long time," Armand concluded.

"How many of us are there?" Susannah asked.

"Three hundred fifty on our plane, three hundred twelve on Swissair."

"Where was Swissair going?" Susannah asked.

"New York. They must have suspected trouble. I understand it was delayed several hours in Zurich while they searched," Sharon said.

"Then how did the hijackers get by security?"

"They looked just like everyone else. Two pistols were hidden in the woman's high-wedge shoes. The Swissair crew put up quite a fight. She was wounded in the struggle and left here late last night. Our own lady hijacker is a tougher dame altogether. She was the one who shot the steward."

They were silent a minute, their eyes turning around the camp until they located the girl. Armed with a submachine gun like the other guerrillas, Asha was in her late twenties, perhaps even thirty. She wore a khaki fatigue shirt, pants and combat boots. Her face was bare of makeup, and her hair was raked back into a severe knot on her head. A heavy watch mounted on a wide leather band was her only jewelry. She had a voluptuous figure, but there was nothing soft or feminine about her.

"I wouldn't say she was beautiful," Susannah observed, almost to herself.

"I don't know," Armand said, his brown eyes glinting. "Some men *like* the type." His eyes followed the girl's figure as she paced her beat around the prisoners. "She has much to recommend her. But I would venture to suggest to you that she actually is quite plain and only the eyes of the world press will find her beautiful. Now, does that make you feel better?"

Susannah had to laugh. The others joined in.

When she felt the sun burning her face, Susannah ducked back under her covering. Monotonously, the hours ticked by. The passengers became more restive as time passed without food, water or relief of any kind. Several women sobbed piteously, and a child wailed incessantly. Others fainted in the sun, and an impromptu first-aid station was organized. Dr. Weisenstein had his opportunity after all. A passenger on Swissair, he manned the station while his colleague from TWA went through the crowd seeking those in greatest distress. There were quite a few. The Palestinians did not interfere. They tramped continuously around and around, their weapons hooked loosely over their arms, their own faces and necks covered by caps and hats. It was blazing hot.

At three in the afternoon, a jeep and two armored cars approached through the mirages shimmering across the desert. The jeep bore Red Cross markings and was sandwiched between the personnel carriers: a prisoner under escort to Freedom Field. Mahoud stepped out to meet them. Today he wore a bandolier of bullets across one shoulder and a pair of pistols in leather holsters. From a distance, they looked like police revolvers. A headcloth protected him from the sun.

A man got out of the jeep. Slim, bronzed, impeccable in a white tropical suit, he made all those who saw him feel hot and gauche. Two aides accompanied him, but he did his own talking. There apparently was no need for an interpreter.

"Who is that?" Susannah asked.

"I believe he represents the International Red Cross in this area. I don't know his name. He's good, though."

Silently, they watched. Around them, the crowd was shifting restlessly, trying to see and hear. The guerrillas

gestured them into a sullen silence. The child was cry-
ing again.

The initial session lasted an hour. When it was done,
the negotiator left Mahoud and his Palestinians and
came to the perimeter of the campground. He strode
past the guards as though they did not exist. Even now,
after an hour in the heat, he looked cool. His skin was
very bronzed, his eyes bright blue. The two pilots
stepped up to talk to him.

Their conference lasted only ten minutes. When it
was over, the Red Cross representative laughed, shook
hands with the pilots and walked back to his jeep. He
lifted a casual hand to Mahoud. The Arab made no
response and, in a moment, turned toward Colonel
Melinsky's tent.

Susannah watched him go. Just before the negotiator
arrived, she had seen the Russian vanish into a tent that
stood a little apart from the main encampment. A guerrilla lounged casually before the closed flap. He seemed
to be loafing, but he was too watchful, his gun too close
to his hand, for relaxation. Now, as Mahoud dismissed
the guard and opened the flap, Susannah realized that
the Russian presence at Freedom Field was indeed being
kept secret. It did not bode well for negotiations. Or for
her. Her spirits sagged. They were not helped by a
secondhand version of what had taken place in Mahoud's meeting.

The Palestinians were demanding the release of two
hundred fifty prisoners held by seven countries—Israel,
Greece, Turkey, Switzerland, England, West Germany
and South Africa. If they were not freed within thirty-six
hours, ten hostages would be executed for every day of
delay. Israelis and Jews would be first. As Sharon had
expected, Mahoud wanted the Red Cross to negotiate
separately for the Israelis. When he was refused, he demanded an additional fifty prisoners, making three hun-

dred in all. In return, he agreed to the supply of amenities to the passengers, the removal of the sick and injured to the capital and the release of those nationals considered friendly to the Palestinian cause. As soon as the supplies arrived, supper would be served to the captives. Cheers were heard, first from one clump of people and then from another as they received news of the comforts. They were short-lived, however. The deadline was too imminent.

Susannah and Armand turned to Sharon. "Would they?" Susannah asked, her eyes showing her fear for him.

"They would."

"My God." She reached for his hand and clasped it hard. Under his tan, his face was white.

"We won't worry about it now," he said with a stiff smile. "They are only bluffing." But his voice carried no conviction whatsoever.

By seven o'clock, the first phase of the agreement had been fulfilled. The ambulances came first, their klaxons sounding strangely lost in the desert. They departed quickly, taking five passengers who had suffered heat stroke and the two who had broken bones in the precipitate dive of the TWA liner. Then the trucks arrived, carrying food, water, portable toilets, disposable cleansing supplies. When they left, twenty-two Arabs and East Europeans rode in the back, clutching their newly returned travel documents and darting smug glances over their shoulders. Silently, the prisoners at Freedom Field watched them go. Army rations and cups of steaming-hot tea assuaged their hunger, but not the depression that fell over them as the second night in captivity began.

Chapter 25

JUST AFTER NIGHTFALL, the Red Cross representative returned. This meeting was brief, its ending wintry. The negotiator stalked away from Mahoud, his back rigid. He glanced just once toward the captives as he climbed into the jeep. He didn't have to say anything. They all knew his offer had been summarily rejected.

"I wonder how many Israeli nationals are here," Sharon mused.

"I'll come with you if you want to find out," Armand said quietly. Sharon nodded. Susannah watched them go. She controlled her tears until Sharon was out of hearing and she was secluded under her jacket.

Sharon and Armand didn't return until the guards enforced curfew. Then they came quickly, bringing a third man with them. He was about forty, already graying, with a prominent beaked nose. He spoke only halting English, but his handshake was genuine as he greeted Susannah. She liked Abraham Berenson immediately. A colonel in the Israeli Air Force Reserve, he was a native of Haifa. From him Susannah learned for the first time of Sharon's association with the Israeli Beth Shin Secret Service. No wonder he had known about the diplomatic pouches. She looked at Sharon with new respect. She knew little about Israeli intelligence except that it was very, very good.

Tonight there were blankets to guard against the cold, medicated paper washcloths and toothbrushes.

Feeling a little refreshed, they wrapped themselves in the blankets and lay down, arms behind their heads. An odor of burning jet fuel, plastics, synthetic fibers and rubber still hung over Freedom Field. Only a few stars could be seen through the haze of smoke. They talked in whispers.

"I am not just going to let myself be taken," Sharon muttered.

"Nor I," Berenson echoed.

"What then?" Armand whispered.

"There's not much we can do in the open like this. If we overcame any of the guards, the others would fire into the crowd."

"They are keeping their distance," Berenson said. "That is some help."

Susannah was getting sleepy. "Whatever you decide to do," she whispered. "I'll help."

"And what can you do, little one?" Sharon asked. The smile in his voice removed the sting from the words.

"I worked for the CIA. I learned a dirty trick or two."

Berenson hadn't followed all she had said. Sharon translated. At the older man's reply, Sharon laughed outright.

"What did he say?" Susannah asked.

"It can't be translated exactly, and I wouldn't if I could, but I assure you it was most complimentary of you."

"I hope so," Susannah said. "Wake me up when you know what you want to do."

"Sleep well. We won't decide anything tonight."

Susannah lay on her side between Sharon and Armand, her eyes following the guards as they patrolled. They had erected tents for themselves, and now they took turns at guard duty. Reinforcements had increased

their number to more than a hundred—enough to foil
any effort of Sharon's. Yet she couldn't fault him for
planning. There wasn't any honor in being a victim.
Her gaze rested reflectively on the female guerrilla.
Asha was tireless. She had been on duty constantly
since the plane had been hijacked. Susannah hadn't
even see her eat.

It was still dark when wild cries from the Palestinians
and shots fired indiscriminately into the air jolted everyone awake. Floodlights had been set up, and the white
glare blinded them. They reminded Susannah unpleasantly of those other lights in Sofia.

"Now what?" was the tenor of the grumbles around
them as the passengers were ordered to their feet and
into a long line. The rifles prodded them into a giant
ring and forced them to march around the campground.
They went slowly, trudging a little. One of the braver
ones called a question to The Lieutenant.

"What is the reason for this?"

"Your exercise for the day. Shut up and march,"
was the curt reply.

It was cold. Most of the hostages huddled into blankets. The men weren't allowed to help the old women
through the loose sand. Mahoud tormented a particularly fat woman, shooting around her feet while she
capered and cried in terror. No one was allowed to
aid her. Periodically, the plodding line was halted and
a passenger was forced out at the point of a gun,
scrutinized by guards, questioned briefly and then
shoved back into line. Several fell.

"What *is* this?" Susannah demanded of Sharon, just
behind her.

"Probably picking the first ten."

"Oh, my God!"

The lights and the circle formation made it easy to
see those who were selected. Most of them were young

men. Not all were Jewish. One was the American who had followed Susannah.

"That's your friend, isn't it?" Sharon said.

"I think so."

"He's not an Israeli, or a Jew either."

"Neither were some of the others."

"I wonder why they are interested in him. Do you mind if I ask him?"

"Not if you don't bring him around."

"Does he make you that nervous?"

"Yes."

"And what are *you* hiding?"

"An aversion to obnoxious men."

Sharon's ringing laugh sounded good there in the desert. But it attracted attention. The line was stopped.

"You there. Fall out."

Sharon stepped forward.

"Not you. We know you, Jew Boy. The woman."

"Susannah!" Sharon exclaimed in shock as Susannah stepped forward. Seeing her sudden apprehension, he stayed by her side, his hand on her wrist.

"What is your name?" snapped the guard.

"Clarke. Susannah Clarke."

"Nationality?"

"American."

"What country of America?"

"The United States of America."

There was silence.

"That is all."

Susannah stepped back into place. Her knees were weak, and she was grateful for Sharon's hand on her arm. The line dragged on. Sharon walked beside her now, and no one stopped him.

"You shouldn't have stood there with me," Susannah said sharply.

"I couldn't leave you alone."

"I thought we agreed you were going to be inconspicuous. Why did you have to call attention to yourself?"

"You heard what they said. I'm known already. I can't lie low now."

"Caleb . . . please . . ."

"All right. I'll be careful."

"You must."

In a while, the lights were turned off and the travelers were ordered back to bed. The four stood a moment, waiting for the crowds to disperse so they could return to the patch of ground they had staked out for themselves. Susannah's eyes avoided the littered campsite and turned instead to the open desert.

A dog was running across the horizon. He moved lightly, buoyantly for all his great size. His giant paws flashed stylishly against the white sand. His ears stood upright. It was a black Doberman pinscher.

Suddenly chilled with omniscience, Susannah searched the faces of their captors until she found him, standing alone not two hundred yards away. He too wore khakis, but unlike the others, he was trim in shirt and slacks. His sleeves were rolled to the elbow in spite of the cold. His head was thrown back, his profile clear as he watched the dog. It was Colonel Azarov.

As Susannah stared, he turned and looked full into her eyes. For a long moment, neither moved. Then he stirred and whistled for the dog.

Ivan came at once, and they started toward a nearby tent. Azarov's head was bent. He didn't seem to notice the dog bounding playfully about him, his tail wagging eagerly. He didn't look up at all until Asha stepped from the shadows and spoke to him. Then he listened carefully. She seemed to be giving a report. When she had finished. Azarov patted her shoulder and nodded approvingly. Then he and the dog went on into the tent.

When he had gone, the woman smiled to herself and hefted the machine gun in a quick, rather joyous movement. There suddenly was a seductive little swing in her walk.

Thoughtfully, Susannah followed the others. Azarov had given no sign whatsoever, but Susannah knew that he had recognized her.

Chapter 26

THE SECOND DAY was like the first. They learned that the Red Cross representative's name was Maurice St. Cleaux and that he was a Swiss from Geneva. He arrived early with more trucks of supplies and spent the day closeted with Mahoud. Susannah suffered under her blanket. In spite of her precautions, her face and neck were painfully burned. Today, only Armand wandered through the crowd. A guard had been assigned to watch Susannah, Sharon and Berenson. He kept his distance and even seemed uninterested, yet when they sought to move, he stopped them. The orders must not have included Armand, however, for no effort was made to curtail his freedom.

Three o'clock came and went with no announcement from Mahoud's tent. Sharon was tense. He, Berenson and two elderly women going to the United States to visit grandsons were the only Israeli citizens on the two flights.

At five o'clock, Mahoud came out. Susannah watched carefully as he crossed the patch of open ground—not to Melinsky's tent, but to Azarov's. Within fifteen minutes, he emerged to speak again briefly with St. Cleaux. When the negotiator left, he was smiling. The two Jewish grandmothers went with him.

Sharon and Berenson were elated. They felt that the release—totally unexpected so early in the negotiations —was a very promising development. Susannah was not so sure. She felt that her fate rested on the two Russians, and so she watched them closely. Just minutes after the Red Cross jeep drove away, she had seen Melinsky storm to Azarov's quarters. His protest must have drawn an unsympathetic response, for his scowl was even blacker when he emerged.

The incident revealed that Azarov was in command, but still, Susannah was not encouraged. Even though she had heeded his warning, she was caught in the tremendous blackmail effort in the desert. Azarov would not help her again. And if TWA 430 had been hijacked because of her presence on board, he would hound her into exposing Absalom. Political expediency had freed two old ladies who might not survive the heat, but that was not leniency or genuine conciliation. There was no softening in the guerrillas' position. The deadline had been reiterated. The postponement they had prayed for had been denied.

With only a few more hours to go, Armand went again among the crowd looking for someone willing to participate in a small commando-type operation. Sharon and Berenson fretted restlessly while they waited for his return. When he did come, the American and a small Oriental were with him. The former greeted Susannah jovially.

"If I can't meet you one way, I can another. Chuck Clayton, Detroit."

Susannah's greeting was cool. She didn't trust Chuck Clayton. Her dislike was based on instinct, and his inclusion in the ten marked for execution did little to arouse her sympathy. Now, when they themselves were so closely circumscribed, she found Clayton's freedom to move about suspect. A protest rose to her lips. Sharon's eager expression quelled her objection. Chuck had been a Green Beret in Vietnam, and he was enthusiastic over Sharon's idea. His exuberance encouraged the others, although it almost gave them away. Kim Soong was from Seoul. He had been a Marine.

That afternoon marked the last of the camp's comparative freedom. At six o'clock a car arrived, driving fast across the desert, stirring up clouds of sand and dust as it came. A man got out. Small, rather thin, with disproportionately long arms and legs, he resembled nothing so much as a spider. He greeted Melinsky as an equal, but looked blankly through Mahoud. The Arab was crushed. He seemed to wilt as he meekly stood aside and let them precede him into Azarov's tent. The Lieutenant solemnly followed Mahoud and, being the most junior, was the first to emerge. He brought new orders for the guards.

The heretofore rather casual atmosphere of the camp was abruptly shattered. Guards were doubled. Talking among prisoners was forbidden. If anyone wished to use the toilet, he had to ask permission. Guards flanked the toilets and washstands and lined the paths to the mess tables and the first-aid station. Suddenly, it was an armed prison camp in every sense.

When the orders had been carried out and a frightened silence prevailed, the four conducted a military-type inspection. The guerrillas, always alert and watchful, now snapped to attention. Their habitual slouches and scowls were replaced by rigid shoulders and expressionless faces. Slowly, with Mahoud tramping a pace or two behind, the four circled the camp. They went to the field kitchen and stood to one side while the passengers were lined up to receive their evening rations. Once or twice they stopped someone and asked a question. Mahoud said something particularly threatening to a pregnant young woman and then laughed wolfishly when she burst into hysterical tears. The unknown man's smile could only be described as sinister.

Susannah feared to pass them, but there was no way

to avoid it. She tried to keep her body turned, her head down, to avoid notice. Melinsky and Azarov both knew of her presence at Freedom Field, but she was reluctant to forgo the slight chance that they would forget her. There were hundreds ahead of her, yet the line moved all too rapidly. Army rations and tea were not difficult to dispense.

For a while, the newcomer examined the approaching faces with interest. A sadistic little smile played on his lips, and he seemed to enjoy Mahoud's badgering of the passengers. Then suddenly he tired of the bedraggled procession. Beckoning peremptorily to the others, he indicated his readiness to leave. Swiftly the quartet marched past the line of travelers. Susannah turned aside, but not before Azarov's eyes raked her face, took in the dusty disheveled appearance, the wrinkled clothes, the virulent sunburn, Sharon still at her shoulder. His expression didn't change. He passed her as though he had never seen her before. The dog, however, paused uncertainly and took a tentative step toward Susannah, nose extended questioningly. A commanding snap of Azarov's fingers called him promptly to heel and the four went on. The newcomer looked back, puzzled, without being quite able to define why.

"Who *are* they?" Sharon muttered.

Susannah wanted to tell him, but Clayton was close enough to overhear. They all shook their heads slightly, then turned to watch the little man's departure. His presence at Freedom Field had boded no good.

Immediately after supper, the passengers were ordered to bed. Tonight guards not only patrolled the perimeter, but moved among them, canteens clanking a little on their hips, guns cocked for instant firing. Susannah lay quietly, her head on her crossed arms, looking into the open desert. Azarov was out there, exercising the dog, scuffing his feet a little in the sand as he walked. Periodically, he paused to light a cigarette, chain smoking.

She was about to drift off to sleep when a woman fell into step with Azarov. Intrigued, Susannah propped herself up for a better view. Asha still wore her fatigues, but her hair was loose and free around her shoulders. She had tucked her shirttails into her pants, and the wide belt accentuated her figure. Her shirt was unbuttoned an extra button, and she carried her gun slung casually across her shoulders. The stance stretched the fabric taut over her breasts.

For some time they walked together. The woman made no overt moves, but to any observer, she was available to Azarov. Finally, the Russian looked at his watch and recalled the dog. Her hand outstretched, Asha tried to delay him, but Azarov shook his head and, lifting his hand in a friendly little wave, started alone toward his tent.

The woman watched him go. Her expression, her posture, her attitude as she shifted the gun into a more ready position betrayed a murderous anger. It was clear that in that moment, she hated Azarov. She hated him enough to kill him.

Chapter 27

THE THIRTY-SIXTH HOUR passed quietly, without extraordinary disturbance in the camp. Sharon was restless, impatient with the slow passage of the night. This time it was Susannah who drew his head down on her breast and held him close until he slept.

The third day was even hotter than the preceding ones. The sun was molten copper. The guards were relentless. It was a particular hell for them all. A mirage shimmered beside the charred tail of the Swissair DC-8; people fainted and suffered heat strokes. There was nothing to do except endure. After a while, even those who sobbed fell silent.

Although talking was forbidden, a curious prison-type whisper from motionless lips passed word through the camp in multiple languages that the deadline had been reset. Ten hostages would be picked at noon. Others might wonder and discuss quietly among themselves who they would be, but Susannah and her friends already knew. Exactly ten had been called out of the plodding circle in the night and identified for future reference.

Hopes for an early settlement had to be abandoned. The governments of Israel and South Africa refused to be blackmailed. What was more, it was now apparent that the Palestinian freedom fighters did not represent the main Palestinian organization. They were merely a small fanatical splinter group, unskilled in negotiation. Their sudden and unexpected generosity in releasing the two elderly women had so alarmed the parent organization that it had taken over the bargaining for the Palestinian side.

That information suggested the identity of the reptilian little visitor. Sharon and Berenson believed him to be the brains behind the Palestinian effort. A shadowy figure whose antecedents were vague and who avoided the political spotlight like a true power behind the throne, he was known only as The Chairman. It was believed that he was Syrian, but no one really knew. His presence at Freedom Field implied an implacable bargaining position. He had been persuaded to postpone the first deadline twenty-four hours so that St. Cleaux could notify the governments involved of the change in negotiating partners, but he vowed to uphold the second deadline.

Sharon and Berenson were calm, even resigned as they waited. Now it was Susannah who was jittery. Armand had found a member of Carter's Worldwide Tours who remembered seeing Azarov in Sofia. Susannah had seen several of her former traveling companions and had even spoken to the Abbotts and Miss Tillie Cary. To her relief, they had formed friendships with others and did not expect her to be sociable. But Miss McMillan—observant, articulate and curious—was different. Armand's acquaintance with her would inevitably reveal Susannah's relationship with Azarov. That would lead to questions, and while she was willing to confide to Sharon and Berenson and even to Armand and Kim Soong that she knew Azarov and Melinsky both, she didn't want to speak of them before Clayton. Not now —not when he was so close to proving that she was Absalom's messenger.

It had happened that morning. The guards' policy of escorting ten to the toilet at a time had left Susannah behind with Clayton. She had ducked under the blanket to wait her turn, but he had followed and, clasping her tightly in his arms, pressed her into the ground so that she could not escape. The blanket shielded them from view.

"Do you still have it?" he demanded in a fierce whisper.

She was so taken aback she almost said Yes. "What are you talking about?" she managed. "Get *off* of me." Her heart was beating so hard he could hear it.

"You know damn well. Do you have it with you?"

"I'm sorry. I don't know . . ."

"Listen. The agency sent me to meet you. You've been playing coy. I was Jess Simpson's assistant. I took over when he died. Absalom's information is too valuable to have it wandering around unprotected. When we get out of this, I'll escort you back to Langley. We're to report directly to the General."

"What is this all about? Who is Absalom?"

"I am not at liberty to say."

"I don't have any information."

"Then God help Absalom."

"God help him, then."

"What's the *matter* with you?"

"Nothing! Now let *go* of me!"

With a muttered oath, Clayton rolled aside, his hand pulling irritably at his shirt. As he stood up, it fell open. For one instant, something swung from his neck, then was covered quickly with his hand and stuffed back inside. He preceded Susannah in the line. There was no more conversation between them.

Susannah was thankful he couldn't see her face. It was beaded with cold sweat, and her hands were clammy. Clayton was wearing a CIA badge. It was exactly as she remembered. The white code letter identified a member of the agency's clandestine division. Strung on a dog-tag chain with a spring clip, the badge appeared to be authentic in every way. It was its presence here in the desert that alerted Susannah. No CIA employee, certainly not a clandestine one, ever traveled abroad with his Langley Headquarters badge. It was always left behind, locked carefully away in an agency safe.

Precisely at noon, the guards came for them. They approached unhesitatingly, knowing exactly where they camped.

"You. You. And you. On your feet."

"What for?" Berenson asked.

"You are the first. Up, now. Bring your blankets and eating gear."

Slowly, Sharon, Berenson and Susannah rose.

"You must take me too," Armand said suddenly.

"Jacques! No!"

"It's not necessary for you to get involved, old chap," Clayton said.

"We all go or we none of us go," Kim Soong said clearly. He too had risen to his feet. Although diminutive in stature, he was magnificently commanding in presence. The guerrillas were caught off guard. They looked at each other uncertainly. Then the senior guerrilla shrugged.

"If you all want to die like Jew dogs, it's no affair of mine. It won't spare any of those already selected. But the termite stays behind." He gestured at the little Oriental.

"I die with my friends," Kim Soong said simply. He picked up his tin plate and blanket and fell into line behind Susannah.

There was a cheer from the passengers who heard. Then silence.

Chapter 28

INCARCERATED IN ONE OF THE camp's few tents, the six congratulated themselves on being isolated from the other passengers. Then they gathered close to hear Sharon's whispered instructions. A watch, rotated every two hours, would be kept. Berenson and Sharon would decide if any of the hostages who might join them later should be included in the operation. Whoever spoke the requisite languages would describe the scheme to the newcomers. This decided, they settled down to wait. It was a relief to be out of the glaring sun.

Other hostages were brought quickly. Wiesynski, from Bonn, was sixty and overweight. Miller was wiry and short, a scrapper from Brooklyn with a cauliflower ear and a knife scar on his neck. Aaron, from Zurich, was a caricature of a Swiss gnome. Even now, after three days in the desert, his business suit was tidy. Bishop was a loudmouth salesman from Nebraska, included only because his temper had irritated the guards. And the two captains, Grant of TWA and Wilson of Swissair, were both handsome, graying men whose hours aloft showed in the fine wrinkles at the corners of their eyes and their tendency to squint, even in the shade. Of the six newcomers, only Miller was invited into the group. Sharon spoke to him in a whisper, his eye on the captains, who, for reasons of diplomacy rather than any judgment of their fitness, had to be excluded. Miller nodded.

"I was hoping someone would think of that," he said.

212

"Good. Are you agreed to wait until after the next negotiating session before deciding when to move?"

"Seems sensible. Who gives the word?"

"I do."

"Whatever you say, chief. I wish I had something solid to hold in my hand."

"What for?"

"Makes more impact in the fist."

Miller was going to be a good man.

At three o'clock, a press conference was scheduled. The busload of reporters, newsmen and crewmen arrived early, and while technicians strung radio and television cables to the camp's portable power units, the commentators were allowed to question selected Palestinian guerrillas. Asha was in demand. Even from a distance, Susannah could see that she was a fiery witness.

Shortly before three o'clock, a small truck backed up to the tent. Uneasy glances passed among the hostages.

"Nothing to worry about," Captain Grant said breezily. "They're just going to make a spectacle of us."

"You were told so?" Sharon asked tensely.

"Yes. They used prettier words, but that's what they meant."

But Grant and Wilson hadn't been told all of the Palestinians' plans. The truckbed contained leg irons and bulky handcuffs of the kind once used by prison chain gangs. Eighteen guards supervised their application to the hostages.

"The hell you will!" Miller snarled savagely as the guards approached with the set designated for him. A rifle butt slammed against his cheekbone, forestalling further argument. He bled copiously.

A sense of unreality descended on Susannah. As long as they were able to move about, to talk and plan in whispers, as long as they were relatively free of the guards' scrutiny, captivity had been bearable. Even their designation as hostages had an element of triumph in the opportunity it afforded to enact Sharon's plan. But this! This made her see them as they actually were, with dust and dirt on their clothes and ugly stubble on their faces. Now she saw how fatigue and worry etched deeper lines around their mouths and how the irons reduced them from men to animals. They shuffled along stoop-shouldered and in their awkwardness seemed less intelligent, less adept, less worthy than those who walked freely. There was particular pain in Sharon's eyes as the Palestinians locked the leg irons on Susannah. Heavy for a man, they were almost impossible for a woman, and the despair Susannah felt was visible on her face.

"Shall we do our tricks like good bears or shall we claw the tourists' eyes out?" Sharon asked.

Susannah smiled faintly.

"So," Kim said softly. He was as encumbered as Susannah.

"Move, now," barked the guard.

Two columns of armed guards escorted them into the glaring sun. The noise of the camp, of the media crews, suddenly stilled. The sound of dragging chains carried clearly.

It was several hundred yards to the place where reporters were seated behind tables with microphones. They had not gone a quarter of the way when Susannah stumbled and fell. Sharon reached to help her, but was rudely stopped by the guards; she had to struggle up alone. The second time, her legs shaking from the unaccustomed weight, it was almost beyond her strength. Groping blindly for help, she grasped the hand extended to her. A hard palm.

She looked up. Azarov had stepped through the line of guards and was lifting her to her feet. He took no notice of her as a person. He didn't look into her face at all. When she was upright, he released her abruptly.

"Which of you is in command?" he asked the guards in Arabic.

"I am, sir." He was a young man, very thin.

"These chains were placed on the prisoners by your orders?"

"Yes, sir."

"Why?"

"I was told to secure the prisoners in such a way that escape would be impossible."

"I see. And who told you?"

"The Chairman, sir."

"The Chairman quite appropriately wished to create sympathy for the prisoners to force their governments to meet our demands. But this is too much. The world will think the freedom fighters and the Palestinian Front are not fit to join the membership of nations. It will turn world opinion against our cause. You should have known that. The key, please."

Silently, shamefacedly, it was handed to him. Azarov knelt at Susannah's feet, unlocked the irons and put them aside so that she stood free.

"Do you have handcuffs?" Azarov asked the guerrilla.

"In the truck."

"Get them."

While they were being fetched, Azarov unlocked Susannah's wrist chains. They fell to the ground with a heavy clank. Her wrists were already red and raw. The Russian handed the key to another guard and ordered him to release the men.

The handcuffs were American police issue, light but strong. Azarov formed the prisoners into a line and then handcuffed each man's left wrist to his neighbor's right wrist. They thus formed a human chain, relatively unencumbered, but awkward enough in its entirety to make escape suicidal. He put Susannah on the end, next to Kim Soong. His hand lingered on her sore wrist for a moment as he latched the cuff into place. Then it fell to his side.

"Thank you," Susannah murmured softly.

He jerked around and looked at her sharply. A muscle worked in his cheek. For a second, the grimness left his glance. An expression of wonder came into his eyes. It was quickly suppressed. Abruptly, he turned away.

"When the press conference is over, release the two pilots. Then, when you have returned the other prisoners to their quarters, remove the handcuffs," he ordered the guerrilla. "It will be sufficient to satisfy yourself that the guards around their tent are adequate in number and weapons. Now, move the prisoners."

Susannah looked behind her once as they marched to the crude platform erected for them. Azarov was climbing into a jeep, his dog beside him in the front seat. Depression and fear assaulted her as she watched them drive away. His departure meant that once again Melinsky was the ranking Russian in the camp, and she feared him far more than Azarov.

Her fears were well grounded. Colonel Azarov did not return for that travesty of a press conference, nor was he seen afterward, when the passengers were lined up for their rations and evening exercise. But Melinsky and The Chairman were there, taunting the captives. This time, the Russian saw Susannah. An expression of triumph crossed his face. He went up to her. Feet wide apart, his hands behind his back, he surveyed her coldly.

"She has a body like a child's," he said in Russian to The Chairman.

"So find one to your taste."

"There's something I want to know." He stepped

closer and, reaching out, clasped her breasts, squeezing them like melons. It hurt, and Susannah slapped his hands away. Sharon started forward. There was a little scuffle as guards held him back.

Melinsky grabbed her chin, jerking her head up to face him. She tried to wrest herself away, but he held her tightly, his thumb digging painfully into the tender place under her chin. His breath was rank.

"Tell me," Melinsky said softly in his own tongue, "was there a Russian in your baker's dozen?"

"Let me go!" Susannah rasped in English.

"Not quite yet." Deliberately, he drew his fist back and slammed it against her nose.

Susannah cried out in pain and anger as she stumbled against a guard. He dumped her into the dirt at Melinsky's feet.

"Bring her to my tent tonight," Melinsky ordered. "I'd like to question her."

He turned away then and, followed by The Chairman, found another passenger to torment. Haltingly, Susannah struggled to her feet, her nose running blood, her lip crushed painfully against her teeth.

"Susannah!"

The guards released Sharon, and now he gathered her into his arms. Aaron handed him a handkerchief, still folded, still clean. Tenderly, carefully, Sharon wiped away the dirt and blood.

"You'll be all right, I think. Bruised and sore, but all right. What I wouldn't like to . . ."

"Just stay by me, Caleb. Just for a little while. It's all I want right now."

He nodded. His arm around her shoulders, he guided her back to the tent. For a precious moment, they were alone together. Susannah studied Sharon's face, then quickly made her decision.

"Caleb . . ." she whispered. He bent close to hear.

"Caleb . . . that man just now . . . he's a Russian. I think a member of the GRU, tht Soviet Army Intelligence. And the one who helped me this afternoon . . . he's a colonel in the KGB."

"How do you know that?"

"I've just been in Bulgaria. A . . . a friend told me."

"My God! We knew they aided the terrorists, but this is the first time they've been so open about it."

"Not so open. I just happen to know who they are."

He looked at her quickly, his face somber. "Yes. I guess you're right. Who are you working for? Your government?"

She nodded.

"Are you in trouble?"

"Yes. But right now, we're all in trouble. I think Clayton is a Communist agent."

"Are you sure?"

"I believe so. Don't . . ." But she couldn't finish. The others were returning. Under the watchful gaze of the guards, they ate their rations.

Susannah wasn't hungry. She lay quietly on her blanket, her face hidden under her hand. Her nose throbbed. Her lip was numb. She was very tired. But she couldn't rest. Silently, to herself, she cursed Colonel Melinsky. Meticulously, deliberately, she thought of all the words she knew and used them against him. It was all she could do. Her hate must be strong enough to sustain her through their next encounter.

Chapter 29

ST. CLEAUX WAS LATE for the evening session. When he arrived, he looked tired. His shoulders slumped, and the white suit was rumpled. Still, the usual polite smile was on his face when he greeted Mahoud.

They were closeted together for only a few minutes before the Arab hurried from his tent to Melinsky's quarters. Their meeting too was brief. In long tense strides, Mahoud returned to St. Cleaux. Watching anxiously from the darkness of their tent, Susannah and her friends exchanged glances. There were no grounds for hope in the stubborn set of Mahoud's jaw.

St. Cleaux emerged first from their meeting. A single cheer was heard. Then the camp exploded with cheering, drowning out the official announcement. It was done! Capitulation! Incredulously at first, the hostages too joined in, shouting and dancing and clapping one another on the shoulders. It was over. They were safe.

St. Cleaux stood a moment, the microphone still in his hand, graciously acknowledging the outpouring of gratitude. Then he slowly laid it down and stepped off the platform. His feet were dragging as he approached the tent where Susannah and the other hostages waited. They greeted him eagerly.

St. Cleaux's face did not relax. He did not smile. Gradually they became still. Susannah voiced their sudden fear.

"Isn't it over?" she asked.

The handsome face was gray. He sank into the tent's only chair and lit a cigarette. "No," he admitted finally.

"What do you mean?" Anxiously, they clustered closer.

He took a deep breath. "It's over for everyone but you."

Sharon nodded a little, as though he expected it.

"But why?" Susannah asked incredulously.

"The Israeli government holds the greatest percentage of imprisoned Palestinians. It won't give in. The Palestinian Front agreed to release everyone but you."

"And the deadline?" Berenson asked softly. "What of it?"

"Postponed again."

"How long?"

"Thirty-six hours. That will take you until three P.M. day after tomorrow."

"And then?"

"By then I hope to have another—a better—answer from Israel. An important cabinet meeting is scheduled tomorrow, as are party meetings and a session of the Knesset. Perhaps something favorable will come of it. I can't promise you anything. I think you know that."

Sharon nodded again. "And these others? Miss Clarke? Mr. Kim? Jacques Armand? They aren't involved in any way."

"When they allied themselves with you, they became part of the first ten. The guerrillas have refused to release them."

They watched him closely, their faces bleak. Susannah had never thought it would come to that absolute a showdown, a firing squad. She hadn't even expected the chains. But one by one, the alternatives were being eliminated. Israel's policy on blackmail was well known. She too should have expected it.

St. Cleaux extinguished his cigarette in the sand.

"Well. I must go. A plane will be here within the hour to take the first group. They will be going to Beirut, fortunately. It will be easier to get them on to their destinations from there. There will be six planes—two tonight before it gets dark, the other shortly after daybreak tomorrow morning." He rose, straightened his shoulders and shook hands all around. Silently, they followed him to the door of the tent.

"Well, I guess that is all," he said, and started to duck under the low opening. Then he stopped and turned back to them.

"There's a quotation I have been trying to recall," he said. "It is something to the effect that the Lord helps those who help themselves. Perhaps you know it more exactly."

Sharon nodded, his eyes suddenly very bright. "I think we do. We appreciate your efforts in our behalf. You were kind to come and tell us the news yourself." The guard outside was listening.

"It was the least I could do."

St. Cleaux left them. Sharon put his arm around Susannah and led her into the deep shadow of the tent, away from the door. The others watched until St. Cleaux had gone, and then they too returned to their usual places on the ground. Wiesynski was picking up sand and letting it run through his fingers dejectedly. Occasionally, he cleared his throat huskily.

There was silence for some little time. Sharon finally crooked his finger at Berenson, whose turn it was at the peephole. Abraham crossed the tent and sat close beside them.

"Does that quotation mean what I took it to mean?" Sharon whispered.

"I think so."

Sharon's voice dropped even lower. "Then we'll have

our chance after all. But we can't use the plan we discussed."

"Why not?"

"Someone may have told it."

Berenson's face whitened. He glanced hastily around. "Are you sure?" he murmured, turning to face Sharon once again.

Sharon nodded. "We'll have to improvise. Susannah and I will devise something. You take your cue from us, but concentrate on getting weapons. You might tell Miller. But not the others. As far as they're concerned, the operation is off."

Berenson nodded.

"I sure could do with a drink," Sharon said fervently, out loud. Clayton was watching.

"I wish I had a cold beer," Clayton agreed. "Say, what are you whispering about? There can be no secrets among hostages."

"No secrets among friends. I was just hoping they had something to read," Berenson said. "Doesn't anybody have anything?"

No one did. But the question initiated a discussion on books and movies, and Berenson moved away, toward Miller, on the other side of the tent. Clayton's eyes remained suspiciously narrowed, but no one was going to tell him anything. He subsided, but his glance followed the others as they talked.

"Custer's Last Stand," Susannah said caustically to Sharon under her breath.

"How many of your Western movies have you seen in your lifetime?"

"Dozens. What does that have to do with our problem?"

"I have seen a few too. Do you know what happens when the wagon train is surrounded by Indians and the settlers are down to their last rounds of ammunition?"

"The cavalry arrives, flags flying and bugles blowing. And everybody in the theater cheers."

"I always did like a good movie."

Susannah studied his face, the little smile lurking, the quiet assurance that had replaced the tension of a few moments ago.

"I thought the International Red Cross was supposed to be neutral."

"Of course it is. I didn't hear anything that wasn't strictly what it was supposed to be. Did you?"

"No. No, I didn't." In spite of the bruises, her smile was brilliant.

The guerrillas must have feared that the hostages would make a break for freedom. Shortly before the first plane landed, twenty-four guards marched them into the open desert, to a small rise overlooking the camp. There they were forced to sit in a tight circle, their backs to one another, their wrists handcuffed together. No talking was permitted, but words were not necessary to convey the torment they all felt as they watched the first passengers receiving their travel documents and lining up for departure.

An American military hospital plane arrived first. Although there were no injured passengers left in the camp, an appalling number were ill with heat and sunburn. They were loaded quickly. Within minutes of their departure, the second plane landed. Although it too loaded without delay, night had come before it was ready to take off. Its lights bathed the hard-packed strip in stark whiteness as it rose and circled the camp. A wing dipped—perhaps in farewell, perhaps in encouragement to those left behind. They watched until it vanished.

Even though there would be no more departures tonight, the hostages were not allowed to return to their tent. They sat savoring the coolness while the guards paced and smoked restlessly. Long after the camp had been quieted for the night, they were freed and ordered to their feet. Stiffly, rubbing their wrists, they marched down the hill to the makeshift command post. There they had to wait while the officer-in-charge made his report. Nearby, Azarov's tent was open to the breeze. The Russian had returned. Now he sat at a crude table, talking with Melinsky. Papers were strewn before him and he toyed with a pen, occasionally jotting a note as Melinsky harangued. His revolver lay within easy reach. A cigarette smoked in an ashtray. As Susannah watched, he put down his pen and rubbed his eyes. The dog at his feet nudged him, and bending, he tugged its ears gently before turning his attention back to Melinsky. Once, he looked out. He didn't see her. Thankfully, Susannah slipped silently by. Her sleep that night was troubled by nightmares and imaginings, but no one bothered her. There would be ample opportunity to interrogate Susannah Clarke when all the passengers who were being released had gone.

Chapter 30

IN THE CONFUSION of the new day, no one had ordered the hostages into the desert. They watched from their tent, not speaking—fearing that even a chance word would call attention to them. Now it was noon. The sixth plane had come and gone. All but twelve of the other passengers had been taken away. Through some miscalculation, these few had been left behind to wait for a plane to be sent back for them. Now they sat forlornly by the runway, oblivious of the broiling sun, unwilling to return to the littered camp behind them.

The guerrillas ignored the mess. Already some of them had left, climbing joyously into jeeps and the back of trucks to return home. Most of them were young, and the stint in the desert was as much a confinement for them as it was for the captives. Sharon and Berenson exchanged glances as the ranks of their guards thinned. The time was coming.

Susannah and Kim Soong were at the peepholes as the seventh plane buzzed the runway. Then, more deliberately, it approached for landing. It set down carefully and taxied to the end of the airstrip. There it waited, its propellers spinning slowly. Suddenly, Susannah felt a warning.

"Caleb," she called softly.

He came to stand at her shoulder. His lips were very close to her ear as he looked out. "There will be commandos on that plane. They'll be hoping for a diversion so they can land. Run out and scream for the guards. Say that we're fighting. I'll neutralize our friend. Count to five. Then go."

Susannah counted as Sharon passed behind Berenson, unceremoniously jabbing him in the rump as he went. Now he approached Clayton, who lounged easily against the wall.

Susannah darted from the tent. "Guards! Guards!" she screamed. "A fight! Stop them! *Stop* them!" Behind her, Sharon said something to Clayton. His fist struck the American solidly in the stomach.

It worked. The two nearest guards promptly ducked into the tent—to be struck from behind by Berenson and Miller. Miller had found something solid to hold in his hand, and the crack of the guards' necks snapping told of its effectiveness. By the time other guards rushed in, Kim Soong and Aaron had snatched up the fallen men's weapons and were ready.

The volley of firing did not deter Azarov, arriving seconds later with more guards. The hostages' gunfire was accurate and deadly. Stumbling over one another, the guerrillas were cut down before they could aim. Seeing Susannah huddling against the wall of the tent, Azarov hauled her up and clasped her in front of him. Gradually, the others realized what he had done. The shooting became ragged and then stopped altogether. In the rear corner of the tent, Sharon and Clayton were locked in a vicious grip. They were evenly matched. Muscles quivering, breathing in rasping grunts, they jockeyed for a decisive blow. Suddenly, they broke apart. Clayton lashed out.

Azarov's gun roared once. Susannah shuddered.

It was not Sharon as she had feared. It was Clayton who clasped a bloody wound in his stomach and toppled slowly.

He seemed to catch himself. "You . . . you're . . ." he gurgled.

Azarov fired again. Clayton took one step and fell forward, face down. He was still.

Now they became aware of gunfire outside and the crash of heavier-gauge weapons. The Russian heard it too. He backed away, his arm still around Susannah's ribs, taking her with him.

"Give me sixty seconds . . ." he rasped. It was not necessary to finish the threat. His gun was too close to Susannah's breast.

They were six to one, but they let him go.

Once outside, Azarov grasped Susannah's wrist. "Run," he commanded. Dragging her with him, he raced for the landing strip.

They didn't reach it. Commandos pouring off the aircraft had hastily erected a makeshift barricade just ahead. It blocked their way. With a muttered curse, Azarov left Susannah behind a stack of packing crates and carefully, the dog at his heels, worked himself toward an opening in the storage area, seeking desperately to avoid the withering crossfire that pinned him there in an exposed position. In a sudden lull in the shooting, Susannah peered cautiously over the top of the crates. In that brief instant, the commando saw her and with thumb and forefinger formed an "OK" signal. She ducked down again as firing resumed. Azarov hadn't moved. The dog hugged the ground at his side, poised to run.

Behind them, Sharon and the other hostages, all of them armed now, were fighting their way forward, toward the commandos, closing the pincers on Azarov. Then, suddenly, his escape route opened. The Palestinians, desperate to recapture their escaping hostages, rushed to eliminate Sharon's line of hostile fire. It was a fatal gamble. The commandos cut them down, but not before Asha and Melinsky had found cover behind an abandoned jeep.

Azarov saw them. Thinking his flank was protected, he glanced first at Sharon, now approaching rapidly from his right, and then at the commandos behind the barricade on his left. Behind him, Asha raised her weapon. Her eyes glittered.

"Watch out behind you! Aleksei . . ."

He heard her and whirled, but it was too late. Asha fired.

Azarov spun and fell.

With a roar, the dog leaped for the woman, fangs bared, fury in its black eyes. Asha fired again, and Melinsky too. The machine-gun bullets caught the animal in midair and hurled him over backward. He fell on his back, twisted awkwardly, and with his last strength crawled, whimpering pitifully, toward Azarov. He died, fingers away, his nose outstretched to be a little nearer his master.

Azarov was groping painfully up onto his elbows, his revolver in his hand. His vision must have blurred or his hand trembled, for he steadied the gun with both hands.

In that moment, the commandos charged the remnant of the Palestinian line. Melinsky and Asha showed themselves just long enough to aim and fire. Azarov squeezed the trigger.

Melinsky fell over backward, a startled expression on his face, as the gun dropped from Azarov's hands. He collapsed into the sand and was still.

Susannah ran.

It was not far, but by the time she reached him and snatched up his revolver, Asha had vanished. The commandos poured over the place where the Palestinians had been, closed the line with Sharon's dusty forces and turned to face the remaining guerrillas. Then a commando, teeth flashing a wide grin in his powder-darkened face, came toward Susannah.

"It's over. Don't shoot!" he called.

Susannah nodded. The heavy weapon fell from her hand.

Unceremoniously, the commando grasped Azarov's hair and lifted his head from the sand.

"There's nothing you can do to help him now. Better go board the plane."

Susannah lingered, her eyes on the still form, the outstretched hand, the dog three feet away.

"Go on. You are only in the way while we clean up the rest of them."

As he spoke, there was sporadic gunfire to the west. It was quickly silenced. A cry died away and a sudden, eerie stillness fell. Numbly, Susannah nodded. Oblivious of the danger, she walked the remaining distance to the airstrip and the waiting plane. Mounting the steps, she noticed in a detached way that it bore no markings of country of origin, and she remembered that the commandos too had been in civilian khakis rather than uniforms. A volunteer effort, probably of Israelis, had freed her.

Some were already there. Others came quickly. Without fanfare, the plane taxied and took off. As it banked steeply over the camp, Susannah looked down, searching for the place where Azarov lay. He had dogged her steps, plagued her thoughts, threatened her life. But she wasn't glad he was dead. She wasn't glad at all.

Chapter 31

THEY WERE FLOWN TO BEIRUT, put onto a bus and driven to the Inter-Continental Hotel. A cheer burst from the crowds waiting to meet them. An explosion of flashbulbs, microphones thrust into their faces and a cacophony of questions in many languages impeded their progress into the lobby. Susannah put her head down and, with Caleb's hand on her arm, went through the crowd without looking or speaking to anyone.

"Caleb!"

The joyous cry rang through the lobby. Susannah stepped aside as a woman broke from the crowd and threw herself into Sharon's arms. His shining eyes as he lifted her off her feet and clasped her close told Susannah all she needed to know. Distance and religion would have separated them. Even so, she would always have a special feeling for Caleb Sharon.

The two seemed oblivious of their surroundings. But when Susannah started to pass them and go with the others, Sharon reached out and stopped her.

"Susannah . . . wait. Rebekah . . . Rebekah, this is Susannah Clarke from Washington. Susannah, my wife."

He was so proud of her, they were so obviously in love with each other, Rebekah was so lovely that Sussannah's regret fell away. She put out her hand, and the other woman clasped it with both of hers. Her smile was warm.

"Have dinner with us tomorrow night, Susannah, before you go?" Caleb invited.

"Well . . . I . . ."

"Please," Rebekah urged.

"Then, yes. Thank you very much. If we're still here, I'd like that."

"You'll still be here. They won't let us go that fast. Seven o'clock. We'll meet you in the lobby."

"I'll look forward to it. Until then." But they had already turned away.

She told them the story—most of it. At first, she had hesitated to speak before Rebekah.

"It's classified, isn't it?" Sharon asked shrewdly.

Susannah nodded.

"You can trust Rebekah. Her clearances are higher than mine." His smile was fond.

Susannah considered it. Rebekah was as fine, as staunch a person as her husband. She sensed it of her, as she had known it of him. So haltingly at first, leaving out most of the names, she spoke of Azarov and Melinsky, and of John Novak.

"So now you must go to your President?" Sharon asked when she had finished. "That must be a difficult assignment. Will your friend Maryanne be able to arrange it?"

"I hope so," Susannah said, her voice suddenly revealing the doubt she felt.

"And if she can't?"

"I don't know. I suppose the next-best route is through his political party. Perhaps through the Senate. I might try one of the senators on the Armed Services Subcommittee that oversees the CIA."

"But there's the leak. Can you trust them?"

"I'll have to trust somebody. I can't just walk into the White House and expect to be admitted to the President's office."

"What about David?" Rebekah asked Caleb softly. "Can't you give her a letter of introduction to him?"

"Yes, I can. I was thinking he might help."

"Who is David?" Susannah asked.

"David Ben David is a close friend in the diplomatic corps. Presently, he is serving in Washington on the Ambassador's personal staff. He himself couldn't get an appointment with your President, but the Ambassador probably could. It's an alternative channel that might be useful to you. And there won't be any leaks! What time does your plane leave?"

"Midnight."

"It's almost that now." He beckoned to the waiter, asked for pen and writing paper and wrote to David Ben David. Then he slipped the letter into an envelope and handed it to Susannah, flap unsealed.

"If there is difficulty, take this to David. If there isn't, take it to him anyway. He and his wife are charming and I think you'll like them."

Susannah's eyes suddenly were full of tears. "Caleb, how can I ever thank you . . ."

"Hush. Don't bother. What are friends for?"

She smiled shakily, and they rose. It was time to go.

They took her to the airport. Rebekah waited in the taxi.

"Aren't you coming to wave me off?" Susannah asked.

"No. You and Caleb have things to say to each other. There will be other partings, I know. I'll come then."

"Rebekah . . . thank you . . . for everything." It was all she could say.

But after all, there wasn't much to say to him. At the customs gate, Susannah turned. He took her hand and held it tightly.

"Rebekah was right," he said softly. "We can't let you walk out of our lives. You'll write?"

"If you'll promise the same."

"I do. The conference I was supposed to attend in Washington is an annual event. Rebekah will come with me next time. We want to see you."

"You must plan to visit me in Virginia."

"We'll count on it."

Wordlessly then, he drew her into his arms. A long, quiet moment passed. He released her reluctantly.

"Good luck, little one."

"You too."

She went quickly to the customs gate and handed her passport, dusty and greasy now, to the swarthy official. He opened it.

"What's this?" he demanded brusquely, pointing to the gaudy stamp of "Freedom Field" on it.

He didn't understand why the American woman broke into choking sobs.

Kim Soong was in the transit lounge. He rose immediately and led her to a seat beside him.

"So," he said softly. "I think it will be a relief to be home again."

"Home? But Washington isn't your home."

"But it is. I am with our embassy there. Didn't I tell you?"

"No, Soong. You didn't tell us much at all."

"It's not always necessary to talk. They are calling our flight. Shall we go?"

Chapter 32

IT WAS NOON when she finally landed in Washington. Quickly, eyes alert for any surveillance, Susannah hurried to the main lobby, where she called Maryanne. Switchboard operators, secretaries and assistants spoke to her before Maryanne's familiar voice finally came on the line.

"Susannah! Where are you?"

"I'm at Dulles Airport. I've just come from overseas. Maryanne, I need your help. Can I come to your office right away?"

"Now? Is it that urgent?"

"Yes, Maryanne, it is."

"Well, sure. Come on now. I'll clear you at the gate."

"If I'm not there in an hour and a half, call the police."

Maryanne laughed. "Are you kidding?"

"I've never been more serious in my life," Susannah answered, and quickly hung up.

But no one followed her. The taxi took her directly to the White House, and soon she reached Maryanne's outer office. Decorated in antiques and porcelains, it was more like a living room than an office. It was restful just to sit there, sipping the coffee handed her by a secretary. Minutes passed before Maryanne hurried in.

"Hello!" she exclaimed. "Sorry I wasn't here, but this has been quite a day. Come in and tell me about this mysterious business that can't wait. I thought your spying days were over."

Susannah followed and closed the office door firmly behind her. Maryanne had already settled into an armchair at her desk. Stacks of invitations threatened to topple onto the floor.

"They're not," Susannah said quietly. "That's why I need your help."

She had Maryanne's full attention. The teasing grin faded from her face. "So?" she said simply.

"I have to see the President."

"But that's impossible! You can't just see the President. His appointments are set up for weeks, months in advance."

"I know. But I must see him, and I must see him alone. It won't take long. And it can't be anyone else. Most emphatically, it can't be anyone else. It's urgent. And it's dangerous, too. My life . . ."

"I think you had better tell me what it is."

"Can't you take it on faith?"

"No. Not entirely."

Susannah paused and took a short breath. "I met one of our agents while I was in Bulgaria. He was assassinated. I have what he wanted to deliver to the President. He gave me a name to use to gain his attention if it proved necessary."

Maryanne rubbed her chin reflectively. "Well . . . how about the First Lady? Will you entrust her with it?"

"I'll entrust her with the name. Let the President decide whether he wants to see me."

"Fair enough. They'll be meeting a delegation in the Rose Garden in about an hour. There's time. I'll tell her. What is the name?"

"Absalom."

"Absalom?" Maryanne smiled and repeated it to herself once more. "Absalom."

"Yes. One more word of caution: no one must over-hear you speak the name."

"I'll be careful. Wait here. There's more coffee, and if you wish, there's something stronger in the cabinet there."

Maryanne was gone some time. Then, in a rush, she was back. "Come quickly," she said.

"Already?"

"Not yet. She said come to the garden, just in case."

The garden baked in a heavy scent of tea roses as the dignitaries assembled. Some of them were from Congress. Most were unknown to Susannah. They chatted and joked and tried to appear nonchalant, but the way their eyes turned toward the White House and the al-most palpable air of expectation revealed that they did not meet the President every day. Beside them their wives waited, a little breathless in the heat. They were so carefully groomed that Susannah was suddenly con-scious of her own appearance. Her suit had been cleaned in Beirut, but the stint in the desert sun had ruined it. Faded and limp now, it hung from her shoul-ders, mute testimony to the weight she had lost. Make-up could not disguise the bruises, the peeling skin, the heavy shadows under her eyes. Her ordeal showed in her tired and travel-worn face.

Preceded by a stir of anticipation, the President came into the garden, looking a little like an apparition, so familiar was his face. He wasn't tall, yet his head and shoulders gave the impression of a massive man. Serene as ever, the First Lady walked beside him. As the Presi-dent moved through the crowd, his wife saw Maryanne and beckoned them to her side. The President turned abruptly.

"Miss Clarke?"

"Yes, Mr. President."

"You have something for me?"

Susannah took the watch from her neck and put it into his hand. "It's wedged in the back. You may have to break the hinge to open it. This goes with it." The letter was worn and faded from being against her skin in the heat. "I was told to give it to you and to no one else."

"I understand." The President closed his hand over the watch and slid the letter into his inside breast pocket. Then, with a little nod of thanks and farewell, he stepped back and was instantly surrounded by a crowd of Senators and their wives.

Bemused, Susannah watched the President as he chatted with the guests. He smiled and seemed serene, supremely confident. A single trace of tension betrayed him. In his pocket, his hand was knotted into a fist, clenched tightly around her watch.

Chapter 33

THE DAYS SLIPPED BY. Susannah was welcomed joyously by her family. Her brothers had all gathered, and for one long, hectic weekend she smiled and accepted the congratulations, telling and retelling the story of the hijacking. But her movements felt mechanical and her smile forced. She was depressed and nervous, and it was a relief when they had gone and she could resume the routine of daily life. Her shop had done well; sales during her absence had exceeded her expectations, and she was pleased. In time, she took Caleb's letter to David Ben David and, as he had predicted, found warm friends in him and his wife, Sara. She wrote thanking Caleb and Rebekah, and they replied. Kim Soong and his beautiful wife, Teea, invited her to an elegantly formal dinner party and provided a personable escort for the evening. Benjamin Brock was generous in his attention afterward, but as with everything else, Susannah had difficulty in being interested. The obligations of family, business and social life had become a burden that interfered with her desire to be alone.

Weeks passed. It was late August when Maryanne Knowles called. "Susannah! Come up and have dinner with me. There's someone who wants to see you."

"Who?"

"Someone you'll want to dress for. Come Tuesday night and meet me here at the office at six. We'll run across to the Sans Souci for dinner and go from there."

"Thanks, Maryanne, but . . ."

"Don't argue. Be there."

"Why the mystery?" Susannah asked when she and Maryanne were seated at the restaurant.

"The President wants to talk to you privately, without the usual horde of people knowing about it."

"You mean . . ."

"Of course. But don't ask me any more. At nine o'clock I'll introduce you to the attaché who will take you there."

Precisely at nine, Richard Morris slid a key into the ignition of an unmarked car and drove Susannah to Andrews Air Force Base. There he helped her into a helicopter for the flight to Camp David. A few more steps took her to the comfortable living room where a small fire burned on the hearth.

The President was smiling as he crossed the room, his hand outstretched to greet her. Susannah leaped to her feet. He looked relaxed. No tension marred his demeanor tonight.

"Miss Clarke, you have picked my favorite spot by the fire," he said, seating himself in the armchair opposite her. "Have you wondered at the silence?"

"A little. The newspapers haven't been very informative."

"Thanks to Absalom, they're in the dark for once. They had it all, but didn't see the significance of it."

He took a clipping from his pocket and handed it to her. It was an obituary for a man whose name was unknown to Susannah. A CIA employee, he had been killed in a single-car smashup on the George Washington Parkway, not far from the CIA-Langley turnoff.

Susannah shook her head. "I must confess, I don't either," she said, returning it to him.

"I'll tell you in a minute. But first I want your story, Miss Clarke. I have yet to hear it."

"There isn't a great deal to tell, Mr. President. I had known John Novak when I worked for the Central Intelligence Agency. I knew he was abroad on assignment, but I didn't know where until I saw him in Sofia. That afternoon, he came to my hotel room and asked me to collect some information for him. He planned to wait for me, but he said that if I couldn't return it to him, I was to bring it directly to you. John Novak was shot to death in front of my hotel a few minutes after I returned. So I did as he asked."

"Did anyone try to stop you?"

Susannah smiled. "Yes."

"Tell me all of it."

She had read that he didn't like long, rambling discourses, so her account was concise. The President listened attentively, his head to one side, his chin propped thoughtfully on his hand.

"And how much of the operation were you able to piece together, Miss Clarke?" he asked when she had finished.

"Almost none of it. John Novak was our agent. His superior at the agency was Jess Simpson. Novak believed his death was murder. Chuck Clayton, whom I met in the desert, claimed he was Simpson's replacement, but I felt that he might be a plant instead. He mentioned taking me to the General at CIA, but gave no name. Vladimir Voorhies implied he worked for the CIA. I doubted him until he was murdered. Now, I don't know."

"Vladimir Voorhies," the President murmured. "You are correct in all your assumptions except the one on Vladimir Voorhies. He was a double agent, loyal to no one except the next paymaster. And the Communists you met? Tell me about them."

"Voorhies told me Aleksei Azarov was a colonel in the KGB, and my knowledge of him confirms that. I believe Colonel Melinsky was a functionary of Soviet Army Intelligence, the GRU. There was a definite rivalry between the two men. Melinsky seemed to have the upper hand in Sofia, although Azarov controlled the hijacking operation. All of these people are dead now."

"Except you."

"Yes. Except me."

The President stared into the fire while Susannah sat quietly, absorbing the impact of his words. Then he rose and dropped a small log on the dying blaze.

"Do you have any theories as to Absalom's identity?" he asked when he had resumed his seat.

"No. I have wondered if it's anyone I know."

The President smiled a little. "I will tell you about Absalom Utz, Miss Clarke. He is a remarkable man."

The President's narrative began slowly, but gathered momentum as he talked. "He was born in 1933 in a tiny village not too far from Moscow. His father's family had been village officials before 1900. His mother was an educated woman, the daughter of servants to nobility in Moscow before 1917. Absalom was their only surviving son, born late in their lives, while they were in the village kolkhoz—the collective farm.

"The year of his birth was the year of famine in Russia. Starvation was endemic in the kolkhozes, and Absalom's mother died. The boy lived only because his father stole from the kolkhoz food supplies to feed him. Once he was caught, and to save himself he killed the official who discovered him.

"Life was hard, but the boy and his father survived. In 1938, the Great Purge saw Absalom's three uncles arrested and deported to Siberia. They were never heard from again. Absalom's father was spared because he supported Communism, yet he came to consider the

Purge a betrayal. The suffering of the upper classes had been predicted by the Revolution, but not that of the masses. They had merely exchanged one set of bonds for another. In his disappointment with the bankruptcy of the Revolution for which he had worked, the father began creating doubt in his son's mind. That was a great risk. He was trusting a five-year-old's discretion at a time when children were under tremendous pressure in school to report on their families and friends.

"Well, Absalom kept silent. In 1940, at the age of fifty-three, his father was drafted. Absalom was seven. Without his father to fight for him, he faced starvation in the kolkhoz. He ran away, and although he haunted the army camps, he never found or heard from his father again.

"He did find food, however. New recruits were not permitted to keep food brought from home. It was thrown over encampment fences, where children and adults scrambled for it. Absalom still bears the scars of struggling for bits of bread and sausage against the barbed wire of those encampments. But again, he survived. He ingratiated himself with the officers, ran their errands, did their chores, located women and entertainment for them, all in exchange for rations. A family took him into their hovel, but he killed one of the sons in a quarrel over a loaf of bread. He was eight when that happened. He moved to another military base and repeated the process. He killed his first adult at nine, his second a year later. He was small, undernourished and cruel, by his own admission.

"In 1944, an NKVD officer named Mikhail Sergeyev noticed that he was a hustler and, when the war was over, took him to Leningrad and enrolled him in the exclusive NKVD schools. Ultimately, he graduated with distinction from the KGB's supreme espionage college, the Institute of International Relations. Sergeyev stayed somewhat in the background of Absalom's life at first, but as the years passed and the young man proved himself, Sergeyev became a friend and, finally, almost an adoptive father. Under his patronage, Absalom advanced rapidly in the KGB. He was unusually bright, with a particular aptitude for languages. At the Institute of Foreign Languages, he became proficient in almost a dozen, mostly Slavic dialects. He also demonstrated what was, to Party officials, a disturbing tendency toward individual thought and action, but as it never went against the Party, nothing much was done about it. His record was brilliant, and so he was groomed for more responsible positions.

"Hungary was his first foreign tour of duty. He was attached to the Soviet Embassy there in 1955. The depth of hatred the Hungarians felt for the Soviets shocked him. It made him think. He began to notice the discrepancy between what the Party said and what was reality. Equally telling, he fell in love with a Hungarian girl who publicly spat in his face. She participated actively in the Revolution, and when she died under the treads of a Soviet tank, Absalom's emotions became explosive. Yet he owed everything to the Party. He quashed his feelings and pushed for a punitive line in Budapest.

"The Party was pleased with him. He was promoted and returned to Leningrad. By 1960, East Germany was losing so much of its population that its economy was threatened. Absalom was offered a post in East Berlin. Since Soviet policy stipulates that only married men can be assigned to cities in or near the West, Absalom obediently married Katerina Petrovna, a highly educated Party member from a family well placed in Party circles. She was a rather pretty young woman, but she was a hardliner. Absalom, on the other hand, was a moderate and a strong supporter of Khrushchev.

"Their marriage wasn't very successful, but while they were in East Germany a son was born. Absalom doted on the boy. He was a truly beautiful child, but he was frail, and tuberculosis was suspected. At the age of two and a half, he contracted pneumonia. The skill and drugs that might have saved him were in West Berlin, and Absalom begged for permission to take him there. The Party refused. Two days later, the boy died in his father's arms.

"A divorce soon followed. In time, Absalom returned to Moscow. Khrushchev was in power. The country was advancing economically. Small but important freedoms were being granted to individuals. Absalom, as a rising member of the KGB, lived well.

"Khrushchev's fall was followed by a resurgence of neo-Stalinism that Absalom found distressing. In 1966 two things happened that illustrated rather forcefully the nature of the changes. The first was a new law that enabled the regime to jail people for as much as three years for anti-Soviet jokes. This was an effort to cope with a growing tide of malicious humor in the USSR, but for Absalom it was particularly personal. He had a sense of humor and had already been reminded of the dangers of levity in Party matters. Secondly, the KGB and military police brutally dispersed a minor religious demonstration in Moscow. The fact that the people had felt secure enough to demonstrate at all indicated the progress the country had made under Khrushchev. Their arrest and imprisonment for five years at hard labor was an indication of the growing dominance of the KGB and the police-state mentality.

"Absalom might have experienced an intellectual crisis then, but he was assigned to Czechoslovakia. There he witnessed the excitement of Czechoslovakia's rush for freedom and the crushing disappointment when the Soviets snuffed it out. This time, he was a mature man. His analytical ability was superb. He saw what was happening in Prague, and he understood the logical outcome of his own feelings. Almost in panic, he requested permanent reassignment in Moscow.

"His friend Sergeyev asked him the reason for his rather precipitate return. Absalom's description of the events he had just witnessed was properly clinical, but having been our informant for years, Sergeyev sensed his protégé's real concern. Cautiously, he hinted at an alternative. Absalom made no comment, but little by little he began to speak more freely to his friend. Sergeyev, of course, passed the additional information on to us.

"Sergeyev was in the scientific hierarchy of the KGB, so it was immediately apparent when he began speaking for a second source elsewhere in the organization. We questioned him, but he would say only that the information was reliable. We found it to be infallible. But Sergeyev refused to direct inquiries to his source, so we could only guess at his position in the government.

"Meanwhile, the KGB had discovered Absalom's real talent. He was assigned to the Osbdenny Otdyel Section of the KGB. The Soviets call it the Dirty Water Department, and that's an apt description. Blackmail, terror and assassination are its responsibility. He was put in charge of obtaining the release of Communists imprisoned around the world. Hijacking as a device for blackmailing governments was not originally his idea, but he developed it into a fine art. He was promoted to colonel.

"Inevitably, the Party learned of Sergeyev's activities. At his last meeting with us, he told us Absalom's identity and gave us a will, leaving the Swiss bank account he had accumulated in our service to Absalom should he ever defect. Then he went home, destroyed all the evidence of his association with us and committed suicide. Had he lived to be arrested, suspicion might have fallen more directly on Absalom. Instead, the Communists were able to convince themselves that Sergeyev had acted alone, and they closed the case. Days, even weeks passed. While we were considering how best to approach Absalom, or whether to approach him at all, he contacted us and volunteered.

"I think at first Absalom wanted revenge—for his son, his friend, his youth, for everything the Party had taken from him. But somewhere along the line, his purpose changed. Perhaps it was the friendships he formed with our people. Perhaps it was his ever-increasing knowledge of our principles and life as opposed to life and conditions in the Soviet Union. Perhaps it's because basically, he's not a mean-spirited man. Whatever it was, it was not money. We established a Swiss bank account for him, too, but he's not interested in it. He's never even asked about it. He's asked nothing for his brilliant service, and seems to expect nothing. He has been courageous, knowledgeable, inventive. No risk was too great for him. The information he's given us has been wide-ranging and first rate. The message you brought was his most valuable."

"I'm glad," Susannah murmured. "I wondered."

The President read her thoughts. "Yes, it was worth it. It was the name of a person in our government who was giving information to the Russians. The leak has almost become a way of life these days, but by and large, the CIA has been blameless. This man was in the CIA. Not only was he *in* the CIA, he was high up in the CIA, on the Director's personal staff. He regularly attended U.S. Intelligence Board and Watch Committee meetings or read the results of those meetings. He was in a position to see every national intelligence estimate and to know of every intelligence-gathering operation, whether electronic or clandestine."

Susannah's face whitened as she thought of the consequences of this man's treason.

"Exactly," the President said. "He could have been extremely damaging. He was damaging enough without divulging everything he knew. He was selective, very selective. And careful, too. He probably was in actual contact with the Soviets only two or three times in all. We know now that he handed over our SALT negotiating position to a Soviet Embassy official. He blew the whistle on the Gamma Gupy limousine traffic by talking to the press. That hurt, more even than losing SALT. The Soviets did not scramble the telephones in their official limousines, so anyone with the equipment and know-how could intercept the conversations. You can imagine how prolific and useful it was. There are other things that he gave away that I won't mention, all of them valuable."

Susannah's face was registering her shock. "Was he the one who betrayed Jess Simpson and John Novak?" she asked.

"Yes, and Absalom as well. The message from Absalom that you brought was his last."

"I felt that it was. Where is Absalom now? Were you able to get him to safety?"

"Yes. Had we waited for your letter, however, it would have been too late. We knew, he knew, that he was under suspicion. That was why we were using the rather circuitous route through Bulgaria. When John Novak was killed, it became simply a question of time, and whether there was enough of it to extricate our man. Thanks to his boldness, there was. He *made* the time."

"He has defected, then?"

"Oh, yes. He has defected. He won't be going back to Russia."

"His identity will be classified information?"

"Absolutely. But would you like to meet him, as my representative? He's arriving tonight."

"Yes, indeed I would. I'd consider it an honor."

"I'll give you only one word of caution. Make him welcome, but say as little as possible. He has been severely wounded, and the only reason we risk moving him at all is that he urgently needs medical attention. You'll be taken from here by helicopter to an airstrip we use occasionally. There you'll meet Adam Ross. He'll be known to Absalom. Ross will take him to the CIA's country house, and as soon as he can stand it he'll have surgery for his wounds. Infection has set in. If he survives, and right now there's some doubt, he'll be given a new identity, a new face and a new life. He has lived in Eastern Europe and traveled in the West. Adapting will be somewhat less rocky for him than for others. He'll always be a Russian, however—inhibited about money and a comfortable life. Russia's informer system tends to isolate individuals from one another, and he'll probably always feel that isolation. Freedom may even make him uneasy. The crucial difference will be whether he wants to adjust or not."

The President looked at his watch. "And now you had better go. There's just time for you to meet his plane. Thank you for coming tonight to talk to me."

"I am the one to say thank you, Mr. President. I'm grateful to know."

"I wanted to tell you this, Miss Clarke, for two reasons. In the first place, you deserved to know the importance of your contribution. You have rendered a critical service to your country, and we can do nothing to honor you for it.

"The second reason is a personal one. Meeting this man may entail obligations for you. You should know now the things in his past that he'll never be able to tell you."

He smiled a little at her expression, but didn't choose to tell her more. He took her watch from his pocket and carefully compared the time on its face with the clock on the desk.

"I had it repaired. It is keeping good time, so I hope I didn't damage it too much."

"That was very kind of you. My great-great-grand-father would have been proud that you used it."

The President smiled and walked with her to the helicopter pad. At the step, he shook her hand.

"Thank you for telling me, Mr. President."

"You're welcome. I'm grateful, and very proud of you."

The President handed Susannah into the helicopter, then stepped back and waited as the rotating blades bit into the air and lifted the ungainly aircraft from the pad. He waved once more and turned back to the house. He seemed tired now—his head bowed, his hands clasped behind him. Susannah looked after him until darkness closed him from view. Then she gazed out at the countryside below and wondered how it would be for Absalom.

Chapter 34

THE HELICOPTER SET Susannah down in an empty field. "Please wait," the aide said. "It looks like the middle of nowhere, but you'll be met." With a quick wave, Susannah ran out of the range of its blades, and the helicopter lifted off, clattering and rattling. Quickly it vanished, and then the only sound was the wind in the grass.

A dark figure rose from a nearby ditch. "Miss Clarke?" he called softly.

"Yes?"

"This way, please. We'll go into the barn."

From the outside, it was a huge tobacco barn. Inside, it was an airplane hangar. The man laughed at her expression. "And the silo is the control tower," he said. "We won't have long to wait. I'm Adam Ross."

"How do you do, Mr. Ross."

"Very well indeed, thank you. Cigarette?"

They smoked companionably and in silence. Ross declined to discuss the defector; Susannah's first question brought only a guarded, "wait and see" reply. But he was eager, impatient, fidgeting, almost like a small boy in his excitement.

"How are you going to take our friend from here?" Susannah asked in a second attempt to develop some conversation on the Russian.

Ross gestured to a small green-and-white panel truck parked in a front corner of the barn. Its sign read WHITE'S WASHING AND DRY CLEANING SERVICE. "It's an ambulance," Ross said. "What do you think of the paint job?"

"As long as no one stops you, it's perfect," Susannah said, grinning.

"No danger of that."

Outside, the hum of an engine was heard.

"Come and watch," Ross invited, and led her out through a small door. He shut it quickly behind them, closing in the light. They stood with their backs to the wooden siding. It was still faintly warm from the day's sun.

Just once, as the plane emerged over the edge of the trees, runway lights flashed and went out. The craft touched down easily on the grass strip and rolled to a stop. Then, with only its revolving lights to show the way, it taxied to the barn. There a man in the overalls of a farmer, two flashlights in hand, directed the pilot through the great doors in to the darkened interior. Susannah and Ross were in place inside when the plane stopped and the pilot cut the engines. Light flooded the hangar again. A steward opened the door of the aircraft but turned back inside.

"Should we get on?" Susannah asked Ross.

"They'll bring him down," Ross said. He suddenly looked worried.

In a moment, the steward came down the steps, followed closely by a nurse in uniform. They came over to Ross.

"He wants to walk," the nurse said.

"But . . ." Ross began.

"I know. We can't do anything with him. He's adamant."

"He's crazy!" the steward said with feeling.

Susannah didn't say anything. She thought she understood.

A moment more they waited, standing in the shadows

so that he wouldn't think they were hovering. Then the man appeared in the door and took his first, cautious step down the stairs. He looked ill and he moved slowly, like a man in great pain. He was neatly dressed in American clothes, but the blue shirt he wore only emphasized his pallor and the cords in his neck. His complexion was gray, his cheeks hollow, his hair liberally sprinkled with white. His mouth was set. Step by painful step, he came down the stairs. Halfway down, he turned a little and the light fell more fully on his face.

"Oh, my God . . ." Susannah whispered.

Ross said something, but Susannah didn't hear it. She was staring ahead, trying to see the defector's face more clearly. On the bottom step, the Russian paused and looked up, perhaps wondering why no one was there to meet him.

Ross said something, but Susannah didn't hear it. She moved forward to the foot of the stairs. He saw her coming, and as he recognized her, an expression of greater pain crossed his face. He gripped the rail to keep from falling and waited for her to make the first move. Her eyes on his, Susannah groped for his free hand. It was hard, harder than she remembered. It shook in her palm, and she felt the stinging of tears.

"Welcome home," she said huskily.

He made a sound deep in his throat and stumbled off the last step into her arms.

She held him until her arms quivered from his weight. Then, murmuring his name, she stepped back and looked up at him. He was haggard, his face damp with an unhealthy perspiration, but he was smiling.

"Susannah . . ."

"I thought you were dead."

"Until just now I felt dead. Who told you I was coming?"

"The President."

"Himself?"

"He sent me to meet you."

"He did that for me? I didn't expect . . . anything. I . . . what happens now?"

"When you've rested, surgery to heal your wounds."

"Can you stay with me?"

"No."

"Then when will I see you?"

"When it's safe. They'll tell you when. You might know about that better than I."

His expression was suddenly bleak. "It could be a long time . . . months . . . Susannah, if you knew how I thought of you, wondered about you—your life, your feelings, your thoughts. Lying in that room, I tried to picture what kind of life had created a person like you."

She smiled. "Was it so much a puzzle?"

"To me it was. You were so decent, so civilized, so *polite* to me, even when you were most afraid. Do you remember that first night when we talked? You were afraid of me. I could feel it. Yet you thanked me for the slivova. Then when we parted . . . and again in the desert . . . I have never met anyone like you. I . . . are you still afraid of me?"

"No."

"When did you stop fearing?"

"The precise minute?"

He nodded. She saw that her answer was important to him. He hadn't moved, nor had his expression altered, but his eyes betrayed his need.

"I think . . . I think it was in the desert. You were walking your dog one night and scuffling your feet in the sand." A little smile appeared on her lips.

He was mystified. "That was important?"

"To me it was."

He let himself take in her expression, the smile, the warmth in her eyes. Slowly, the tension, the ache, some of the pain faded from his face. Hesitantly, he reached for her and folded her into his arms. They stood clasped for long moments, her head on his chest, his cheek on her hair, quiet, savoring the closeness and his relief at being safe and forgiven. Then he turned her face up to his and searched her eyes.

"Will you wait for me?"

"I'll wait."

"It won't be easy."

"No."

"Could you . . . would you . . . risk it?"

"It's no risk. You kept your word."

"My word?"

"To keep me . . . alive."

"You remembered," he murmured. His hands touched her face, cupping it tenderly. Very softly, as though he feared his touch would hurt her, he bent his head and kissed her.

Her eyes were wet when he stepped back, but he could build his life on her smile. She slipped an arm around his waist and helped him to the ambulance, where Ross waited. The two men shook hands. The Russian immediately turned back to Susannah.

"This is as far as I can go with you," she said. "Mr. Ross is in charge from now on."

"How will I find you?"

"You kept my card?"

He shook his head. "It wasn't safe. I destroyed it. I memorized the address."

"Then I'll be there . . . when you come."

Once more he reached out for her and held her close. Then, painfully, he climbed into the truck. Ross jumped in after him and reached to shut the door. Susannah stopped him.

"Mr. Ross . . . can you get word to me . . . how he does?"

"No news will be good news, Miss Clarke."

She nodded her understanding. Behind him, the Russian had already lain down on the stretcher. The nurse was covering him. Susannah heard his tired sigh. Then the door slammed shut. The barn lights went out, the big door slid aside and the van started forward. Susannah followed it to the exit. There she stood and watched as it drove down the lane and turned onto the road. In a moment, its red taillights winked out and the Maryland countryside was dark.

YOGA
FOR ALL AGES

Relax wound up nerves and muscles. Maintain youthful vitality and looks. And do it all in just a few minutes a day—with the world's fastest-growing way to physical well-being.

Fitness for the whole family

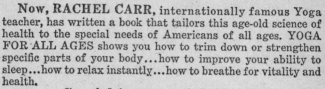

Now, **RACHEL CARR**, internationally famous Yoga teacher, has written a book that tailors this age-old science of health to the special needs of Americans of all ages. YOGA FOR ALL AGES shows you how to trim down or strengthen specific parts of your body...how to improve your ability to sleep...how to relax instantly...how to breathe for vitality and health.

Special features of this book:

—Rachel Carr's Six-Week Yoga Course. Acquire a basic mastery of physical yoga to help keep you fit for the rest of your life.

—Yoga exercises you can do in a chair. Ideal for office workers, old people, and the handicapped.

—Yoga for children. The Rooster, The Cobra, The Swan and other exercises which children find great fun.

—Simple steps in relaxing.

—Concentration and Meditation. An introduction to the mental and spiritual aspects of yoga.

—Lavishly illustrated with more than 250 step-by-step photographs and drawings.

At your bookstore or mail this NO RISK coupon

S 81/3